CALLS ACROSS THE PACIFIC

ALSO BY ZOE ROY

Butterfly Tears
The Long March Home

CALLS ACROSS THE PACIFIC

a novel by

Zoë S. Roy

INANNA PUBLICATIONS AND EDUCATION INC.
TORONTO, CANADA

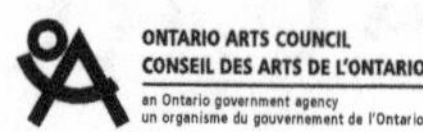

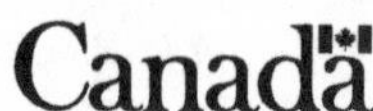

We gratefully acknowledge the support of the Canada Council for the Arts and the Ontario Arts Council for our publishing program. We also acknowledge the financial support of the Government of Canada through the Canada Book Fund.

Cover design: Val Fullard

Library and Archives Canada Cataloguing in Publication

Roy, Zoë S., 1953–, author
Calls across the Pacific : a novel / by Zoë S. Roy.

(Inanna poetry & fiction series)
Issued in print and electronic formats.
ISBN 978-1-77133-229-3 (paperback).--ISBN 978-1-77133-230-9 (epub).--
ISBN 978-1-77133-232-3 (pdf)

I. Title. II. Series: Inanna poetry and fiction series

PS8635.O94C34 2015 C813'.6 C2015-904999-7
C2015-905000-6

Printed and bound in Canada

Inanna Publications and Education Inc.
210 Founders College, York University
4700 Keele Street, Toronto, Ontario, Canada M3J 1P3
Telephone: (416) 736-5356 Fax: (416) 736-5765
Email: inanna.publications@inanna.ca Website: www.inanna.ca

MIX
Paper from responsible sources
FSC® C004071

To the sent-down youth and to those
who appreciate freedom in the New World

CONTENTS

1.

MILITARY FARM

DUSK, LIKE A THICK CURTAIN, concealed the quiet fields of Number Five Military Farm near Jinghong County in Yunnan Province, China in 1969. The hot, damp air of an August evening hovered over the rows of soybean plants and clung to the barb-wired fields. Rusted iron posts stood alongside the trees and bushes, outlining a path that sprawled into the faraway woods. Under a massive fir tree, a young man and woman, both about twenty years old, stood silently.

"Nina, why don't you say something?"

The woman bit her lip. "What else can I say?" She lifted her head and fixed her gaze on his eyes. "Do you love me, Dahai?"

"Yes, but I can't go with you." Dahai's hand fanned mosquitoes away from Nina's face. "Love isn't everything. I must go to Vietnam." He paused and then added, "I just don't think it's right to sneak across the border into Hong Kong."

"You have to sneak across the border to get to Vietnam," Nina said and grasped his hand. *The Viet Cong are communists, too.* She shook her head ruefully. "Think twice about this, Dahai. I am afraid you will regret this decision."

"I want to be recognized as a revolutionary," said Dahai. "It's that simple."

"And I can't live under the repression of the Cultural Revolution anymore. The land across the Pacific Ocean means freedom to me," she said, her hands on his chest, her eyes imploring him to change his mind.

"Maybe we are both wrong. Who knows?" Dahai's eyes locked with Nina's, and a twinge of sadness pierced his heart. He pulled Nina toward him gently and embraced her. "I'm sorry to have kept you waiting. I've thought it over and I cannot follow the path my parents took before me." His parents had been labelled enemies of the Communist Party, but Dahai fervently believed in communism. "Maybe I can prove it's wrong to say, 'the hero father raises a revolutionary son, and a reactionary father raises an anti-revolutionary bastard.' I need to prove that I'm a revolutionary, and the only way I can do this is to join the Viet Cong in the anti-American war."

"You're so headstrong." Nina quavered and withdrew herself from his arms. "What's the use of proving you are different from your parents? Nobody treats us like human beings here because of our family backgrounds. Since the Cultural Revolution, we've been branded as evil." She shook her head, her bobbed hair swinging back and forth. "We've been trying hard to remould ourselves here, but because of our backgrounds we will always be second-class citizens. I'd rather take my chances someplace where I can be free."

Dahai nodded. "I understand. Listen, in case..."

"In case what?" Nina stared into his brown eyes, and abruptly pulled away.

"If I die, and if you ever see them again, tell my brother and sister my story."

"Well, if I die, go and find my mother but don't say a word about me," Nina said, irritated.

"Enough, stop." Dahai hesitated, but reached out his arms again to draw Nina close. At the prospect of leaving her, his heart sank into a dark well, but he could not relinquish his plan to go to Vietnam — his only chance to prove himself.

Nina clenched her fists and punched his chest. "I will blame you forever," she sobbed, unable to speak anymore.

Dahai held Nina tighter to him. "Forgive me. But we both need to do what we must."

She stopped weeping, vehemently rubbing the tears from her cheeks. Leaning her head on his chest, Nina was calmed by the beating of his heart against her ear. "We deserve a better life," she said. "Something is wrong with this society, not us. I know I will regret it if I don't try to escape and I'm sorry that you aren't coming with me."

A gust of wind wrapped itself around their bodies and they shivered under the darkening sky. The sound of a dog's barking brought the reality of their future steps closer. Nina remembered she was supposed to meet with her girlfriend, Zeng, to plan for the next day's trip to Kunming. "I've got to go," she whispered with a sudden urgency.

"You go." Dahai clasped her head with his palms, and his lips covered hers. His mother's words echoed in his ears, and despite his usual aversion to the sentiment, he repeated it now. "God bless you."

Nina drew back from him, and with a muffled "Goodbye," she hurried away toward the end of the path. When she turned her head, she could barely distinguish his lanky figure; the darkness had engulfed him.

Watching Nina fade away, Dahai almost called out, "Wait! I'll come with you." He felt frozen, heartbroken. That he might never see her again in his life was a tangible reality. He covered his eyes with his hand, but could not stop the tears, and they dripped through his fingers. Like a puppet on strings, he shambled back to the hut he shared with twelve other young farm workers.

After breakfast the following morning, Nina did not follow the other workers out to the field to pick ears of corn. She gripped the fictitious telegram sent by her cousin, Rei, in Guangzhou, and exited the dormitory. She was in her yellow-green uniform: a worn-out shirt and pants with patched knees. It was so hot that she had to roll up the shirt's long sleeves and the hem of the pants as she headed over to the head office of the military farm. A middle-aged army officer sat at a desk, his greying head bent over a newspaper.

"Good morning, Chairman Yang," she greeted him politely. "I'm sorry to disturb you. May I ask for a personal leave? It's not the busy season now."

Yang lifted his head from the paper in his hands and noticed her red-rimmed eyes and puffy eyelids. "What's wrong, Nina?"

"My mother's been hospitalized." Nina handed her telegram to him. "Look at this."

"'Return home. Mother's sick.'" Yang read it aloud and then scrutinized the date. "Well, it looks like you haven't been home since you came here a year ago." Yang seemed to mull over the issue though his face expressed no emotion or reaction.

Nina prayed that he would not reject her request. She could hardly breathe while he turned the note over and over again in his hands until, finally, he agreed. "Okay, I will give you permission, but you are ordered to return in three weeks."

"Thank you so much!" Nina was surprised to find her hands were trembling.

"Being away from the farm doesn't mean you should stop reforming your thoughts. Follow Mao's directives every day," Yang said, his voice clipped, his fingers tapping the desk hard.

"Yes, Chairman Yang," Nina replied meekly. She bowed and hurriedly left the office, walking quickly back to her dorm room, a spring in her step.

Nina packed her belongings hastily and left the compound before anyone returned from the fields. She carried a worn green canvas handbag over her left shoulder and gripped the handles of a dark blue duffel bag with her right hand as she trudged along the road to Jinghong County. She narrowed her eyes to shield them from the stark midday sun and surveyed the green crops blanketing the fields like huge rugs. A profound sadness filled her chest when she thought about Dahai. But she did not turn her head; she was afraid she would lose the courage.

Nina had walked about ten minutes when she heard a horse's

hooves clacking on the ground behind her. Zeng had arrived in a horse-drawn cart just as expected. Zeng lived with her parents who were local peasants. She borrowed the horse-drawn cart from her commune.

"Get in," said Zeng, as she deftly guided the horse to a stop. Her two long braids swung down in front of her as she reached down to take Nina's bags. She flung them into the back and then pulled Nina up over the side of the cart.

Nina dropped onto the hard seat and felt the exhaustion of a sleepless night fall over like a darkened tent. Gradually, the rocking motion of the cart and clocking rhythm of the horse's hooves pounding the dirt road helped her drift off to sleep.

After a few hours of restless slumber, she finally opened her eyes. Night had fallen. There was no moon, only the silvery light of a star-filled sky. The horse's snorting reminded her she was in the cart that had stopped at the roadside.

"Zeng?"

"We're close to Kunming," said Zeng as she handed her an open canister. "Here's something for you to eat. I've just had something, too."

"Thanks." Nina grabbed a steamed bun from the canister. Her growling stomach betrayed her hunger. She wasn't satisfied until she had gobbled down three buns. After quaffing water from a canteen, Nina asked, "Do you think your boyfriend will be on duty with today's train?"

"I'm not sure," Zeng said with a shrug. "His schedule changes all the time and you are a couple of days late. I had no way to reach him and let him know you were still coming."

"I'm sorry," said Nina, holding back the tears that unexpectedly clouded her eyes. She had waited to leave, hoping that Dahai would change his mind. She could not explain all this to her friend. There wasn't time. "What do you think I should do? Should I try to find him?"

"Get on the train by yourself at first. Only try to find him if you get caught without a ticket."

"Okay, that's what I will do." Nina grasped Zeng's hand. "I really appreciate your help and will repay you in the future."

"Our moms are old friends, so I think of you as my sister, Nina. I am glad to help and I wish you the best," Zeng said with a warm smile on her face.

The horse-drawn cart resumed its way to the Kunming West Railway Station. The feeling of leaving her friends forever and facing an uncertain future came flooding back to Nina. She wept like a little girl under night's curtains.

Finally, Zeng parked her cart near the station where a lonesome train whistle broke the quiet of dawn. Nina climbed out of the cart then caught her bags as Zeng tossed them over the side. She rummaged through her handbag and pulled out a package covered in newspaper, which she then placed in Zeng's hand. "This is for you; a silk scarf to remember me by. Be careful on your way back."

Zeng hugged the package to her chest, holding back tears. "Don't worry about me. You must be careful, too."

Nina patted Zeng's hand reassuringly, although she herself felt uncertain and afraid. "Goodbye! And thank you," she said. Then, she turned and spotted a side entrance to the station under a dim streetlamp where train workers came and went. She headed in that direction. Through the station window she could see a man resting his head on the table, clearly asleep. Without hesitation, Nina scampered past the security booth where a whiff of cigarette smoke drifted from the small opening and mingled with the odour of diesel.

When she reached the barren platform, she used her travel bag as a stool, and waited.

The train arrived an hour later. When she boarded, nobody asked to see her ticket, but she could not find anywhere to sit. Wading through car after car, and nudging the people standing in the aisles, she finally spotted an empty space near an elderly and kind-looking woman. She squeezed in her luggage and plunked herself on top of it. By the time she settled, many passengers had awakened. Some stretched their arms or legs, and others stumbled across the crowded aisle to the washroom or the dining car. Nina watched as a few crew members hurried past. She was determined not to ask about Zeng's boyfriend unless she was in a real pinch.

About an hour later, a loudspeaker announced a ticket check, which required the passengers' full co-operation. Nina stood with her bags and walked hastily into a nearby washroom, locking the door securely behind her. The damp stench of voided bowels mixed with smoke fumes blanketed her nose. Even with the window ajar, the smell penetrated the air. The noise of people shuffling, questioning, and arguing lasted ten minutes, and then receded. Relieved, she left and returned to her spot.

"I thought you'd got a seat somewhere else," the elderly woman said, drawing back her legs to leave Nina some space.

"Thank you. I went to the washroom. I have a terrible stomach ache." She could not reveal the real reason behind her retreat.

"A lad was fined fifty yuan for not having a ticket. That's a lot of money," the woman sighed.

Nina drew in a breath. *My eight yuan would not have gotten me far.* At least she had not needed to call on Zeng's boyfriend, and put him at risk, too.

Three days later, Nina slept soundly in a dust-layered room on Lujing Road in Guangzhou City. In her dream, she was a child again, and her mother sat beside her in bed. Her mother's warm hand gently stroked Nina's hair. Before she could look directly into her mother's face, her childhood faded like a shred of cloud dissipating in the sky.

She opened her eyes to dust particles dancing in the afternoon sunshine that had slipped through the gaps of the window curtains. She heard a knock on the door, and someone approached with caution. "Who is it?" she asked.

Nina was relieved when she heard her eighteen-year-old cousin, Rei, answer. He pushed the door open and walked in.

"What time can we leave?" he asked.

"I... I..." Nina stammered. "I want to say goodbye to my mother, but I am afraid of getting us into trouble."

"It's not a good idea," Rei said, looking somewhat alarmed. "She might be charged with aiding our escape. It's better if she knows nothing about it. If we fail, she will see us behind bars."

"You're right," Nina said, reaching for her clothes on the chair next to the bed. Rei turned his eyes away and squatted to arrange his items in the corner: a pack with an air pump, two deflated basketballs, a knife, plastic cords, and a couple of string shopping bags.

That evening, Nina and Rei paced back and forth on Yuexiu Street North, gazing up at a building across the street. When Nina finally noticed a blurred figure in the lit window, she drew a deep breath.

"Goodbye, dear Mother," she whispered. Nina turned her head and strode purposefully toward Rei. "I am ready to go now."

They walked briskly to the end of the street and disappeared.

2.

KELP IN HONG KONG

BY TRAIN, Nina and Rei arrived in Shenzhen, where Rei paid his contact to help arrange for their escape. At night, with the help of a map, they reached Defence Road in Sha Tau Kok and hid in a nearby ditch. Both Nina and Rei had a basketball tucked inside a string shopping bag that was then tied to their waists to help them float if they had to swim. The shore in the distance was invisible in the thickening darkness, but they could hear waves lapping the beach and smell sea-grass. Time passed at an excruciatingly slow pace but they dared not budge until the People's Liberation Army patrol team had stridden past.

They jumped out of the ditch to cross Defence Road and scampered along the shore to the reef, where they found a boat camouflaged with seaweed. Nina pulled away the seaweed as Rei cut the mooring rope. As they climbed into the boat, the blinking lights far across the sea beckoned to them.

"Be sure your wallet remains tied to your waist," Rei said as he dipped the oars into the water. "How's your basketball? Is it securely tied?"

"It's in the right place," answered Nina, sitting across from him at the other end of the boat. Her hands were clasped tightly around the ball strapped around her waist. Her voice quavered with fear. "What should I do?"

"Keep an eye open for anything suspicious." Rei propelled the boat smoothly and glided toward the east.

The sky darkened, and the oars creaked occasionally. About twenty minutes later, they could see the faintly-lit sky over the New Territories of Hong Kong, and Nina could feel the pounding of her heart slow down as she regained control of her edgy nerves.

Suddenly, an engine rumbled from the northeast. Nina felt her limbs suddenly go weak. "An army patrol boat is coming straight at us," she gasped. Rei's arms pulled the oars through the water as fast as they could muster.

The sound of the engine grew louder, indicating that a boat was speeding toward them. "What are we going to do?" asked Nina, panicked.

"Push the ball onto your back now, drop into the water, and then swim east. That's Starling Inlet over there," Rei said, pointing. Then he stopped rowing. "Hurry!"

Nina felt her body stiffen as she dropped into the water. She swallowed a mouthful of water and choked, but with Rei's voice echoing in her ears, she forced herself to propel her arms through the water in the direction he had pointed to. Turning her head slightly, she noticed Rei's rowboat moving in the opposite direction and heard the engine rattle away. Nina ploughed through the water until she touched several reeds on shore.

Bang! Bang! Shots erupted in the distance. She shivered and knelt into the sand. A chill spread through her limbs. Her eyes wide open, she peered into the dark, but could see nothing. Darkness blanketed the water and engulfed Rei's boat and the terrifying sound of the engine.

Nina wiped the water from her face and listened carefully but heard nothing suspicious. She detached the netted basketball and plodded through the reeds. *Is Rei dead or alive?*

As she staggered to the weedy shore, it began to rain. She waded through mud and bushes and darkness for what seemed like forever. About a hundred metres away several scattered houses loomed ahead of her, and she shuffled over to one of them. The rain was pouring heavily by the time she reached some kind of wall. Just as she was about to lean her weary body against the wall, a huge dog darted out from a corner and jumped on her, growling and angry.

"My God!" Nina's shriek held the dog back only momentarily; it flinched and then attacked her again. She stooped, groping at the ground with shaking hands. Before she could grab a rock, she saw a faint flash of fangs and felt the dog bite her leg. She screamed as she grasped the rock and hit the dog's head with all her might.

The attacker finally yelped and galloped away, its tail drooping. Nina touched her leg and felt the warmth of her sticky blood mixing with the cool rain. Then she collapsed.

"Momma!" a child's voice called out. "She's moving!"

Nina slowly opened her eyes. She found herself lying on a low bed in a strange room with a little boy staring into her face. She blinked hard and tried to remember what had happened.

"Don't be afraid." A woman in her thirties, with a bowl in her hand, walked over to Nina. "Did you slip through the border?"

Before Nina could respond, the woman continued, "Last night, I heard a dog barking and then somebody shrieking. I rushed out and found you lying on the ground."

Nina sat up and felt a pain in her left leg. She lifted the sheet draped over her leg and saw a bandage wrapped tightly around her calf, which triggered the memory of the dog's assault. Looking up the woman, Nina asked, "Did you bandage my leg?"

The woman nodded.

"Where am I?"

"We're near Wu Kau Tang Village," answered the woman, as she sat down on a chair next to the bed.

"Is this your home?"

"Yes," said the woman. "Me and my husband escaped the Mainland two years ago. Now he works on an oyster farm."

She handed a bowl, with a spoon, to Nina. "You must be starving. Have some congee."

Nina took the bowl gratefully. The warmth of the congee spread to her heart, which was still heavy with last night's nightmare. She burst into tears. *What's happened to Rei? How is Dahai?*

"Don't weep." The woman patted her shoulder. "You'll feel better after you eat."

"Thank you for helping me," Nina said, wiping away her tears. "What should I call you?"

"Everybody calls me 'Gui's Wife' or 'Gui's,' because my husband's family name is Gui."

Nina nodded, aware that in the rural areas of her homeland it was customary to address a married woman by her husband's name. A married woman belonged to her husband.

"My name's Nina," she told Gui's Wife.

"That's a strange name."

"Yes, it's Russian."

"You city people are always funny. Aren't you afraid of being called a 'running dog'? The radio is always critical of the Russians."

"When my parents named me, the Soviet Union was our fraternal country," Nina said. She knew that since the Sino-Soviet split, the Chinese media was critical of the Russians as modern revisionists driving home the point that the Soviet Union was now China's enemy, even though many people, including herself, did not really understand what being a Russian revisionist meant.

Nina spooned the congee into her mouth, devouring it as she had not eaten a home-cooked meal since she had gone to live on the military farm. The pork congee tasted salty and sweet and was full of Chinese cabbage and lotus root.

Seeing Nina gulp the food, Gui's Wife asked with a chuckle, "Want another bowl?"

"Yes, please. It's delicious."

"Momma, I want a bowl of congee," said the boy.

"Go and get it yourself, Bean." The mother smiled.

Nina felt better after she swallowed her second serving. No longer dizzy, she was eager to get out of bed. "Where're my jacket and pants?"

"Not dry yet. Try mine," said Gui's Wife as she pulled a blouse and a pair of slacks out of a closet.

"You are very kind," said Nina hugging the clothes to her chest. "Do you know how to get to the Office of the Residents' Affairs?"

"You'll have to ask Gui when he comes home. Don't worry; you'll get a resident card. The Hong Kong government is kind. Why don't you get dressed now and join me in the kitchen."

Nina took a few steps and was thankful that the pain from the bite was bearable. She pulled on the baggy clothes and peered around the door. "Gui's Wife, can I help you with anything?"

"My goodness!" Gui's Wife slapped her thigh, a broad grin lighting up her face. "I forgot I was hanging kelp."

Nina followed her into a walled yard. Numerous pieces of half-dried kelp hung on bamboo sticks across the low walls, waving in the breeze that blew in salty air from the ocean. Gui's Wife stooped over a vat to pick up kelp, piece by piece, and along with her, Nina hung the kelp on available bamboo sticks. With a deep breath, Nina felt the sea again, and its familiar odour aroused more memories.

Five-year-old Nina enjoyed ambling on the beach with her mother, where she had gathered seashells and colourful pebbles into the toy bucket she carried. She spied sails on the choppy sea and thought about her father, who was always busy working on a naval base in Hainan Province, and who only returned home once or twice a month. She wondered which one was her father's navy vessel and asked, "When will Daddy come home?"

"Perhaps in a week," answered her mother. "Someday, we'll let you see what a navy vessel looks like."

"It must be big. Like this?" Little Nina tilted her head, and her arms stretched widely toward the far-away sails. The pail in her hand fell, spilling the shells and pebbles all over the sand.

"Much bigger," answered her mother, with a wide smile on her face. She helped refill Nina's pail. "You'll see."

Nina did not see her father often, let alone his vessel. She was ten when she finally got the long-awaited opportunity to visit her father on the vessel along with her mother.

Nina climbed with her parents on a warship anchored at a military port. The ship looked like a three-storey building floating over the water. Together, they had a seafood meal in a light blue dining hall. Nina imagined the table would shake if the currents pushed the ship, so she jumped hard on the floor, but nothing budged.

After supper, the family strolled along a path in the compound. Holding her mother's hand on one side and her father's on the other, Nina bounced along, kicking up tiny rocks with joy. She raised her head to look at a number of dark green, basketball-sized objects in the high palm trees. "My heavens, what are those balls?"

Amused by her old-fashioned exclamation, her father laughed out loud. "Oh, my silly girl. They're coconuts."

"But I've never seen big coconuts like these." She pulled at her father's hand.

"Nina, take a break." Gui's Wife's loud voice called her back to the present. Nina turned around, found the vat empty, and all the kelp already on the sticks. Back in the kitchen, Gui's Wife brewed a pot of herbal tea.

"Are you hot?" Gui's Wife asked as she soaked the tea pot in a basin of cold water. "In ten minutes, we'll drink cold tea. It's really good."

"You work really hard."

"I learned to do all kinds of chores as a little girl. Kids in the country start working early, not like city kids."

"I didn't learn about the hard life of farmers until I lived on the military farm."

"Tea's ready." Gui's Wife handed a tall glass to Nina. "Let's forget the past. We have a better life here. When Gui comes home, you can ask him anything you want about Hong Kong."

The following day, Nina went into town with the family. Gui was about forty years old. His suntanned skin indicated he worked outdoors. He sat with his son on the bus, and Nina sat with his wife. When the boy became excited about the view, a satisfied smile filled the deep creases at the corners of Gui's eyes. As soon as they arrived downtown, Gui led Nina to the Office of the Residents' Affairs while his wife took their son to a department store. By the time they met again, Nina had received her resident card, and Gui had bought himself rubber boots, his wife her favourite floral cloth, and Bean, a toy gun.

Gui's family offered her a room and Nina decided to stay.

Two days later, Nina visited the American Consulate on Garden Street and requested an application for political asylum. On the same trip, she bought a Chinese-English dictionary from a bookstore. With the help of the dictionary, she worked on the application form and filled it out with the following information:

Applicant: Nina Huang, born in 1949. Student, 1956-68. Thought reform on the Number Five Military Farm, 1968-1969. Arrived in Hong Kong on August 28, 1969.

Father: Jim Huang, born in 1924. Studied at the U.S. West Point Academy, 1946-48. Returned to China and worked in the Nationalist Army, 1948-1949. Joined the People's Liberation Army in 1949. Served in the

Chinese Navy, 1955-1966. Persecuted because of his training in the U.S. and died in October 1966.

Mother: Min Liao, born in 1925. Medical doctor at Guangzhou Children's Hospital, 1950-1967. The May Seventh Cadre School, 1967-69. Under house arrest, 1969-present.

She attached two additional pages describing why she was applying for political asylum and then sent the package by registered mail.

During the week, Nina helped Gui's Wife pick kelp on the beach. The collected kelp was then dried in the yard, and later, packed and stored. Every other week, Gui's Wife sold the kelp packages to a vendor. In the evening, Nina taught Bean how to read and write.

Several weeks later, she returned to the American Consulate for an interview.

She had written to Rei's grandmother in Guangzhou to ask about Rei but she had not heard back. Her letter may have been intercepted or Rei's grandmother may not have dared answer. The word "death" haunted her so much that she could not help but sob. Gui's Wife would pat her shoulder and say in a tender voice, "Crying is no help." But she wept along with Nina, wiping her tears with the corner of her apron.

Often, Nina wondered about Dahai. *How would he be punished if caught crossing the border? Has he gotten to Vietnam?* The questions were like worms eating away at her heart. She felt hollow, but she could not contact Dahai or Zeng for answers. Any letter from outside of China, to either of them, would create suspicion and cause problems for them. All she could do was pray that Dahai and Rei had survived.

Nina began to follow the Voice of America's "English 900" program on the radio. Listening to the English conversations provided her with glimpses into American society and culture. She imagined her future and felt happy. She would not be forced to read Mao's or anybody else's works; she would not be afraid of expressing a different opinion; she would not be judged by her family background and be regarded as the offspring of the revolution's enemies. She would have the right to make choices in her own life.

When, six months later, a package arrived from the American Consulate, Nina opened it with trembling hands. She had been granted a visa to enter the United States. The visa stamp showed March 17, 1970, as the entry date into the United States. Relieved, Nina could not keep her hand, which held her passport, from shaking.

"Don't go. Those blue-eyed and high-nosed people are scary." Gui's Wife pleaded. "Stay here, with us."

Nina raised her head and looked deeply into Gui's Wife's eyes, knowing with certainty that she could not stay. The green sheet of the paper that had unfolded in front of her, granting her asylum, looked shiny, as if a sparkling star had emerged in a starless sky.

"Don't worry about me," Nina said.

She gazed at the visa and wished someday, somewhere, that she might meet Dahai again.

3.

DEAR UNCLE SAM

On a sunny afternoon in March 1970, a Pan Am airliner landed at Augusta State Airport in Maine. *The land of freedom and opportunity,* Nina thought as she stepped onto Uncle Sam's soil. A carry-on bag in her hand, she walked among the passengers to the baggage carousel. She looked around, her face beaming with excitement even though she felt groggy after the twenty-hour journey.

She finally spied her suitcase. It was navy blue canvas with white stripes, colours she enjoyed because they reminded her of her father's uniform. She pulled it from the carousel and placed it and her satchel in a buggy, then pushed it to the nearest exit. The interpreter at San Francisco International Airport's Customs Office had said that someone from the Catholic Church Refugee Settlement in Brunswick, Maine, would meet her. The image of a nun in a traditional habit, her solemn face under a white coif covered by a black scarf like she had seen in the movies, crossed her mind.

She eyed the crowd around her as she moved her buggy. She passed two young men in black suit jackets and noticed that one of them was looking at her intently. Her eyes met his and then widened as she saw her name printed in Chinese on his placard. Before she could say anything, the other young man turned to her and asked in fluent Chinese, "Are you Nina Huang?"

"Yes," she answered, very surprised to hear the familiar

Chinese words from a Caucasian man here in America. "Are you from the Church Refugee Settlement?" she asked.

"Yes, I'm Jim. I'm here to help with translating," he replied, turning to his companion. "And this is George."

George shook hands with Nina and took her buggy. "Follow us. We'll drive you to your host family." He led them out of the airport and into a parking garage.

Nina tried to speak in English, but some words became Chinese. Jim translated for her: "I'm surprised to see snow in spring!"

George, in English, and Jim, in Chinese, replied at the same time, "I'm surprised to see you without a coat."

Nina chuckled with them as the three settled into a dark blue Ford and George pulled the vehicle onto Interstate 95. Nina looked out the window from her back seat. Pine and spruce trees lined the road. Half-melted snow banks on the road's shoulder glistened in the sunlight. George talked about the services of the Church Refugee Settlement, while Jim interpreted for Nina. "Mr. and Mrs. Duncan are your host family. Mr. Duncan is a veteran, and his wife, a retired schoolteacher. They volunteer with the Settlement and are willing to accommodate you for free." Jim told Nina that if she needed translation services in the future, she could ask for this at the office where they were going.

Two hours later, they arrived at the building that housed the Catholic Church Refugee Settlement in Brunswick.

George led them inside an office where an American couple in their sixties sat on a bench waiting. "This is Mr. and Mrs. Duncan." George introduced Nina to the couple and then wished her good luck. Nina thanked George and Jim as they turned to leave, then approached the couple.

The woman smiled and said, "You can call me Eileen and him Bruce." Nina was surprised that they would invite her to call them by their first names. In China, it was customary to call a couple of her parents' generation, "aunt" and "uncle," or address them by their title and family name, as a gesture of respect. Nina smiled back. *Calling them by their first names makes me equal to them, like we're friends. Maybe this is the equal spirit of Americans.* With Eileen's help, Nina filled out the necessary forms, handed them to the secretary at the desk, and then followed the couple to their car.

It was a short drive to their home, a two-storey house on a peaceful street with a steep gabled roof decorated in gingerbread trim, different from the block-like buildings she was used to seeing. It was the kind of house Nina had once seen in a picture book of Hans Christian Andersen's fairy tales, surrounded by big leafy trees and a manicured garden with tidy flowers along the edge of the walkway. Eileen and Bruce lived in the house by themselves, their daughter having married and moved to another city. A spacious bedroom on the second floor had been prepared for Nina's arrival. Here, with renewed energy and excitement, she would start a new life.

Eileen helped Nina settle into the house, and into the country. Nina began to attend English as a Second Language classes that were sponsored by the church in the evenings and on the weekend. *If I learn to speak English, I can explore this new world,* she thought and remembered the awkward moments when she could not understand what people said to her. She also registered in two credit courses — math and physics — at an adult school. She would receive her high-school diploma in a year if she passed all the examinations. She had been seventeen years old, an eleventh grader, when the Cultural Revolution broke out in 1966 and the education of high school and college students all over the country had suddenly come to an end. Now, she wanted to make up for everything she had missed.

Everything in America was different. Nina had never had cold milk for breakfast, so at first she heated milk in a small pot on a stove. Then she poured the warm milk into a bowl and added a teaspoonful of sugar — the way she did in China.

Cornflakes were new to her. After mixing them into the warm milk, and eating the odd-tasting hot cereal, she thought that later she would try to eat the cereal in cold milk as Eileen did. She had never had a sandwich either. Eileen taught her how to make tuna or egg sandwiches for lunch. They, too, were a novelty.

Nina had never lived in a place where it snowed. It seemed strange to her that it could snow in March when it should be spring, but she enjoyed being surrounded by fresh and crisp snowflakes. In the early morning, she helped Bruce shovel snow off the driveway. She even learned how to use a chainsaw to cut wood for the fireplace. Like a sponge, she quickly absorbed all the new foods and customs and day to day activities of life in this new land.

Several weeks later, on a Friday, after Nina had come home from school, Eileen entered the kitchen with two pots of flowers, placing one in the centre of the table. Nina remembered what she had learned from her ESL class and asked, "Is this an Easter flower? It's very nice and so delicate."

"Yes. It's an Easter lily, the flower of the Resurrection and of the Virgin."

"Easter lily?" Nina said. "I didn't know it was so symbolic."

"Its specific name is 'Madonna lily,'" Eileen replied, using a wet paper towel to wipe smudges of soil off some of the leaves.

"It's a pretty flower. I have seen them in China, too," Nina said as Eileen placed the second pot on the windowsill. "Where did you get them?"

Eileen dusted the table. "I got them from Hannaford Supermarket. Does the lily have any special meaning for you?"

"I know its bulb can be used as medicine," Nina said, trying to remember what she knew about the bulb's medicinal applications.

"Interesting. Yes, I can see that it might," Eileen sighed as she gazed at the white buds. Her face clouded while she murmured, "Two years."

"Two years?" asked Nina. "Do you mean this lily is two years old?"

"No, no," Eileen said, shaking her head. She hesitated, as if a fish bone had stuck in her throat.

Nina understood not to press her with more questions.

On Easter Sunday, the family invited Nina to join them for dinner. At the table, she sat with the couple and their visitors: their daughter, Emma, son-in-law, Mike, grandson, Timmy, and granddaughter, Alicia, from Bangor, a town about 100 miles away.

In the centre of the oval table, an Easter candle's flames danced around the wick. A cross on the candle glistened under the light of the chandelier. Everyone around the table held hands and bowed their heads as Bruce said grace: "Dear Lord, thank you for this food...."

Nina's thoughts returned to a night three years earlier when she had stared at a painting of *The Last Supper*, which depicted Jesus and his disciples sitting at a long dining table.

It was 1967. Nina had been looking for her shoes when she found a book under the bed. Most of the books in her home had been burned during some ransacking by the Red Guards. She had been sitting on the floor, flipping through the pages one by one when an illustration caught her eye. While she gazed at *The Last Supper*, she had contemplated why such an abrupt turmoil had engulfed her family. Her father, an officer of the People's Liberation Army, had been branded as an American spy because he had graduated from the United States Military Academy at West Point; and her mother, a paediatrician, had also been considered an enemy of the revolution since she had no intention of denouncing her husband. With her eyes fixed on the painting, she had wondered: *Why did Judas betray Jesus?*

Somehow, that painting had brought to mind the ways the Cultural Revolution in China had encouraged people to turn on their neighbours and friends, and she had felt anguish for her father, and her mother, and everything they had gone through, despairing at how their ordinary lives had been betrayed and taken away from them.

Nina returned to the present when she heard, "Through Christ, our Lord, we pray." She bowed her head and said, "Amen," along with the others. At that moment, a sense of well-being filled her and as she looked at the happy faces of the people at the dinner table around her, she realized she was among friends who would not betray her, but friends who had welcomed her into their lives, and who were helping her find her own way in this new life and new land.

Nina nibbled on the roast turkey with sweet-and-sour cranberry sauce for the first time. She thought of the turkey with a grey head and scarlet wattles that she had seen at the zoo and smiled to herself. She had never imagined such a creature could taste so good. She eyed the creamy mashed potatoes with gravy, the green beans sautéed with sliced almonds, and the hot cross buns and fruitcake, and knew that those dishes would be delicious too. A motherly smile on her face, Eileen said, "Try our food. It's prepared in a kind of Scottish-style. I think you'll like it."

After the dinner, Mike played the piano, while the others sang a traditional Easter song, "The World Itself." Nina leaned back on the couch and mused on the lyric, "*The Lord of all things lives anew.*" Releasing a deep breath, she was grateful she did not die during her escape.

Eileen and Bruce's granddaughter was sitting next to Nina, a pink stuffed bunny lying on her lap. "Why don't you sing with them?" Alicia asked, her hand patting Nina's arm.

"I'm not familiar with these songs, but I'm listening," answered Nina. "Do you enjoy singing?"

"I like to sing at school." The little girl cradled the smiling, toothy bunny. "My bunny's sleeping now. Tomorrow morning, we're going to roll Easter eggs down the hill. Do you want to join us?"

"What are Easter eggs?" Nina was curious.

Alicia scampered to the kitchen and returned with a basket full of hard-boiled eggs that had been painted red, yellow, green and blue. "Here they are. We like the Easter Monday egg roll. We'll climb to the top of the hill behind the house."

"Thanks for showing me." Nina carried the basket to the table and laid it there, wondering if the eggs would be eaten after they were rolled down the hill.

Mike was playing the piano. Emma was singing a song composed by Loretta Lynn, a country music singer:

Dear Uncle Sam, I just got your telegram,
And I can't believe that it is me shakin' like I am,
For it said, "I'm sorry to inform you..."

Nina noticed that Bruce and Eileen, sitting on the loveseat, were holding hands and looking at each other with big sad eyes. Emma was leaning against the piano, singing in a deep and mournful tone, and staring into the distance.

Alicia turned to Nina and whispered, "Did you know my uncle?"

"No," Nina said and shook her head. "Where is your uncle?" she asked.

"In heaven."

Nina's heart sank. "What happened?"

"Mom said the Viet Cong killed him."

Nina felt a shiver run down her back. She understood now the sadness in the room and she nodded sympathetically in Bruce and Eileen's direction. That must have been what Eileen had meant earlier when she mentioned something about two years having passed. She couldn't help but also think of Dahai. *Is he still with the Viet Cong?* she wondered. She was still perplexed that he could be so convinced his mother and the Americans were the enemies. She sighed and thought, *He was brainwashed.* But, immersed in thought, Nina had another question: *Why did the Americans go to the war in Vietnam?*

"Are you okay?" Eileen asked, coming to sit next to Nina.

"I didn't know you had a son."

"He died in Vietnam two years ago. We don't want the war, but as a soldier, he had to follow orders."

Nina held Eileen's hand. "I'm so sorry for your loss."

Eileen said, "He's resting in peace. We hope the war will end soon so no more sons will die."

Mike stopped playing the piano and looked at Nina. He seemed to have perceived the question in her head. "America entered the Vietnam War to stop the spread of communism," he said. Then looking at her curiously, he asked, "You escaped the communist regime, didn't you?"

"I was raised in communism. But after the Cultural Revolution began, especially when my father was jailed, I rejected it." Nina breathed deeply and told her new friends about her family. "In the end, my father took his own life," she said. She had lost her father to the revolution on the land across the Pacific. Eileen and Bruce had lost their son in the war across the Pacific, too. These two realities, she felt, created a bond between them that warmed her.

That night, Nina tossed and turned. Dahai was in her dreams. He was staring into the distance, as if he were trying to see through the world. Then he turned and said, "I'm confused."

Nina imagined Dahai running through bamboo-blanketed hills, a rifle in his hands, bullets criss-crossing over his head, and bombs exploding. Dahai fell, struggling to raise his blood-soaked face to ask for help. In her dream, Nina stretched out her arms but was unable to touch him. She tried to say, "You're a lost sheep," but she could not utter a sound. Then she watched as a lamb collapsed on the grass. Its face was stained with blood, and its feet struggled to stand. Snow-white clouds inched across the crystal-clear sky and cast shadows on the yellow-green grass.

Her knees weak, Nina fell on the grass too, her hands covering her tear-filled eyes. Then the words of a woman from her

Bible study group resounded in her ears: "God is watching our journey. If we're lost, God will call us again and again until we're back on the right path." Nina prayed to God to guide Dahai and save him.

The following morning, Nina brooded over her dream. She hoped that Dahai was well. She would not understand the meaning of her dream until years later.

4.

UNCLE TOM'S CABIN

SCHOOL ENDED IN JUNE. Nina looked out her window and noticed the tree in the backyard full of thumb-sized apples. *Summer is coming,* she thought with relief. She was excited to have just gotten a full-time job at a potato chip factory that would help her earn tuition fees.

On her first day of work, she arrived at the one-storey building on a second-hand bicycle. She met with a middle-aged foreman who gave her instructions and a uniform. After putting the white uniform on and tucking her bobbed hair into a net, she got her card punched and followed the foreman into a workshop. She surveyed the equipment: two long conveyer belts starting in the hall and extending into another room. Rows of seats flanked the belts. An aroma of potato chips flavoured with barbecue or sour cream or vinegar and pepper hovered in the air.

"You work at this section," the foreman said. "Pick out potatoes with dark spots." He pointed at the green boxes along the conveyer. "Put them there. Simple?"

"Yes, sir," Nina answered, heading over to the workers already standing by the conveyer belt.

The foreman told Nina, "Follow the others. You'll learn quickly enough what to do." He glanced up at the clock on the wall, turned on a switch, and the machines hummed.

The first group of peeled potatoes on the grey belt eventually moved in front of Nina. Next to her was an African-American, introduced to her as Jasmine, who quickly picked up a potato and placed it into a green box on a stool beside her. Nina caught one but did not see any black spots, so she put it back.

"Look! Get that one," said Jasmine, one hand catching a potato and the other pointing to yet another potato right before Nina's very eyes.

Nina caught it and thanked Jasmine. She realized she needed more practice. Amazed by Jasmine's sharp sight, Nina wondered how soon she would be able to easily spot the unwanted potatoes. Meanwhile, she tried her best to catch up with the other seasoned workers. The moving potatoes passed her like a bubbling brook. Her arms moved up and down as if she were ploughing through the bubbles, and the undesirable potatoes eventually filled the box.

At lunchtime, Nina followed the others into a multi-purpose room. Sandwich boxes and coffee cups were scattered on the tables. Chatter filled the room. Some workers lit cigarettes. Nina sat down, and the blonde girl next to her said, "Hi! I'm Carol. Are you new here?"

"Yes. I'm Nina. How about you?" Nina asked, smiling at Carol.

"I've been here about a year," Carol said. "I finished high school last year but have to make some money to help my family. I'm going go to college in September. Are you in college?"

Nina shook her head and told her she was in an adult high school. "How do you like working here?"

"Boring, but I don't think I can find a better paying job," Carol mumbled as she chewed on her sandwich. "Unless I have a diploma or degree."

"What are you going to study?"

"Occupational Therapy, but I'm not a hundred percent sure if I can get through it." Carol bit her lip. "My mom's always under the weather."

Puzzled, Nina asked, "Do you mean she feels cold?"

Carol chuckled. "I mean, she's ill." She noticed Nina's embarrassment, and added, "Your English isn't too bad."

Nina felt a hand on her shoulder and heard a woman's voice say, "I thought you couldn't speak English."

"Why?" asked Nina, turning her head.

Jasmine stood behind her. "Aren't you Chinese? I thought Chinese people didn't speak English." Jasmine gave her friendly, toothy smile, then nodded and said, "Back to work."

Not knowing what to say, Nina nodded and mumbled, "Nice meeting you."

The afternoon slipped by. All the potatoes with flaws did their best to roll away, but Nina learned to spot and catch them.

Two weeks later Nina got her first pay cheque: $140. She was elated. She could put food on the table now. She always got an uneasy feeling when she had to line up with the elderly and children for the donated canned food and staples distributed by the church, which she brought back to the house so she wouldn't use up all of Eileen and Bruce's own supplies. She placed the cheque in her wallet and thought that someday she would also be able to pay them some rent for her room. After work, she got on her bicycle and rode to Hannaford Supermarket where she had been with Eileen. In the supermarket, she was always amazed at the variety of fresh and frozen food and almost got lost among the shelves fully loaded with tons of colourful packages. She picked some meat, vegetables, and fruit, and then pushed her buggy into an aisle of canned food. She gaped at the tins with pictures of dogs and cats. She was stupefied until she picked up a tin and understood that the food was meant for pets. She chuckled but was still astonished at the attractive pet food packaging. *These cans look nicer than any cans of food for people in China,* she thought.

That evening, when Nina sat at the desk in her room, she rubbed her sore hand and reached for a grade eleven textbook from the pile of books. Visions of flowing potatoes still flashed in her head. She told herself she must try harder while recalling a Chinese myth about a young man preparing for the ancient imperial exams who had to keep himself awake by jabbing his bottom with a gimlet and tying his long hair to a beam. *I don't need to do that,* Nina thought, shaking her head. She just needed to forget watching TV and focus on her studies. Her plan was to graduate from high school within the next year. She drummed her fingers on the desk and imagined the day she would receive her diploma. After receiving her diploma, she would be able to get a better full-time job, and she would be able to live a simple and much better life than the one she had lived on the military farm. *Do I know what I want eventually to do?* she wondered, remembering her letter to Gui's Wife, which briefly outlined the details of her new life. She had not been able to specifically articulate what she hoped to do when she graduated and she wondered if Gui understood all that Nina hoped for in this new land.

The text on the page suddenly blurred in front of her and her mind wandered. The past flashed in front of her, sucking her in tight and deep as though it were a dark and endless hole. She could hardly breathe. *How is Mother?* she thought. *Did she get my letter? Is Dahai in Vietnam or in jail? Is Rei alive or dead?* She was haunted by these questions and worrying about her family and friends made it difficult to focus on her reading.

She was interrupted by a knock on her door, followed quickly by another. Eileen's voice rose. "Nina, can you join us?"

Relieved to be called away from what was bothering her, Nina opened the door. Eileen beckoned her to follow. Downstairs, in the living room, on the table in front of them, was a cake lit up by a multitude of candles. The overhead light went off, and the candles flickered. With wide smiles on their faces, the couple sang, "Happy birthday to you!"

I'm twenty-one years old! Nina counted. She had forgotten her own birthday. She was not even sure of the last time it had been celebrated. Her memories of birthdays had been erased by the Cultural Revolution. Such celebrations had been criticized and abandoned because they were considered part of a bourgeois lifestyle. Staring at the flames dancing on the wicks of the cake's candles, Nina found her eyes blurred by tears. *They are celebrating my birthday!*

"Make your wish," Eileen reminded her.

I wish I could go to university. She blew out the flame. The illusion of candlelight remained in her head like a star guiding her path. She suddenly realized that going to university was what she really wanted to do, despite the fact that educated people are targeted in the Cultural Revolution and the horror of that reality still lived somewhere deep inside her. Now, she fervently hoped that getting a better education in this free world would help her find answers to her questions about China and the Cultural Revolution that had shaped her life.

"What did you used to do to celebrate a birthday?" Eileen asked, her tone revealing her curiosity.

"My mom used to cook some noodles with fried eggs for me," Nina replied. Joyful memories crossed her mind. "Sometimes we went out for a meal and ice cream."

"Food seems to be part of birthday celebrations everywhere," Eileen said with a chuckle.

Sweet cake and pleasant chat erased, for now, Nina's gloomy feelings about her shadowy slowly passed as the aim of going to university became clearer to her.

Nina befriended Carol. From her, she learned about various colleges and universities, and also admission procedures. She was delighted to know that there was no family background check required for any applicants. In China, candidates with undesirable family backgrounds, such as landowners, the wealthy, anti-revolutionaries, and rightists, would not be accepted to universities.

One Saturday, Carol took Nina to visit Bowdoin College where Nina had dreamed of pursuing her higher education. When she drove along Federal Street, Carol pointed at a beautiful two-storey Colonial-style building, which Carol told her had been built in 1806. It was painted white, had large windows adorned with black shutters, and a red brick chimney on its roof. "Have you heard about this house?"

The sign read: "Harriet Beecher Stowe House." Nina shook her head. "What about it? It looks like an inn."

"It is now. But it was the house in which Stowe lived and completed a well-known novel," Carol said with an elated tone. "Have you heard about her?"

"No. I know about Mark Twain and Jack London. What's her novel about?" Nina asked, her eyes fixed on the house. She wondered if this woman's book was something like *Jane Eyre* or *Wuthering Heights*. Those novels were banned during the Cultural Revolution, but young people enjoyed reading them secretly. Nina had read many foreign novels translated into Chinese.

"It's called *Uncle Tom's Cabin.*"

"Oh!" Surprised, Nina said, "I've read it before! It's about a slave in the South, who finally escapes to the North. I didn't remember the name of the author."

"Wow! Did you read it in China?" Carol glanced at Nina.

"Yes. A Chinese version."

"I read it when I was in in the eighth grade," Carol said.

"Have you ever heard about the war epic, *Romance of the Three Kingdoms* or *Dream of Red Chamber*?" Nina wondered whether these Chinese classical novels were known to Americans.

"No," Carol replied as she parked the car. "But I did read *A Many-Splendoured Thing* by Han Suyin and *The Good Earth* by Pearl S. Buck. Their books are about China."

"I don't know anything about those books." Nina sighed, realizing the red door of China had been closed too tightly for too long. She got out of the car and she and Carol headed over to the campus. "Is it expensive to study here?" she asked.

"A private college is usually much more expensive than a

state university," Carol explained, her ponytail swaying as she walked. "That's why I'm going to Lewiston-Auburn College, part of the University of Southern Maine. The tuition is considerably less." Carol paused in front of a building. "Look. The Admissions Office is in there. If you need any information, you can go inside to ask."

The campus visit helped Nina form a clear picture of her future in which there would be new mountains to climb and new rivers and lakes to cross. Some days it would be sunny, other days cloudy or rainy. But she was ready. She felt challenged and excited and she could hardly wait.

The next day at lunch, Nina sat with Jasmine, who asked, "Do you go to church?"

"Yes, on Sunday. You?"

"Of course. I'm rich because I have God in my life," Jasmine said, her face lighting up.

Nina asked, "Have you heard of *Uncle Tom's Cabin*?"

"Definitely. It's about my people, but I don't know how much she understood us." Jasmine shrugged her shoulders. "She didn't walk in our shoes."

"Do you mean the author?" Nina asked.

Jasmine nodded, and then opened her lunch box.

"Well, how about Lincoln then?" Nina said. "He wasn't black, but he helped abolish slavery."

"Lincoln's grandma was black," Jasmine said as she started to pull out her food and then line it up on the table in front of her.

"Are you sure?" Nina was puzzled; she had not known that. She decided to add Lincoln's biography to her reading list.

"I'm positive." A proud look on her face, Jasmine added, "Did you know that Jesus was black too?"

Nina was astonished. "Really?"

"I know what I'm talking about." Jasmine unwrapped a fish cake, then picked it up with her fork and placed it into Nina's container. "Try it."

Nina chewed the fish cake and nodded. "This tastes really good."

"I made them myself," Jasmine said. "Hey, aren't you in high school?" Before Nina could answer, Jasmine asked, "Can you find some math tests for my son? He'll be in grade ten in September. I think he should work on his math this summer." Jasmine moved her head from left to right as though she were shaking something off. "It's no good if you don't have education. You can't get a job without education. And without a job, you can't survive in this world."

"Sure! I'll find some tests for your son to practise on. He'll be fine if he practises. Martin Luther King, Jr. had a Ph.D. you know."

"But he was murdered," Jasmine said. "I wish he were still alive. God bless him," Jasmine sighed, her hands closing her lunchbox. "Time for work."

Nina followed her out of the lounge and back to the conveyer. After the foreman's hand flicked the switch, the assembly line moved again. Nina was now close to picking out unwanted potatoes as fast as Jasmine could. At the end of the humming belt, the machine packed tons of bags of Humpty Dumpty potato chips. Nina pictured the smiling egg-shaped face on the pack, its hat off and hand waving. Then, she envisioned a group of students entering a two-storey building that looked like the one at Bowdoin College.

Could I be one of them? she wondered.

5.

FRANKLIN'S FISH AND CHIPS

THE SUMMER DREW to a close, and Nina resumed her high-school courses as a full-time student in September. In order to save money for college, she found a part-time job as a kitchen helper in Franklin's Fish and Chips restaurant.

She reached the establishment just before four-thirty p.m. A tall man her age was in the kitchen. *A young boss,* she thought. "Are you Mr. Franklin?"

"No," the young man answered. "I'm his assistant. Call me Bob. Meet Reno." Bob pointed to another young man who was bending over to pick out some sacks in a corner. *Piles of stuff,* Nina thought. *It's a busy restaurant.*

"They're potatoes, carrots, and onions," Bob said, "Your job is to peel and cut them. When you have nothing to do, you can help Reno wash dishes, okay?"

Reno pulled a couple of sacks to the floor and placed them between the cutting table and dishwasher. He raised his head and pointed at the kitchen utensils hanging on the wall hooks. "Get a peeler over there," he said. "There are stools under the table." He placed several large bowls on the table, and then added, "Let's do potatoes first. Once they are peeled, please put them in the bowls." He sat on the stool that Nina had passed to him and said, "You can sit down, too."

Nina gripped a vegetable peeler in her hand. She picked up yet another potato. *Boring!* She remembered the word Carol had used about the job at the potato chip plant.

As soon as they had filled one of the bowls with peeled potatoes, Reno began to slice them with a machine that was at the other end of the table. Nina continued with the carrots. An hour later, the boss, Kent Franklin, a rotund, middle-aged man, arrived and started to cook with Bob. Soon, the delicious aromas of fried fish and French fries spread throughout the kitchen.

Nina thought the bowls filled to the brim with potatoes and sliced carrots looked like blooming white-and-orange flowers. Meanwhile, dirty dishes and cutlery started piling up in a mound next to the dishwasher. Reno filled the dishwasher then switched it on. Nina took over his job of chopping the vegetables. The pungent smell of onion rings made her weep like a mourner at a grave surrounded by flowers.

The waitress placed order slips on the ledge of the kitchen window adjacent to the dining hall. Kent prepared the orders one after another, never missing a beat. *The boss works harder than us,* Nina thought.

Nina enjoyed her break and the bits of fish and chips that Kent handed to her and to Reno. *Who says there's no free meal? I'm getting one now!* She smiled at her thought.

"Fish and chips are much cheaper in my country," Reno mumbled as he chewed the food. "How about in your country?" he asked Nina.

"I have never seen such a meal before," Nina replied. "Which country do you come from?"

"Can you guess?" Reno grinned, a small piece of onion dropping from the corner of his mouth.

"Mexico?"

"You're wrong!" He seemed upset. "I am from Cuba!"

"Ha! Chairman Castro."

"You know something." With this thick eyebrows raised, he looked pleased. "You're Chinese, right? Mao Zedong."

"Right, but I hate Mao and Castro."

"What?" Reno pursed his lips. "Why?"

"Both are dictators."

"Maybe Castro is better than Mao!" He raised his tone. "I love my country."

"Then why did you come to America?"

"We're poor back home." His voice lowered. "I want to make some money."

Puzzled, Nina had not understood, or had never considered the idea that not everybody from a communist country hated a dictatorship the way she did. *Which is more attractive in the States?* she asked herself. *Freedom or money?*

In the last hour of their shift, Reno shifted the stack of plates in and out of the dishwasher. Nina selected unclean ones and used a knife to scrape cheese bits off the plates. As she worked, the words of Karl Marx, which she had memorized in her grade ten Political Studies class, rang in her head: "The capitalist mode of production is *this* repetition of an ongoing process, which is the process of becoming itself." Her teacher had said that workers, exploited by capitalists, had to work at simple and repetitive jobs. *Am I being exploited by Kent, who works even harder than I? If Karl Marx didn't work as a labourer, how did he make a living? Did he exploit others?* She was perplexed.

The kitchen closed at eleven p.m. Nina's hands ached from peeling vegetables and holding hot dishes. However, compared with the work she used to do on the military farm, this work was easy. According to Mao's article, "The Foolish Old Man Who Removed the Mountain," everyone was supposed to work hard like the old man who wanted to move a mountain. *Once I worked like that old man moving a mountain from one place to another,* she thought.

Many times, at the end of the day on the farm, after long hours of transplanting seedlings in the rice paddies, Nina had been unable to straighten her back. Her head would spin and her neck and back were stiff and sore. Sometimes after carrying bundles of wheat stalks with a shoulder pole, back and forth, between the field and the barn, she had felt as though she had become a sack of bones and flesh without a spine. Hunger and thirst had clung to her. It had seemed that in order to get rid of her hunger pangs, she would have to eat an entire pig and swallow all the water from the nearby pond.

Mao's hero was an old fogey, she smirked, *and I was a young fool then.*

Bob handled the knife playfully as if it were a toy. A round cabbage soon turned into a heap of shredded ingredients for coleslaw.

"Why don't you use this?" Nina pointed at the food processor.

"I need to keep myself busy. Besides, cutting is a kind of art form." Bob extended his long arm around Kent's squat neck. "If you wish, I can shave your head with my knife," Bob said to his boss jokingly.

Kent nodded with difficulty since he was in a clinch under Bob's arm. He giggled like a child. "Do what you wish, as long as you please my customers."

Kent isn't only the boss, but also Bob's buddy, Nina thought.

"Ha!" Reno joined in. "You Americans always say, 'Customers are God.' Tomorrow, I'll be your God if I eat here. Right?"

"Yes," Kent and Bob answered concurrently. "We have a saying that customers are always right," Bob added.

"Do you like the president of your country?" Nina took the opportunity to ask a question that had been on her mind for a while.

"Nixon?" Bob asked, and his hand flicked out. "No, I don't like him."

"Why?"

"I don't like the Vietnam War. He sent young men to be slaughtered there," Bob replied, loosening his arm from Kent's shoulder. He turned to Reno. "What do you think?"

"I'm not interested in politics."

"Me neither. Let's work to make money," said Bob. "Tonight,

my girlfriend and I are going to the movies. We are going to see *The Vampire Lovers*."

"Sounds interesting. Nina, do you like going to the movies?" Reno asked eagerly.

"No, I'm too busy," Nina replied, aware that Reno had hoped to ask her to join him.

The next evening, during their break, Bob grabbed three onions and juggled them, his face lighting up and shining under the lights. "Catch them!" Suddenly, he threw one to Kent who was resting in a chair. Kent ducked, but his hand caught the onion. But before Kent could stand up, Bob swung his long leg over Kent's outstretched arm as if he were jumping over a hurdle. Everybody laughed.

Nina visualized Bob throwing his knife bravely at a burglar. She could not help asking, "What would you do if a robber wanted your wallet?"

"Me?" Bob pointed his finger at his chest. "Of course, I'd give it away and run as fast as I can."

"What?" Nina had expected that bold Bob would confront the thug. "You're a coward, then," she said, stifling her laughter.

"Coward? Do you mean I should take a chance by resisting a mugger? No way. My life is worth more than my wallet.

Surprised by Bob's answer, Nina had nothing to say. In China, she had heard many stories in school about fearless youth fighting to protect public property whenever they encountered theft. The schoolchildren were asked to learn from such heroes who had sacrificed their health and lives. Ruminating on Bob's easy surrender, Nina realized life was much more significant than any property or heroism. *Money seems to be more important in the States than in China, but life is a priority over here,* Nina thought.

One afternoon, after writing out a cheque, Nina went to the living room where Eileen was reading various newspapers. "Do you have a minute?"

"Yes, sweetie. Do you need my help?" Eileen laid the paper aside.

"It's been a year since I came to live here. I'd like to pay rent from now on." Nina put the cheque into Eileen's hand. "It's a hundred and fifty dollars."

"I don't want to take this," Eileen said, and withdrew her hand. "You can continue staying with us." She patted the couch. "Come sit here. You need to save that money for college."

"It's very kind of you," Nina said. "I don't know what to do to pay you back for all your kindness," she added, as she sat next to her. She wondered if she would be able to do the same for others one day.

"You remind me of my boy," Eileen said, then told Nina that her son had worked in the evenings to save money for college, but then joined the army after high school. Admiring his father, a veteran from the Korean War, the boy had intended to go to battle for America. His sister had objected, but could do nothing to stop him as military service was compulsory at that time. "I've felt a little bit better about his death since I heard your story, Nina. He did something worthy. I think that he fought to stop communism from spreading all over the world, and that was important."

"I should read about the Korean War," Nina responded. As a schoolgirl, she had learned that the American imperialists had invaded Korea, so Mao had dispatched the Chinese army to resist the invaders.

"I should read some history books, too. One is never too old to learn."

"When my father was persecuted, I started to doubt what I'd been told. After being dispatched to the military farm for re-education, I thought something was terribly wrong with Mao's regime."

"It's good to learn from life. Come. I'll show you something." Eileen stood and led Nina into her bedroom. She gestured to a framed picture on the wall. "This is our son."

Nina gazed at the photograph. A young man in an army uniform smiled at her. "Handsome and admirable," she whispered, remembering the yellowish, wallet-sized graduation photograph of her late father in his uniform taken at West Point twenty-three years earlier.

Every day, Nina repeated the same duties in the restaurant kitchen like a horse endlessly trotting to the promise of hay in the barn. She felt like she had a star lighting her path. At break, Reno reminisced about the halcyon days of his childhood and his absurd stories made everybody laugh. Sometimes, when Bob practised Spanish with him, Nina also caught a few words. Sometimes, if several orders came in simultaneously, Kent and Bob could not stop to take a break.

One afternoon, Kent led a middle-aged man into the kitchen and introduced him. "This is Bogdan, Reno's replacement."

"What happened to Reno?" Nina asked.

"He returned home to tie the knot."

Tie the knot? Nina asked, "What kind of knot?"

"He's getting married," Kent explained.

"Will he be back in three weeks?" Bogdan asked as he took an apron off a hook on the wall.

Kent patted him on the shoulder. "Maybe yes or maybe never. Who knows the policy in a communist country?" He turned to Nina. "Show him what he's supposed to do."

"I will." She pulled two sacks off the top of the pile in the corner, dragging them to their regular spot near the table, and asked Bogdan to get a pack of onions.

Is Reno happy now that he is back in his country? Nina wondered. Then, she sat down on her stool and started peeling the next batch of potatoes. All she could think about was when she might have the chance to go back to her country and see her mother again.

6.

PING-PONG DIPLOMACY

ON A MONDAY in February of 1972, Nina arrived at West Brunswick Adult High School. She had been in America for almost two years and her command of the English language had improved significantly. Nina was excited by the possibilities and promises of a brighter future. That day, at the beginning of her Social Studies class, the teacher posed a question: "Has anybody heard any important news?" He looked at Nina, who shook her head.

"President Nixon is starting an eight-day visit to China today," answered another student sitting at the back of the class.

"Thank you," the teacher nodded. "His visit could help dispel a quarter-century of mutual antagonism between these two countries," he added, snapping his fingers emphatically. "The mysterious door of China is being opened!" he announced, looking directly at Nina, who squirmed in her seat, agitated and excited by this news.

Nina envisioned a red double door, with rows of decorative brass bosses girded on, slowly pushed ajar; she could even hear the squeaky noise of the hinges as the door swung open. She peeked past the red painted door with the row-by-row brass bosses and saw a sea of human figures in grey and dark green gradually moving forward beneath a cloudy sky. *Is my mother with them?* When she blinked, the red Chinese door vanished, and she saw only her teacher standing in front of the blackboard.

That day, the instructor asked the class to write a two-page essay on what they thought about President Nixon's visit as homework.

After school, Nina went straight home and as soon as she arrived, she hurried into the living room and turned on the television. She listened to the news about Nixon's arrival in Beijing and watched him shaking hands with Mao Zedong, but she was confused. *Why is Nixon visiting the dictator? Does Mao no longer hate Americans?* All the memories of her mother and the friends she left behind came flooding back. One thought was uppermost in her mind: *I'll soon have a chance to see my mother again. And I can finally find out what's happened to Dahai and Rei.*

Day after day she watched the news on television to follow Nixon's visit even though some of the scenes were repeated daily. *How could the Americans befriend a dictator? Could communism admire the path of capitalism?* These questions bothered her even when she was at work. During her break, she ate the fish chowder Bob had prepared for all of the staff, but she did not taste it as her mind remained fixed on Nixon's historic visit to China.

"The chowder is absolutely delicious," Bogdan said to Bob after he licked up every drop in his bowl. "You're the best of the best."

"Sure I am." Bob threw his fork up and caught it in the air. "My training has paid off. I'll open my own restaurant someday," he said, grinning at Kent.

Nina longed only to change the subject. "Anybody hear the news lately?

There was a moment of silence. Kent placed his empty plate on the counter. "Nixon has shaken hands with Mao," he said slowly. "Does that concern you? You're Mongolian, aren't you?"

Before Nina answered, Bogdan chuckled. "She's a fake Russian."

"What are you talking about?" Kent looked puzzled.

"I'm not Mongolian. I came from China." Nina went on to say, "I was given a Russian name because China and the Soviet Union were once brotherly countries."

Bogdan smirked. "I am a *real* Russian. Perhaps my kid should have a Chinese name."

Nina frowned and then grinned. "This is a free country. You can name your kid anything you wish."

"Don't be upset," Kent said as he lifted a metal basket of fries from the fryer to drain it over the rack. "I'm thinking about visiting the Great Wall."

"You should think about opening a restaurant there." Bob scooped shredded onions from a container and placed them into a frying pan on the stove.

"Sure, only if Mao's Red Guards don't arrest me for being a capitalist," said Kent, placing a cup of coleslaw on a plate and passing it through the opening to a waitress.

Every night at home, Nina would write something she had thought about Nixon's visit and its possible impact on China, and how it might affect her own life. By Sunday evening, Nina had finished her school assignment. In the last paragraph, she wrote, "Nixon's visit has brought me some anticipation. Someday, I will no longer be treated as a communist traitor and I will have a chance to see my mother again, the only family member I have left in this world."

Nina also wrote another letter to her mother. When she dropped the envelope into a mailbox, she imagined a pigeon flying first over land and then over ocean. *Will it reach my mother this time?*

There was no school during the March Break. Nina spent the week at the Curtis Memorial Library browsing through the shelves of books and periodicals. One afternoon, a note on a bulletin board caught her eye. It was about a group discussion on China being held in the library at that very moment. Nina strode to the room right away. A speaker, who looked to be in his forties, was seated at a large table and was recalling his recent visit to China in front of many listeners.

"Six years ago was the beginning of the Cultural Revolution. The ocean-going freighter I worked on arrived at Nanjing. We stayed at Xiaguan Wharf."

The storyteller's memoir brought Nina and the audience back to that scorching hot day in July of 1966. Guided by several dock workers, a group of Chinese students had boarded the American freighter, the red arm bands on their short sleeves like flames in the sun. The Red Guards asked the crew to go up to the deck and then gave each member a copy of Mao's *Little Red Book* in English.

One of the Red Guards had led a shout of "Long Live Chairman Mao!" The air was hot and humid; sweat poured out of the marine mechanic's every pore. When he scoured the serious faces of the Red Guards and observed the obedience of the other sailors, he had had to stifle his laughter. A Red Guard had then ordered everyone to open the red books to read Mao's quotations, from the "core of leadership for our cause is the Chinese Communist Party" to "First, do not fear hardship; and secondly, do not fear death."

The voices in both Chinese and English had drifted down the Yangtze River. The mechanic had stared at the red book in his hand, sweat trickling down his cheeks. The sentence, "Political power grows out of the barrel of a gun," had made him feel as if a string of bullets were shooting through his heart. At that moment, dark clouds had cast their shadows over the river, thunderbolts roared, and a drenching rain poured down over the freighter....

The speaker brought his audience back to the present. "That was the revolutionary education I got from China. I think everybody understands what that threatening power means." Nina nodded. She understood well the relationship between the dictator's power and the barrel of a gun. The speaker then suggested added, "Obey the Red Guards if you visit China."

"I have a question," a woman asked. "Do you think Nixon's visit will help slow down the Cultural Revolution?"

Nina was all ears. She had been seeking an answer to a similar question.

"Maybe. Mao's willingness to meet with Nixon could be a signal," answered the speaker. "Any ideas?"

"It seems ping-pong diplomacy plays well. Nixon's China game is working, but I'm wondering how the Red Guards will react to his visit," said another person.

Nina drew in a breath. "I think, at the beginning of the Cultural Revolution, Mao sanctioned the Red Guards. Later on, he sent them down to the countryside for re-education when he didn't need them anymore. Maybe many of the Red Guards have already re-examined their radical behaviours and regretted them."

More questions came up. The subsequent discussion gave Nina another perspective on American society, where people enjoyed the freedom of expressing their ideas. Before leaving the library, she checked out several books, including *Mao and China: From Revolution to Revolution* by Stanley Karnow, and *Mao's Revolution and the Chinese Political Culture* by Richard H. Solomon. She hoped she might learn to understand why China was experiencing all these political movements that had severe consequences on the lives of about a billion people.

Nina went to the library almost every day. One day, as she sat at a table in the reading room, going through a pile of books and periodicals, she raised her head and noticed a familiar face at a table across from her. It was Bob. Several magazines in his hand, he walked over to her and perched himself on a chair beside her. "What're you reading?"

"About the Chinese revolution and American history."

"Tough read. Mine is a no-brainer." Bob showed her the covers of his choices: *Hot Rod*, *Baseball Digest*, and *Gourmet*.

"I wish I had time for such reading."

"You can read these if you want any old time." Bob said, standing up. "I'll leave you to your research."

Nina tried to resume reading, but she could not focus. She went to another shelf and chose a few copies of *Vogue, Photo,* and *Country Music Magazine*. She flipped slowly through the pages of the magazines, absorbed in the stories and photographs that she held in her hands. The eye-catching designs and vivacious colours of so much fashion, as well as the photographs of breathtaking scenery, lightened her spirit. All of the enthusiastic singers and guitar players in the *Country Music Magazine* seemed to come to life. Nina felt as if she could hear the songs playing. *Life is enjoyable,* she thought. *There is time for this kind of reading, too.*

That evening at work, the hours seemed too long. She felt as if she were on an isolated island even though she was surrounded by other people. *What's wrong with me?* A sigh came from her lips.

The last customer left and the kitchen finally quieted. Nina rinsed the containers and food processors, and wiped the cutting board.

"Can you do me a favour?" Bob's voice startled her.

"What favour?" She figured he had yet another task for her before she could leave.

"Are you free in the morning? Maybe we can swap lessons. I thought maybe you could teach me Chinese, and I could help you with your English," Bob said without pausing, as if he didn't have enough time to finish his words.

"I go to school every morning. Today is the last day of my March Break," Nina said as she pulled off a paper towel to dry her hands. "Why are you interested in Chinese, this language that is not easy?"

"Someday, I'm going to open a restaurant in China and I want to learn to speak Chinese. So, I hope I can practise with you." Bob grinned, and his teeth shone.

A nice smile, she thought and felt her heart skip a beat. "What about on the weekends?"

"When can we start?" asked Bob, his voice delighted.

"How about Saturday morning?"

"That's tomorrow. I'll book a room in the library for ten o'clock in the morning. Is that okay with you?"

Nina nodded and took off her apron, hanging it on the hook behind the door. "See you tomorrow," she said softly but cheerfully.

The following morning, Nina put on a light green blouse — her best one. Since her arrival, she had not bought any clothes; her only new clothes had come from church donations and some hand-me-downs from Eileen. She looked through her closet and pulled out a navy skirt that she knew flattered her figure. She looked at herself in the mirror and thought she was more than presentable, but maybe, she should keep up with the times a little bit more. She shrugged her shoulders, slipped into her pumps and left the house with a smile on her face.

As she entered the library, she spotted Bob waiting at a desk. He led her to the room he had reserved. They sat down and Bob placed a page on the table full of handwritten sentences. Then, he took a pen out of his front pocket.

When Nina read the first sentence, "Where is the restaurant?" she asked. "Which restaurant?"

"I'm not asking you the question." Bob shook his head. "I'd like to learn how to ask this question in Chinese. Can you say it slowly?"

Nina said the sentence in Chinese, and Bob pronounced the words slowly, one by one. Then he asked her to say them again. Carefully attentive to her pronunciation, Bob took notes to help him remember the sounds and continued with the other sentences.

Nina read the questions and smiled. She was amazed at how practical Bob was.

"Where is the washroom?" Bob asked, in his hesitant Chinese. "Where is the train station?" "How much does this cost?" and "Do you speak English?" Since he could not always find similar English phonetic sounds, his mispronunciations made Nina giggle.

"What's funny?"

Nina said, "When you said 'restaurant' in Chinese, I heard 'long tube.' And your 'train station' sounds like a 'place for cremations.'"

Eyebrows rising, Bob laughed. "Holy cow! That's the best I can do?"

Nina laughed with him, then asked, "Why are you interested in opening a restaurant in China?"

"I've visited a number of countries on vacation, but haven't been to Asia yet. Opening a restaurant in China would open a window to that entire mysterious continent." He winked at her playfully as his face beamed.

"An exciting idea, but China doesn't accept foreign visitors."

"Someday it will." Bob changed the topic and asked about her studies. When Nina told him she was finishing high school in order to prepare herself for university, he seemed surprised. "Why don't you learn some useful trade skills?" he asked. "I took a cooking program for a year and became a chef. I got a well-paying job right away. We all want to make more money. You know, Bogdan works two jobs so he can send money home."

Nina tried to explain why she wanted to study political science. She told him she wanted to compare all the aspects of different societies and political systems in order to understand what was wrong with the Chinese political system and society. Eager to find the right answer, she discussed her confusion about money and freedom. "I thought, like me, people from communist countries must appreciate freedom more than anything else, but Reno and Bogdan seem to like money more."

Bob listened but appeared baffled by her answer. Finally, he asked, "Do Chinese women have their feet bound?"

"What?" Nina gasped and stretched her feet out under the table. "Can't you see how big my feet are?"

"Ha!" Bob clapped his hands and teased her. "I noticed your big feet on your first day."

Blushing, Nina asked, "Do you play ping-pong?" Then, she thought about the phrase, "ping-pong diplomacy," which she had recently learned.

"Once in a blue moon."

"Do you know about Nixon's ping-pong diplomacy?" asked Nina.

Bob seemed perplexed but then he smirked. "Well, have you ever worn a bikini?"

Nina looked at him and they both burst into laughter. And, at exactly that same time, they both called out, "Never!"

7.

MOON RIVER

IN THE FOLLOWING WEEKS, Nina and Bob continued their tutoring exchange. Bob could speak thirty everyday Chinese sentences now. Meanwhile, Nina finally understood many idiomatic English expressions that had confused her before.

One Saturday morning, Nina taught Bob several new sentences from a book about drinking at a tea house. He repeated the sentences a couple of times, but noticed that Nina appeared distracted. "Is anything bothering you?" he asked gently.

"I got my first rejection letter from a university. I'm worried about other universities not accepting me," Nina sighed, her hand on her forehead as if she were shielding herself from his gaze.

"One rejection isn't too bad. They won't all turn you down. Don't worry." He patted Nina on the shoulder and in Chinese he repeated a phrase he had learned from the book: "Let's go have some tea." He got up from the table and then led Nina to the door.

"Where is the tea house?" she asked, using a question from the book. His smiling face delighted her. *He's right. I still have a chance of being accepted by other universities*, she thought, which made her feel better.

"Tea is..." Bob tried to form his own sentence in Chinese. "Nearby, in the coffee shop," he said and with a flourish of his arm, he escorted her out of the library.

They stepped into the Krispy Kreme on Pleasant Street and

lined up in front of the counter. Nina asked for a cup of hot chocolate; Bob ordered a large coffee and a chocolate chip cookie. Drinks in hand, they sat next to each other at a small table in the corner of the shop.

The hot chocolate warmed Nina. The cloud over her head seemed to have dissolved when Bob said, "The rejection isn't the end of the world. There're so many choices in life." He wrapped his fingers around his cup, and leaning closer, he looked deeply into her eyes. "Do you think going to university is your only choice?"

"I think so," she answered, curving her mouth into a smile. "I'm not used to having many choices but getting an education is my priority."

Bob thought Nina looked lovely when she smiled. He hesitated only a moment, then bent his head to kiss her. But before his mouth touched her lips, she pushed him away in panic. "You have a girlfriend!" Nina sputtered. She had imagined such a romantic moment with Bob for some time now, but she never expected it would actually happen.

"Oh, we broke up a while ago," he said, sitting straight up in his seat. Then he asked, "Do you have a boyfriend?"

"Yes, but I don't know where he is." Nina bit her lip, feeling as if she had been drawn into a dark tunnel.

"What?" He had not anticipated such an answer. He turned to Nina and stared at her grief-stricken face. His heart softened.

He reached out to clasp her hand. His palm covered her fingers, and Nina felt a shiver of warmth spread throughout her body. Then Dahai's face suddenly appeared before her eyes, so she withdrew her hand from Bob's. "His name is Dahai." She took a breath and began to tell Bob about him and how they had parted.

Bob listened attentively to Nina's story. He was surprised at her idea of what it meant to have a boyfriend. "You don't really have a boyfriend," Bob said. "And you don't have him now. You don't even know where he is." Bob pulled his chair closer to Nina and wrapped his arm around her shoulders. "It's time to start a new life."

Again, the warmth from Bob's arm spread along Nina's back, and the image of Dahai disappeared. Nina sighed and leaned her head on his shoulder. "Where is your ex?"

"She's gone to New York."

"Why didn't you go with her?"

"I don't like big cities. Don't think about her. Let's talk about us instead." Gently, Bob's hand lifted her chin. As she stared into his clear blue eyes, his face moved slowly closer, and his mouth covered hers. Her heart pumped quickly. She was kissing another man now. A sense of guilt arose in her; she bent her head.

Bob saw the flicker of worry in her eyes. "What's the matter?"

She did not answer but gave him a shy smile. Holding her cup, she sipped the hot chocolate, her heart still pounding. *Such a sweet kiss,* she thought, admitting to herself that she had enjoyed it though her guilt festered.

He walked her home after they left the coffee shop, and he kissed her again, a slow, lingering kiss that left her breathless, before saying goodbye. Her heart felt full when she saw Bob in the kitchen at work the following day, and suddenly the repetitive peeling and chopping of vegetables became less boring.

On the following Saturday, they met in the library as usual for their weekly tutoring session. Nina interpreted Bob's sentences into Chinese and asked him to repeat them, but Nina could tell his heart wasn't in it.

"What's the problem?" Nina asked, her eyes full of concern.

He shook his head, then tipped her head up so that he could look into her eyes. "I don't understand why you keep yourself for a person you may not see again for the rest of your life."

Nina felt something invisible distancing them. She understood that Bob could not understand the way she had been shaped by a culture and customs so foreign to the American way of life. "Would you listen to a Chinese story that may help you understand me better?"

"Okay," Bob said. "I'm listening." He bent his head to focus on her quiet voice, and with a pen in his hand, he doodled on a piece of paper.

"A long time ago, a girl named Zhu went to school and met Liang, a young man. They fell in love, but Zhu's family didn't approve of her choice since Liang's family was too poor. They arranged for Zhu to marry into a rich and powerful family."

"Was she happy?" Bob asked with interest.

"No. When Liang died from depression and illness, Zhu's heart was broken. On the way to her wedding ceremony, Zhu insisted on visiting Liang's grave."

"Did she find it?" he asked, wondering why Zhu couldn't have simply refused to marry someone else, and why Liang had to die.

"Yes, she did. When she reached his tomb, it unexpectedly opened. Zhu threw herself into it, and the tomb closed over them both."

"Dead people have no more tales," he sighed.

"But the story goes on. Liang and Zhu changed into two beautiful butterflies in their next lives and met every day above the tomb."

Bob's eyes dimmed; a perplexed look came over his face. "Do you mean you want to be with Dahai even if he is dead?"

"No, no," Nina cleared her throat. "I mean, we have different ideas about love," she said hesitantly.

"Tell me what you mean."

"To me, a relationship between a woman and man should last forever or at least for a very long time. I don't understand how you can forget your ex-girlfriend, someone you used to love, so quickly."

"I live in the present," Bob said with a rueful smile. "I live in this moment, but you seem to live in the past. You still imagine that Dahai is somehow with you."

"This is how we are different," she said. "I need a little more time to get over my past."

He placed his hand over hers and nodded. *I can wait,* he thought.

Several weeks later, on a Saturday in early May, Bob took Nina on a ride to Popham Beach State Park. The woods of spruce and pine along the road blanketed the land and stretched to the horizon. Some ponds and lakes that had recently awakened from winter were now steaming in the bright sun. Nina had almost forgotten what it was like to be in nature after spending so much time running around from room to room and from building to building in the city. The sunshine and oxygen-rich air cleared her stress and tiredness and reconnected her with Mother Earth.

While reaching a bend in the road, Bob slowed the car. Nina suddenly screamed in excitement. "Look! There is a big animal wandering along the road!"

"It's a moose. This is a moose zone." Bob slowed the car down almost to stop so they could watch the moose cross in front of them. He was inordinately pleased to see her delighted face, and he grinned along with her.

After they arrived, Bob parked the car in a lot, and they headed to the shoreline. They wandered along the pristine beach, felt the wind skimming over the water, and watched the white caps roll in under the bright sunlight. Seagulls squawked in the air over them; flocks of shorebirds and sanderlings hopped around. They walked hand in hand, stepping over and remarking on the clumps of seaweed mixed with grains of sand, broken lobster traps, missing ballasts or runners, strangely shaped pieces of wood eroded by the tides, pebbles, and seashells that lay scattered along the beach.

The blue-green of the ocean and the salty sea air was refreshing and they were both lulled by the lapping of the waves against the sand. Nina could not deny her affection for Bob, or her attraction to him, which now seemed to swirl around inside her. Dahai was completely forgotten. She stopped to turn, and lifted her face up to Bob's. She looked deeply into his eyes, her lips parted and she drew in a breath. Her desire for him was as keen as the sea breeze that washed lightly over them. When he bent over her, she wrapped her arms around his waist. Bob embraced her tightly. He felt her trembling. "Are you cold?"

"A little bit. How about you?" she asked, her hand caressing his face.

He released her from his arms, pulled off his sweater, and eased it over her. It looked like a sack dangling in the wind on her slight frame. "Let's go back and get my jacket from the car." They trudged like toddlers against the wind, hand in hand, their arms swinging all the way to the car. He put on his jacket and pulled a backpack out of the back seat. "Let's go hiking in the woods. It'll be less windy there." Laden with the pack, he led the way to a hidden path.

"I'll hang off your back if I'm too tired to move," answered Nina with a giggle.

They hiked along the trail covered with fallen pine needles and withered leaves from the previous fall. Warblers sang cheerfully to their mates while sunshine danced through branches.

They returned to the parking lot much later in the afternoon, both tired and hot from the long hike. They threw their empty juice bottles and potato chip bags into the garbage bin. Bob looked up into the sky. "It may rain." He opened the door of the passenger's seat for Nina, and then slid into the driver's seat.

Halfway home, a raging thunderstorm caught them. The downpour fell on the windshield, and the wipers moved up and down quickly, but they were not quick enough to clear the glass. It became difficult to see the road, so Bob slowed the car to check the road signs, and asked Nina to look for a motel on her side of the road. As soon as they spotted one, Bob pulled his car in and stopped at the front door. They got out of the car and rushed to the outdoor hallway. Bob went into the office and checked in. Nina wondered if she should get another room. She hesitated to follow Bob who led the way to a door and opened it with a key in his hand. Bob switched on the light and she was relieved to see there were two beds inside. "Do we have a chance of getting home today?" she asked.

"Are you afraid I'm going to eat you?" He teased her by touching her head. "It's raining too hard to continue right now. Go dry your hair. It's wet." Then he plopped into a chair and turned on the TV.

When she stepped out of the bathroom, Bob pointed at a couple of Pepsi cans, more potato chips, and some May West cakes on the table. "This is all I could get from the motel."

The thunder roared, and the wind blew with rain. Nina sat into the chair next to him. "Well, it's not too bad for our supper."

After Nina called Eileen to explain the delay, she went to the window to pull the curtain shut. "Except for the rain," she said, turning to face him. "I'm enjoying this trip very much."

Bob walked to her and stretched his arms around her back, gently pulling her to him. "I feel the same." He kissed her eyes, cheeks, and neck. "Do you enjoy this?" he asked. As an answer, she kissed him back. "Can I touch you?" he asked and took her silence as permission. His hand explored under her blouse. He felt her body stiffen and then soften. He lifted her and placed her on the bed. He took off his T-shirt and then slowly unbuttoned her clothing.

"No," she whispered.

"Why not if we both enjoy it?" He stopped touching her. "What has the ancient butterfly done to you?"

"It's nothing to do with the butterfly. It's a moral issue." She sat up abruptly.

He sat next to her and gently stroked her hair. "We're both free. I don't see the problem."

"But we're not married," Nina finally said under her breath. "I mean, premarital sex is immoral."

"What?" He stared at her curiously. "What century are you living in? If people don't have sex before they marry, how can they know if they suit each other? I think these so-called rules prevent you from enjoying life." When he noticed the determined set of her jaw and the steely look on her face, he got up and went to lie on the other bed.

A lump swelled in Nina's throat. She had been taught that premarital sex was wrong, but her body yearned for Bob's touch, and in her mind she kept thinking about what Bob had said. "Sex is pleasure that can be equally enjoyed by men and women." She asked herself, *Do I enjoy being with Bob? What's wrong if I make love with him? But what if Dahai is still alive?*

While she debated this with herself, Nina felt her mind grow heavy. She dreamed she was wandering on a riverbank and beneath the moonlight, the surface of the river looked silver white and smooth, floating quietly in front of her. In the distance, she could hear a familiar melody, which she recognized as the song "Moon River," drifting over the water and coming toward her. *That's a beautiful song!*

She sauntered along the bank and bent over the water. Her fingers touched the liquid, and she felt its lukewarm caress. A couple of yellow downy ducklings swam over to her but then turned around before she could touch them. She could not help wading into the stream. Eventually, the water came to her waist and then to her shoulders as she waded forward. Looking around, she did not see any ducklings but found herself naked.

She was anxious to get dressed, but she couldn't find her clothing. She crossed her arms to cover her breasts even though nobody was around, but then she relaxed. Peacefully, she swam in the Moon River, with her arms stretching out and her feet kicking through the smooth surface.

A familiar voice called out, "Nina!" She raised her head and saw a human figure on the river bank, but she couldn't tell if it was Dahai or Bob.

"Wait up!" she cried out.

Feeling a hand touch her forehead, she opened her eyes. "Are you all right?" asked Bob, kneeling on the floor by her bed.

"I had an odd dream," she murmured. "Do you know the song 'Moon River'?"

"You want to talk about a song in the middle of night?" he asked, staring at her flushing cheeks under the dim wall light, but he couldn't speak anymore since his mouth was soon covered by her warm lips.

Nina woke up, her head snuggling on Bob's chest.

He opened his eyes. "Did I hurt you?"

"Not really," she hesitated. "I..."

"What?" he asked and kissed her cheek.

"I enjoyed it."

"I didn't know you were a virgin. You're twenty-three years old. That was a bit shocking. With surprise in his voice, Bob asked, "He never made love to you?"

"No, I didn't want him to."

"Did you love him?" Seeing her nod, he sighed. "How strange! When I love a woman I make love to her." His hands fondled her breasts.

"Have you made love to more than one girl?" she asked in a timid voice, trying to understand his way of loving.

"Yes, to all of my girlfriends. They enjoyed it, too." He noticed a wry smile on her face and felt her withdrawing from him. "Don't get me wrong. I mean at different times. Now, I will only make love to you. I don't have any other women."

"Understood," Nina said, holding his face to look into his eyes, which appeared dark blue in the faint light. "I'm not sure if I agree completely, but I'm learning to enjoy this moment with you."

"That's my girl. Life's short. Don't think too much. Otherwise, your head will explode." He pulled her hair playfully.

"Remember, I'm going to university in September."

"Sure I do. It's the University of Southern Maine, right?"

Nina nodded. "You're okay with that?" She chose a university in a small city knowing that Bob disliked big cities.

"*Esta es la vida*," he said. "This is life." As he held Nina close, the sweet voice of Holly Golightly from *Breakfast at Tiffany's* singing "Moon River" echoed in his mind.

"*Wherever you're going, I'm going your way.*" Nina listened to Bob whistle the melody in the early morning after that unexpected rainstorm.

8.

THE FENIAN CYCLE

ONE SATURDAY AFTERNOON at the end of August 1972, Nina cooked Chinese food for her host family to show her gratitude. Amazed by the different foods displayed on the table, Bruce said he loved the steamed Chinese-style ravioli stuffed with minced beef and celery. Eileen enjoyed the stir-fried sweet-and-sour cabbage. Although the egg and tomato soup was foreign, the couple also ate it with interest. Since Nina couldn't find certain ingredients, such as star anise and ginger, she felt sorry that her dishes were not authentically Chinese.

The following day, Bob came over to pick Nina up and take her and her belongings to Portland. About an hour later, they arrived at the University of Southern Maine. The energetic young faces on campus made Nina regret her youth spent in the chaos of the Cultural Revolution. Some student volunteers helped move Nina's luggage to her two-bedroom suite, which she shared with another freshman named Mabel. After helping unpack Nina's suitcases and boxes, Bob stayed for the evening.

The dormitory visiting hours were over at eleven-thirty p.m., so Nina kissed him goodbye. "Drive carefully. Watch for deer along the road. It's almost the season."

"Yes, Mother," Bob smirked. When he looked at his watch, he sighed. "Time goes too fast when we're together."

Nina saw Bob off to the door. When she turned back, Mabel

made a face at her in the living room. "If he were my boyfriend, I would have asked him to stay another day."

"I don't have as much time as you do," answered Nina. "I have a lot of catching up to do! You're still young and I'm jealous of your age."

Sweetly, Mabel grinned. "I bet you are."

Nina participated in student orientation but didn't join in on the other activities. Instead, she spent most of the week reading in the library.

Her first class, American History, began on a Monday evening. A binder in hand, Nina left the dorm hastily and went straight to the next building. On the second floor, she hurried past the first door on the left and noticed the number was 201. A crowd of students entered the third door on the left. She was sure that was 203. After stepping inside, she found an available seat, and sat down quietly. A young professor spoke enthusiastically, his hand occasionally moving in the air. Instead of using the chair, he leaned against the front of his desk, his voice was cheerful, and his tone was humorous. Laughter rose from the audience. Bob's face appeared in Nina's mind, sometimes smiling and sometimes frowning. She shook the image away and tried to listen attentively. The professor was narrating an Irish legend from the third century, which confused her; why, if this was American History, did she need to know that particular myth?

At break, she hastened to the desk and talked to the professor. "Sorry to bother you. I'm confused about the 'Fenian Cycle.' How is this Irish mythology related to a secret revolutionary organization in the United States in the sixteenth century?"

The professor's gaze fell on this new face, and he answered, "You know some details about modern American history." He clasped his hands. "You also have an excellent imagination. The legend has nothing to do with the Fenian Movement, though the word 'Fenian' was derived from the saga."

"But," Nina asked with hesitation, "why do we have to learn the legend?"

"My answer is simple," the professor responded, taking a tissue from a box to clean his glasses. "Because this course is on Irish Culture. Understood?"

At that moment, Nina realized the blunder she had made. "I'm sorry. I'm in the wrong classroom!" Turning around, Nina fled like a defeated warrior without hearing the professor's question: "Which course are you supposed to take?"

Nina got a part-time job working two hours an evening as a safety escort. Together with a partner, her job was to accompany individual students from their classrooms or computer labs or library to a bus stop near the campus at night. She was glad she would have some income.

One night after work, Nina wearily dragged herself to her apartment. She passed by a multi-purpose hall, and heard a familiar piano melody, which brought back a fond memory. It was "Moscow Nights," the Soviet song composed by Vasily Solovyov-Sedoi with lyrics by Mikhail Matusovsky, which had been popular among Chinese youth before the Cultural Revolution and was subsequently banned, as all foreign songs had been. Some, behind the scenes, had sung it still. She looked into the room and saw a woman playing the piano. The sweet music drifted along while her fingers ran restlessly over the keys. Nina tiptoed in and stood beside the piano. She couldn't help humming along in Russian:

Stillness in the grove, not a rustling sound,
Softly shines the moon clear and bright.
Dear, if you could know how I treasure so
The most beautiful Moscow night.

As the player finished, she turned and looked at Nina with surprise. "How do you know this song?"

"How do you do, comrade?" Nina answered in Russian.

"What?" the woman gaped at her, a puzzled look on her face. "A Russian commie?"

"No," answered Nina. "Are you?"

"No. My grandpa was a White Russian. He fled the communists in the early 1920s."

"I fled the Chinese Communists." Nina wondered how the White Russian, loyal to the Tsar and anti-communists, had escaped from the Soviet Union when the Red Army won the civil war in the Russian Revolution of 1917. "Did you learn the song from your grandfather?"

"No," the woman answered. "He hated the Bolsheviks. I learned the song at school. I love it since it's so romantic."

"I learned Russian at middle school." Nina remembered that every student had been encouraged to learn the language. "I even had a Russian pen pal."

"Really? How interesting," the woman said. "Did you learn this song from your pen pal?"

"I learned it from school, too. In the 1950s, China and Russia were brotherly countries. Everybody, young or old, learned Russian songs and watched Russian movies. We started learning the Russian language in elementary school." She sighed at the memory that the relationship between the two countries had soured by the 1960s.

"Were you a communist? Why did you flee China? Why did the two countries break up?"

"I wasn't a communist. I fled because my parents were persecuted. Russia and China became enemies for political reasons, I think," answered Nina as she looked at her watch. "I've got to go. I have an early class tomorrow."

"Nice meeting you," said the woman.

After the chance encounter with the piano player, the song, "Moscow Nights," echoed in Nina's head for several days.

A thought dawned on her. She decided to explore the relationship between China and the Soviet Union. The topic would be a good one for her group project in her International Relations course.

In the group meeting, the students shared their research results and ideas with one another. One topic was about the roles of the Americans and Soviets during the Korean War; another was about the American government imposing an arms embargo on Cuba; and yet other topics focused on the cultural similarities and close military alliance between Britain and the United States.

Nina focused on the period spanning from the Sino-Soviet Treaty of Friendship, Alliance and Mutual Assistance to the Sino-Soviet split in 1956, when the relationship between China and the Soviet Union became tense. The group discussion enhanced each student's interest in the course, and Nina benefited from this kind of learning process. Finally, one student from the group was chosen to present the group project to the class and they called their presentation, "Friends or Enemies in the Relationship between Countries."

Nina wrote a letter to Eileen and Bruce before Thanksgiving Day:

> *Nov. 19, 1972*
> *Dear Eileen and Bruce,*
>
> *How are you? I'm thinking of you. I still remember last year's Thanksgiving dinner with you. This year, I will work on my assignments and count my blessings at the same time. I've been busy studying and also working part-time, but I've been enjoying my student life so far.*
>
> *I feel grateful for knowing you and for your support. Without your generous and kind help, my dream wouldn't have come true.*
>
> *Happy Thanksgiving!*
> *Nina*

Then Christmas was around the corner; Nina bought a crystal angel figurine for Eileen and a heating pad for Bruce to help with his gout. From the library, she had borrowed books and periodicals to read over the holiday as she only planned to visit Eileen and Bruce as well as Bob in Brunswick for a brief time. The rest of the time she wanted to use for her studies. Bob came to campus to pick her up on Christmas Eve. He insisted that after visiting his parents for dinner, she stay at his place for the rest of the winter break. Unable to resist, Nina agreed with Bob, and with his help, she did laundry and cleaned up her apartment before leaving for the holiday.

By the time they arrived at his parents' house, Bob's brother and sister and their spouses had been there waiting in anticipation to meet Nina. Bob's father hugged his youngest son with a wide smile. "Your girlfriend is lovely," he said, shaking Nina's hand warmly.

Bob's sister hugged Nina. "I hope my kid brother can learn something from you."

After the joyful evening with Bob's family, Nina and Bob left the house. He drove past many houses decorated with colourful lights. Shining reindeer and a smiling Santa Claus on the lawn in front of Bob's apartment building gave Nina a warm feeling of homecoming.

The inside of Bob's apartment provided Nina with a glimpse of Bob's bachelor life-style. A heap of clothing lay in the middle of the living room floor, a pile of takeout boxes were stacked on a kitchen chair, and several unwashed plates were on the table. "Since I had to leave at eight in the morning, I didn't have time to clean up," explained Bob. "You can take a shower and I'll tidy up."

"Let me help you."

"No," he said, his hand steering Nina toward the bathroom. "Go."

The warm water from the showerhead and pleasant scent of Irish Spring soap washed away Nina's stress and she felt her entire body relax. Quietly the door slid open, and Bob stepped in, his firm arms wrapping her from her back. His warm mouth pressed on her nape and then searched for her lips. She turned around and clung to his muscular body. Passionately, they kissed, and their bodies joined. Her fatigue slipped away.

Bob carried her to the bed, and they sank into each other's arms. "Aren't you tired?" Nina asked in a breathless voice. The red-and-green Christmas lights that blinked through the window's glass made her feel dreamy.

"Haven't touched you for more than ... hmmm, I should say forty days exactly." Bob grinned. "You have a gorgeous body that drives me wild."

"You really surprised me," said Nina, her hands on his waist.

"Which part?" Bob muttered, his lips moving from breast to breast.

"In the shower," she whispered, curling herself up.

"Did you enjoy it?" he asked, pulling her closer. He felt himself tighten again.

"Couldn't you tell?" She laid her head on his chest. "Good night."

The following day, Nina went to see her host family and visited with them the whole day. As soon as she returned, she helped Bob with chores. He cooked a simple dinner and she cleared the table after eating. "We make a wonderful partnership just like when we worked at the restaurant," she said, drying the dishes with Bob. When Nina remembered Bob and Kent horsing around in the kitchen, she chuckled. "At that time, I saw you as a funny man."

"But now you know me as part of you deep inside, don't you?" he teased back, tilting his head at her with a big smile.

Nina felt guilty about being away from Bob for the most of the day, so she didn't open any of her books that evening. Instead, she snuggled with Bob on the couch, and they watched TV.

For the rest of the week, Bob had to work at Franklin's Fish and Chips as usual. Nina busied herself with studies, without knowing what time the sun rose and set. She didn't even notice when the snow started or when it stopped. Her world was occupied with historical events and political figures from different countries.

One night, after Bob came home from work, Nina walked to him sluggishly and gave him a hug. "We're like an old couple now."

"What do you mean?" Bob asked.

"We see each other every day and do the same, everyday things."

"Look," he said, taking out a videotape from his jacket pocket. "Let's try something new." It was an erotic film that aroused them both. They tumbled into bed giggling and practising making love in different positions.

Nina enjoyed being with Bob; he was a great lover and a caring man. But he was not always patient when she was busy studying.

Sometimes, Bob slouched on the couch, waiting for Nina to finish with her studies. He gazed at her back and wondered how those books could keep her so engrossed for hours, so that she barely noticed him. He got up slowly and approached her, curious about the book she was taking notes from. He stood behind her, his hand on her shoulder. "Hey there, tell me about the book you're reading."

Nina patted his hand and turned to look up at him. "It's *The Rise and Fall of the Third Reich*."

"It's about Hitler, right?" Bob asked with surprise. "Why do you want to know about him? Is he more interesting than me?" he asked in a teasing tone.

"I'm interested in Hitler's Reich," said Nina, "because I am wondering how his policies led to the Holocaust."

"I don't understand why you're attracted to politics," Bob said. Yawning, he added, "Years ago, at college, I switched from a business program to a simple cooking one because I got bored."

"I think I'll keep going." Nina's mouth twitched into a smile.

His head bent over her face, and he said with a grin, "You are too beautiful and too sexy to have your head inside a book all the time."

She stood up and kissed him as a response.

He wrapped his arms around her and took her to bed. He could not fathom her passion for politics: today it was about the Nazis and the Holocaust, the next day it was about communists in Cuba. He believed his body language told her that life was not only about books and studies.

The holiday passed. It was soon time for Nina to return to school. At the bus terminal, Nina and Bob embraced for a long time, as if they might never see each other again. Bob would not let her go until she promised him she would visit at least one weekend a month.

9.

BUTTERFLY MYTH

TIME FLEW AND THE spring of 1973 arrived. Saturday morning, Nina did some chores, and then, with a stack of books tucked under her arm, she went to a computer lab. An essay was due on Monday, but she was only about halfway done. She struggled through the whole day. At five-thirty p.m., she hurried away from the lab as Bob was coming to take her out to a meal. She had chosen to see him only once a month since she needed to double her efforts to catch up with other students. English was not her first language, and it always took her longer to read the required course texts.

On the way back to her suite, she passed the security office, and a clerk called out, "Nina! Are you available this evening? I can't find anybody else to replace Bill. He's just called in sick." Before she could decline, the worker said again, "Please help. We need escorts for this evening badly."

She looked at his anxious face and had to nod, yes. Her steps slowed as she worried about how she would explain this to Bob. It had been a month since she had last seen him. She knew he was counting on going out with her that night. As she approached her dorm room, she heard Bob's lighthearted laugh from inside. She unlocked the door and saw Bob sitting with his leg crossed over his knee at the table in the living room while Mabel was standing in her doorway, smiling.

"Ah, you're earlier today." Nina dropped her books on the table and opened her arms.

"If you're unhappy, I can leave and come in again," Bob said, standing to hug her.

"She's always as busy as a bee," Mabel said and disappeared into her room.

"Are you hungry?" Nina picked up her books and went into her room. Bob followed.

After he closed the door, he embraced her, and his hand unbuttoned her blouse. "Yes, I'm going to eat you," he said, his lips brushing her breasts.

"Mabel's still here," she said, patting his back.

"If you're quiet, she won't hear us." His hands slid under her clothes and in between her thighs.

She felt tickled at his touch, but she stifled her giggles. "Let's go to supper." She raised her head to kiss him back as she stopped his hands.

He drew in a breath. "Then we'll go to a movie according to your plan."

Nina dreaded telling him she couldn't go to the movie. "Would you mind going to the movie with Mabel?"

"Why should I go with her?" He lifted his head from her face and looked at her warily.

"One of the escorts called in sick." She breathed with a sigh. "They need me to fill the shift. I can't say no."

"Why don't you think about your own needs as well as mine?"

"I do. I decided to be with you," she said, feeling that she wasn't being understood. "Even though I need time to finish my essay, I still bought the tickets for us to be together."

"Okay, my sweetheart." He smoothed his shirt. "Let's grab a bite to eat."

After returning to the apartment, Nina handed him the tickets. "The movie starts at six-thirty. At nine o'clock, I'll be back. The rest of this evening will be ours." She needed to spend some time with Bob before starting to work on her essay. She peeped at the door and said, "Mabel's in her room. I bet she'll be glad to keep you company."

At work, Nina felt anxious and regretted leaving Bob with her roommate, a younger, more charming girl. Also, guilt rose in her heart. *Am I being selfish?*

She arrived home first. Fifteen minutes later, Bob and Mabel walked into the apartment and said goodnight to each other. She opened her door, and he came in, whistling merrily. Nina hugged him. She glanced at his face and noticed a trace of lipstick. "Did you kiss her?"

"She kissed me. Just a friendly kiss, nothing else," he said. "You chose a nice movie. We both enjoyed it." He said the word "both" with a special tone.

"Did you..." Nina hesitated for a second. "Did you kiss her?" She quivered.

He shook his head, and his mouth covered hers. They were together again. Into his kiss she melted.

At the end of April, Nina had five exams. Two of them were very difficult. One night, she dragged herself to the suite after her shift and was surprised to see a note from Bob on her door. It read, "I dropped by and waited for you for two hours, but you didn't show up. I decided to take Mabel for a ride. I left a hamburger for you in the fridge. See you tonight."

She opened the refrigerator and took the food out. With an appreciative feeling for Bob, she ate her late supper at the table. Before she finished it, the door pushed open, and Mabel came in alone. "Where is Bob?" Nina asked.

"How should I know?" grumbled Mabel, raising her eyebrows. "We went to a bar together. Then he drove me back and left. He didn't tell me where he was going. I suppose he went to a nightclub." She entered her room and closed the door.

Nina didn't know what to say. Too weary to do anything else, she went back to her room and lay down on the bed, despondent and anxious.

Later, after recuperating from a brief nap, she looked over her course notes for her very last exam, which was tomorrow morning. A knock on the door interrupted her thoughts. She strode to the living room and opened the door and there was Bob. Rubbing her eyes with her hand, she drew a deep breath. "You're back finally," she said with relief.

"You, too." He smirked. When he followed her into the bedroom, his gaze fell onto the book lying on the table. He muttered, "Am I bothering you, busy girl?"

"Sorry. I didn't expect you to come today," she lowered her voice and closed the door. "After class, I went straight to work." She held his arm with her hand. "Where have you been?"

"Do you care?" he answered. "I met a woman at a bar. Had fun."

"You..." She felt her throat tighten, and she could not speak. Her hand on his arm loosened.

"You're always studying," he added. "Don't blame me."

"I have an exam tomorrow. I can't discuss this now," she said. "You know college is important to me. I don't want to fail."

"So you're going to study tonight," Bob said. "Your dorm will be closed soon. Are you going to come to the motel with me?" Seeing Nina shake her head, Bob left alone, in silence.

The next morning, Nina got up early and thought about phoning Bob at the motel, but she was afraid of waking him up, and besides that, she didn't have much time to talk, so she did not call.

At the motel, Bob could not sleep. He searched his mind and tried to get a clear picture of the past few months. From time to time, he had lowered his expectations of her, anticipating that Nina would soon have more time to be with him. He had not been able to get used to her lifestyle, and he needed more. He made up his mind, picked up a pen, and scribbled a note: "Dear Nina, it's better for us to say goodbye to each other. I don't want to suffer or to wait hopelessly for you to have more time for me. We are through now."

After her exam, Nina returned to her apartment and rushed directly to the telephone. She called Bob, thinking she would invite him to lunch, but nobody answered. When she called the front desk of the motel, she learned that he had checked out. She turned around and spotted a note lying on the floor under the door, almost hidden by the door mat. She read his words twice before she understood what he meant. Her mind went blank; she crumpled the note slowly with her trembling hand, held the wad of paper tightly for a while, and finally tossed it into the garbage bin. Tears trickled down her cheeks. *We are through.* Bob's words resonated, and her head throbbed.

Though she had misspelled a number of words and made a bunch of other mistakes, Nina passed her exam and was thus qualified as a Political Science major for the following school year.

Nina got a full-time summer job as a cashier in a department store located in a shopping centre. On the first day, the manager showed her how to use the cash register. Then she was trained with an experienced cashier.

Two days later, she started to work at the cash register on her own. The store was having a large sale and business was brisk. Registering the discount off the regular price into the cash register slowed her down. *You just need more practice,* she told herself.

After work, she dragged herself home. Wearily, she lay flat on her bed, stretching her sore back and rubbing her stiff fingers. For a few evenings in a row, she reviewed working with the cash register in her head. The visual practice helped her perform better at the actual job and within a couple of weeks she was as fast as her fellow workers.

One morning, after several customers checked out, a young man hastened over to her. Strangely enough, he tossed a pack of pink hairpins on the counter. "How much is this?"

They're nice hairpins for little girls, Nina thought while she pressed a few keys and pulled the hand crank. "That will be one dollar and four cents, please," Nina said, as she looked at the display. The fellow gave her a two-dollar bill. As soon as the drawer of the register popped out, the youth lunged toward the machine and grabbed a few stacks of bills from the register's slots with one hand and pointed a knife at Nina's face with his other hand. Nina froze, her knees weak. The robber dashed away. A thought flashed in her mind: *It's more than three hundred dollars. That's almost two months' rent for me!*

"Stop him!" she shouted, whirling around the counter to chase him.

She sped up but suddenly a hand gripped her arm. "Stop!"

She turned around and saw the manager standing in front of her, panting. "Are you crazy? Money is not that important!"

"What do you mean?" asked Nina.

"Your life and safety are more important!" the manager said. His face was pale, and his eyebrows rose. "I don't want anything to happen to you. Don't do that again!"

At that moment, she remembered Bob's answer to her question about being robbed: "I'll give him my wallet and run away as fast as I can."

Thinking about Bob touched her weak spot, and she felt tears welling up.

"Are you okay?" her boss asked, patting her on the shoulder.

"I'm fine, thanks," Nina said, feeling relieved. "I appreciate your help."

"Don't worry about the money." The manager comforted her. "You don't need to pay for it."

Back inside the store, the manager called the police immediately and reported the robbery.

That night, when she lay down in bed, Nina recalled what had happened during the day. She became frightened all over again when she imagined the robber slashing her throat or even killing her. Bob's words about life being more important than a wallet crossed her mind again.

The next day was Sunday. She hesitated for a moment and lifted the phone receiver. Before she finished dialling, she stopped and perched herself on the edge of the bed for a moment while a memory of Bob flooded her mind. Finally, she picked up the phone and punched his number.

She held her breath as she heard a young female's voice say, "Hello?"

After a second of hesitation, Nina asked, "May I speak to Bob?"

"He's still in bed. May I take a message?" the woman said with a yawn.

"No, thanks," Nina answered and hung up the phone. Flopping onto her bed, she knew she had completely lost him. Pierced by an acute loneliness, she sobbed. Their paths had crossed briefly and the only some nice memories would remain. She reached her hand out to the night table and pulled out a tissue from its box to wipe away her tears.

In September 1973, Nina started her junior year. When she didn't have any classes, she went to the library to read. Sometimes, she took notes for later use from a pile of periodicals. One day, she hurried along the hallway and passed an Asian woman, who spoke to her. "Are you going to the library?"

Nina slowed down and smiled back. "Yes, are you?" The woman was in her forties and looked familiar to her. She scoured her memory for where she had seen her before.

"I work in the library. I often see you in the reading room. Seems you're always busy," the librarian became talkative. "I came from China."

"Me, too," Nina said. "Did you come here a long time ago?"

"My family escaped to Hong Kong after the Communists took over Mainland China. I was just a little girl when the landowners were denounced. I still remember how scared my parents were since they were landowners themselves."

"I don't know much about that period. But I know enough about the political persecution during the Cultural Revolution." Nina then asked, "How do you feel about your life now?"

"I'm quite happy. Now the relations between these two countries have improved. I'd like to visit China someday," said the librarian. "But the Red Guards are really terrifying."

"I think most of them have been sent to the countryside. They were used by Mao to attack his political rivals. They may've learned a lesson by now."

The woman looked at Nina with interest. "Really? That's a relief. There've been too many political movements in China since 1949."

"It's easy to manipulate those who grow up under the red flag. I was a Red Guard, but they threw me out because my father was labelled an American spy and a traitor to the revolution."

"Why was that?"

"He graduated from West Point Academy. Once he worked for Chiang Kai-shek's Nationalist Army before joining the People's Liberation Army."

"So he betrayed Chiang Kai-shek's government but not the communist revolution. The people who persecuted him suffered from a problem in logic," the knowledgeable librarian said as they went into the library. She patted Nina's arm. "It was so nice talking to you. I'll see you around." She walked into an office.

On her way to the reading room, Nina paused at a catalogue cabinet, pulled a drawer out, and searched the cards for books on the Chinese Land Reform Movement. Her mind returned to the elementary school where she had learned that poor peasants were contented to denounce landowners who had exploited them for centuries. But now she had heard a story from the other side — the tale of a landowner's daughter. On a scrap of paper, Nina copied down a couple of call numbers for books she had found. A glance at her watch reminded her that she had to finish the groundwork for her course on American Political Thought before she could explore the politics of China.

She placed the list into her folder, then turned and headed to the bookshelves with a stack of periodicals and government documents in her hands.

10.

BAMBOO STICKS

LATER THAT FALL, Nina attended a presentation in one of the university's multi-purpose halls. Ajax, a fellow student, stood on the podium. He was talking about his personal experiences in the Vietnam War.

"I've never spoken of this until now," Ajax said, starting his story. "I need to get it off my chest. I want people to know what we Vietnam veterans are going through. The Americans may be withdrawing, but the war is still raging and the memories are fresh and painful."

Nina followed his story attentively and pictured a battlefield in the mountain bamboo groves of Vietnam. On a June afternoon, during the late stage of a Tet Offensive in 1969, a group of American soldiers had stooped under the bushes to search for a path to move ahead. Their alert eyes and sticky faces shone in the sun; their heads were hidden under twig wreaths; their uniforms were soaked in sweat mixed with dirt.

"We groped around," Ajax said. "Suddenly, gunshots were fired from behind a hut about twenty metres away. A fellow next to me collapsed, and blood trickled over his face. All of us immediately dropped to the ground, and some of us shot back. I remembered what I'd learned during training, so I felt the pulse of my fellow soldier. He was dead. 'Son of a bitch,' came out of my trembling mouth. I grabbed a grenade and hurled it into the hut. I was fighting for my own life and my fellow soldiers' lives. In the explosion, smoke and fire erupted. You can bet that the sniper's gunfire was silenced, but then I heard a child scream from inside the shelter. One soldier dashed to the burning spot. A minute later, he leapt out of the flames, carrying a little boy under his arms. It was my buddy, Lenard! Before he could place the kid on the ground, he sank into a patch of ankle-high grass. I jumped up and ran over to Lenard to help. I took the child and laid him under a tree, but my buddy was stuck in a punji trap: a couple of sharp bamboo sticks pierced his body. He was soaked in blood, his eyes half open — I have never forgotten that stare. It was a close stare, right in front of my eyes, and yet it looked a thousand yards far away. Pain twisted his face. He mouthed the words, 'Shoot me!'

"I was shaking all over, but I pulled the trigger. I heard the blast of the gunshot, but I dared not open my eyes. I felt as if my own body had been blown apart, as if my own flesh and bone had just been splattered all over the ground. I threw my rifle away in disgust. I fell to the ground and vomited. My empty stomach expelled only water and mucus. The finger that had pulled the trigger went numb. Lenard vanished in my fuzzy vision, and I passed out."

"*Let's sharpen bamboo sticks. We are preparing them for the American enemy.*" Nina remembered these lines from a song she had learned in a music class as a ninth grader in 1965. That year, the Vietnam War had become more intense, and more American combat troops had been dispatched to Vietnam. Since China had sided with Hồ Chí Minh's North Vietnam, all Chinese schoolchildren had been taught songs and poems to support North Vietnam. Nina's class had also performed a show that admired the North Vietnamese soldiers and humiliated the U.S. Army. Nina had acted as a member of a group of Vietnamese women and children making sharp bamboo sticks for punji traps.

Nina trembled from her memory of singing and performing as a Vietnamese fighter. The image of the bloody figure stuck with sharp bamboo sticks made her feel as if she were the killer of Ajax's friend, Lenard. She shook her head incredulously as she thought about the naiveté of her adolescent years. She looked up at the podium and thought Ajax must be about twenty-four years old, her age. She shivered to think that in 1969, only four years ago, Ajax had been thrust into the cruelty of the Vietnam War. *That was the same year Dahai left for Vietnam, if he ever made it there.* The thought startled her. Her fingers pushed through her loose shoulder-length hair, and her hands pressed on her forehead. The student next to her asked with concern, "Are you all right?"

"I'm okay. Thanks." Nina's tension loosened, but a pang of guilt surged through her when she imagined Lenard's bloodied body ripped open by the punji stake.

Ajax's voice brought Nina back to the present. "Before the war, I longed to be a patriot. After surviving the war, I changed. I often ask this question to myself: Should America have entered the Vietnam War?" He paused, eyeing the attentive audience. "And my answer is yes. As in WWI, we used the war to try and stop the war. We wanted to stop the Viet Cong from killing more innocent people. I think we made a difference."

"I disagree!" a student shouted from the audience, her hand up in the air. "If America hadn't gone to the war, thousands of young men like your friend, Lenard, would still be alive. Their families would not have suffered."

More listeners participated in the heated discussion that followed. The war in Vietnam was still raging and the debate questioned whether the Americans had actually done any good. Nina listened intently and finally understood what freedom of opinion and expression meant.

After the presentation, she walked over to Ajax and thanked him for his story. "It reveals so much of what we don't know about the Vietnam War."

Ajax looked at her and asked without hesitation, "Are you from Vietnam?"

"No, I'm from China," Nina answered. "I learned about the war as a schoolgirl. I was told the Americans invaded Vietnam."

"Do you still think so?" Ajax asked.

"No. I've heard different stories from the other side now. In addition, I truly dislike communists from any countries. I think America's participation in the Vietnam War has helped raise awareness of the imperative to put an end to dictatorship and communism."

"Interesting," Ajax said, grinning, the tension in his face dissolving. Then he added, "My friends who died or were injured in Vietnam would be more than happy to hear that."

Another student then approached Ajax, so Nina bid him farewell, feeling much better after having talked to him, even briefly.

Nina took a course of East Asian Politics, and when it was her turn to make a presentation, she talked about her father's death during the Cultural Revolution and her attitude toward communist rule in China. In addition, she talked about her understanding of American policies in the Far East. Many listeners asked questions such as: "Why did your father choose to study at the West Point?", "What is the functional difference between the Nationalist Army and the People's Liberation Army?", "Do you think Nixon's visit to Beijing introduced capitalism to Communist China?" Nina responded as best she could, even though she felt she did not have clear answers to some of those questions.

The enthusiasm and thoughtfulness of Nina's fellow students touched her very much. But what truly made her day was the positive feedback from her professor.

On New Year's Day, 1974, Nina boarded an Amtrak train from Portland for a visit to the United States Military Academy to dig up her father's past. She wanted to understand what had led to the accusations that labelled him as an American spy. Several hours later, she arrived at Penn Station in New York

City. The Academy was located at West Point, some fifty miles away from the city.

The next day, at the archives of the Academy, she presented a letter from her professor and her student I.D. to ask for permission to do her research. An archivist rummaged through the stacks of records from more than two decades ago and placed a copy of *1948 USMA Howitzer Yearbook* on the counter. "You can check the photos of the graduates from that year," he suggested.

She thumbed through the pages of portraits, her fingertips slowly tracing the names under each photograph. Her heart pounded as she scanned each graduate's face, wondering when she would come upon her father. Finally, she shook her head in disappointment. "His photo isn't here."

"Don't give up so soon," said the archivist as he cleaned his lenses. "He may not have sent his photo to school. I'll check other resources for you." He entered a large storeroom. Several minutes later, he returned with a few copies of other journals: *Official Register of the Officers and Cadets in 1946*, and *Pointer View*, Vol. 1, 1946. The archivist pointed at the desks in the hall. "You can take these over there and look them over. If you need any help, please ask me."

She made herself comfortable at a large table, turned open the official register, and examined the listed names of students carefully. When her gaze fell on the name, "Huang," her throat tightened. She narrowed her eyes at the first name. *It's Marvin Tian! My father!* Nina drew in a deep breath, tracing his name with the tips of her fingers.

She had never heard her parents talk about her father's background until a hot September afternoon in 1966. The Red Guards, made up of high-school students, had broken into her home and denounced her father as a traitor to the revolution and an America spy. Before taking her father away, one of them had cut the red band off Nina's left arm. "You no longer deserve to be a Red Guard," he had hissed.

The Red Guards had wreaked havoc through the entire house. Looking for evidence of anti-revolutionary activities, they had opened and trashed the contents of closets, and suitcases and drawers had been turned over and emptied, chairs tossed and broken. Clothing, torn books and magazines, shattered dishes, and broken knick-knacks were scattered all over the floor.

Nina had asked her mother, "Why didn't you tell me about Father's connection with America?"

Her mother had held Nina's shivering shoulders and said, "Because you were too young. We didn't want to confuse you. We assumed working with the People's Liberation Army would have proved his loyalty to the Communist Party. Your father is innocent. Believe me. He's never passed any information to any American even though he graduated from the West Point Academy."

"West Point? It sounds like a spy institution."

"It's a military academy. He majored in engineering." Nina's mother had wiped her tears with a handkerchief.

"But why did he only stay for two years instead of four?"

"He was a student in the Huangpu Military Academy in Guangzhou. When he was a sophomore, he won a scholarship. Thanks to an arrangement between the two academies, he began his studies as a junior." Her mother had gathered and piled a stack of magazines that had been strewn about, and then perched on the only chair that had not been broken. "Do you remember Dr. Xu, the director of my hospital?"

"Sure. She used to tell us kids fairy tales," Nina had said. "What about her?"

"She grew up in America and worked as a medical doctor in Los Angeles. The news of the establishment of New China excited her, so she resigned from her high-paying job and gave up a comfortable lifestyle, because she'd longed to help her motherland — China. A while ago, she was under suspicion for being an American spy and eventually was put behind bars.

I told your father about her arrest, but he never thought the same thing could happen to him."

"Dr. Xu came from the U.S.? She looks like a clerk from a local Chinese herbal store. She is always in plain clothing," Nina had said, her mind working hard to link characters from the few American movies she had watched to images of her father and Dr. Xu, but she had not been able to form any single picture that would indicate they were spies.

Nina's mother continued. "It's true that your father could be considered a traitor to the Nationalist Party but not the Communist Party. The Red Guards need to learn a little bit of modern Chinese history before they label people."

"But why did he betray the Nationalists?"

"When I knew him, he was already working with the PLA. He told me he wanted to help the New China grow stronger."

"Do you think America is our enemy?" Nina had asked again.

"That is a hard question. If we are to believe what we've been told, I should say yes, but personally, I don't think so. There are good people and bad people in any country. Whether a country is friend or foe is a political issue. Have you heard from your Soviet pen pal recently?"

"No. We've been discouraged from corresponding with Soviet students."

"You see, yesterday's friend becomes today's stranger and even enemy." Her mother had paused. "Don't tell anybody what we've talked about. It will definitely cause more trouble for your father and for us." Then, she retreated to the messy kitchen to throw together a simple meal.

After supper, her mother had taken the framed portrait of Mao off the wall, removed the cardboard on the back, and then retrieved a small manila envelope hidden behind the frame. *What's that? Secret codes? Money?* Nina had thought as she kept her eyes on her mother's fingers.

"It's your father's graduation photo," her mother had murmured as she passed it to her. Nina had opened the envelope to reveal a wallet-sized photo of a handsome young man in a grey uniform. On his dress cap was the crest of an eagle with its wings outstretched. The black-and-white photograph had yellowed, but her father's eyes were dark and intense as they looked back at her. That night it seemed that she had grown a few years older and was better able to understand her father.

In the archives, Nina also found a class photograph of the cadets who had graduated in 1948, and her father was among them. After she had made a couple of photocopies, it was already noon. She returned the journals and went out for lunch.

Nina strode along Jefferson Place and found a small café where she bought a chicken sandwich and a carton of milk, and relaxed in a chair at a table near the window. A young man in a green T-shirt sitting at the table next to hers looked familiar, but she could not remember where she had seen him before.

He had also noticed her. "Hi," he said with a friendly smile on his face. "I saw you in the archive earlier. Are you a student?"

"Yes, but not from here," she said, returning his smile. "Are you?"

"I'm too old to be a student here," the man chuckled. "I'm doing some research for a report."

"Are you a journalist?" Nina asked with interest. "I'm from the University of Southern Maine."

"That's in Portland, isn't it?" he said.

He seemed to guess her next question and explained, "I go there often to interview subjects," he said.

"It's a small world," Nina said.

"Indeed, it is," the journalist responded. "What were you looking for in the archives?"

"Information related to my father. He was a graduate of the Academy twenty-six years ago."

"Now that's interesting. Why did he attend the military academy?" The man stood and walked up to her, with his hand stretching out. "I'm Roger Hughes. You are?"

"Nina Huang." She stood up to shake his hand. It was warm

and firm. They sat down, and Nina continued, "As a student at the Huangpu Military Academy in China, my father won a scholarship from the exchange program with the West Point Academy. That's why he spent two years here."

They chatted amiably. Nina told him about her father, and Roger asked more questions about the Cultural Revolution. When they got up to leave, Roger handed his business card to Nina and said, "Call me anytime if you would like to meet and talk again. I wonder also if you might give me your phone number."

"No problem," Nina said, took out a pen, and jotted down her number. He seemed nice, and she would be happy to meet with him again.

Back in the archives, Nina continued to scrutinize other documents. In the end, the archivist asked about her father, so she told him what had happened to her father, and the archivist expressed his sorrow, though he was happy to hear about a graduate from the forbidden country.

Staring absent-mindedly out the window of the Greyhound bus back to Portland, Nina mused over what she had learned from Ajax's presentation, and the research she had done on her father, and the politics of China. *What would my father's view of the American Military Academy at West Point be if he were alive? Would he be proud of it?* As she pondered over these many "what ifs," she noticed nothing outside the train window as it rolled by vast fields and dense forests.

11.

LONG LIVE...

THE CHRISTMAS BREAK was over and school resumed. Nina was too busy to telephone Roger though she often recalled their encounter and interesting conversation. She kept his business card because it reminded her of his smiling face and captivating voice.

Not long after classes had started again, she was pleasantly surprised to receive a phone message left by Roger asking if she would join him for coffee. He gave the name and address of a café near her university and said he would be there between four and five p.m.

She glanced at her watch and worried about her tight schedule. She had only just received the message, and he wanted to meet her that same afternoon. Her last class would end at four-thirty, and she was supposed to start work at her new job in the cafeteria at five-thirty. How on earth could she manage it?

After class, she rushed back to her room. Quickly, she changed into a winter skirt and threw on an overcoat. Then she walked hurriedly down the snow-blanketed alley. Her warm breath broke the brisk air and left a trail of fog behind her. When she stepped into the Dunkin' Donuts, she eyed the tables eagerly.

Roger spotted her first. He walked over to her, took her by the hand and led her to a table by the window. "You finally showed up," he said cheerfully.

"I was afraid I wouldn't find you," Nina said with relief.

They talked as if they were long-time friends, while they

drank coffee and ate donuts. When it was time for her to leave, she hesitated.

Roger noticed her uneasiness. "Is anything wrong?"

Nina shook her head. "No, but I've got to start work at five-thirty at the cafeteria," she said, standing and reaching for her coat. "It's not far from here," she added.

"I'll walk you there," Roger said, then helped her with her coat before donning his own.

They headed to the cafeteria building, laughing and talking all the way there. At the entrance of the cafeteria, Roger gently pulled Nina to him. He kissed her on her mouth. A surge of desire rose in her, and she folded her arms around his neck to return his kiss. A cold wind blew outside, but Nina felt warm inside.

"How are you going home?" she asked.

"Oh?" replied Roger. He seemed to awaken from a sweet dream. "I forgot that my car is at the Dunkin' Donuts. It should be faster than my feet," he said, chuckling.

Nina's heart softened. "I'll call you."

"Promise?"

She nodded.

Nina did not call Roger despite the fact that she had enjoyed spending time with him. She was too busy to date, she told herself. She needed to study. Besides, the break-up with Bob still hurt.

But when reading week was just around the corner, she couldn't shake the image of Roger from her mind or the feeling of his kiss. She remembered her promise to phone him and so, one evening, she worked up the courage to dial his number. A young woman answered the phone. Hesitating only a second, Nina asked for Roger, but the woman said he was not in but she could leave a message if she wanted.

"Please tell him Nina called," she said, then hung up. The excitement of seeing him dissipated.

Who was that woman? she wondered, sitting down on the edge of her bed, anxious and curious.

He didn't return her call, and disappointed, she realized how attracted she was to him.

On Sunday evening the telephone finally rang. Nina picked up the receiver and, upon hearing Roger's voice, her heart skipped a beat. He apologized for being unable to respond earlier since he had been away on assignment for a while. "Can you visit me or shall I come to see you? How about next Saturday?"

Nina hesitated. She was still worried about the woman who had answered the phone in his apartment. "How about if I come over to your place?" She needed to get away from school. In addition, she was longing to see where he lived. Thinking about seeing him excited her, but at the same time, she reminded herself she had no time for a relationship. Finally, she stopped debating with herself and decided to follow her heart.

She read through *The Rise of American Democracy, Politics Among Nations: The Struggle for Peace and Power, Red Star Over China*, and *China's Red Army Marches*, as she worked on a few assignments, waiting for the weekend to come so she could finally see him. Then she started counting down days. Four days. Three days. Two days. *Am I nuts?*

Saturday morning, she took a Greyhound bus to Lewiston. At the bus terminal, Roger, in a dark blue corduroy coat, waited for her. *He is so handsome,* Nina thought. He led her to his car, opened the door of the passenger seat, and gestured her in. When he sat behind the wheel, he asked, "What would you like to see in town?"

Nina replied, "What do you usually do on Saturday mornings?"

"In winter I go cross-country skiing. Would you like to do that?"

"Why not? If you don't mind teaching me," Nina answered.

"Are you sure you want to ski?"

"I grew up in a place without snow. Since I came to Maine, I haven't had a chance to learn."

"No kidding. Well, I can be your instructor," said Roger. He pulled the car over in front of an apartment building. "Let's get some ski gear."

She followed him into his apartment. The living room was tidy and well-organized. A bookshelf stood against the wall, and a newspaper rack sat in front of it. A large desk and chair were placed in front of a grand window that looked out onto the street. Nina imagined sunshine pouring from the window and silhouetting Roger's figure whenever he sat at the desk. The polished hardwood floor shone; several framed pictures hung on the walls; and a brown leather couch faced a TV set. *Warm and clean,* she thought, wanting to ask if he had had help decorating the place, but she did not.

He seemed to know what she was wondering, so he said, "I'd tidied up before my sister came last week." He left momentarily to retrieve two pairs of skis and poles from the balcony."

"Where is your sister?" Nina asked when he came back into the room. *His sister! Not just any girl!* she thought.

"Back in New York City where we grew up," Roger said. "Sometimes, she brings her boyfriend here for a weekend in the peace and quiet of the country. That's why I have extra skis. Can you try on these ski boots?" He pointed at the smaller pair he had taken out of a closet. Then he put the skis up against the wall. With one hand gripping a wax bar, and the other supporting a ski, he gently crayoned the wax on the surface of it. He glanced at Nina. "You must wonder why I don't live in New York. As an unreformed hippie, I prefer a freer, simpler lifestyle. New York is too complicated for me. So I'm here."

She tapped her feet on the floor. "The boots fit me well," she said. But the word "hippie" troubled her. She couldn't help but ask, "So, as a hippie, do you smoke pot?"

"Sometimes. But don't stereotype me," Roger laughed. "I hope you'll get to know me as a person and not as a stereotype." After the skis had been waxed, he asked, "Can you carry these poles? Let's get going. Otherwise, the sun will set on us." He took a winter ski jacket out of the closet and handed it to her. "Wear this. Your coat is no good for skiing." He held all the skis and his jacket in his arms as they walked out of his apartment.

Half an hour later, Roger parked his car at the end of a dirt road. After strapping on their ski boots, they stepped into the woods and onto the ski trail. Nina found it difficult to control her balance. When she aimed to stand, her feet moved in different directions. She wanted to go forward, but she couldn't move. It seemed like her body was being dragged by a horse that she was bound to. She laughed out loud and then looked to Roger for some help. Shrugging her shoulders, she said, "It seems my feet have a mind of their own."

"Bend your knees and move your feet just like you're walking," said Roger, demonstrating by moving one step ahead. "It just takes a bit of practice."

Like a horse stuck in the mud, Nina still had trouble stepping forward in the right direction. Despite all her exertion, she had only managed to slide forward about five metres. Puffing, she slumped onto her poles and looked toward Roger beseechingly. "Hey, wait for me!" she called out.

Roger laughed and skied quickly back to her. He patiently showed her a few simple movements and had her repeat them until she was comfortable. Finally, after falling onto the snow several times, and dissolving into laughter as she awkwardly pushed herself up and brushed the snow off her face and clothes, she managed at last to keep her balance on the skis. More practising made it possible for her to follow Roger's tracks.

Roger moved ahead and then returned to join her. "You've made progress. You're doing great!"

His encouragement and praise made her feel as if she could fly over the snow like a spring swallow. Nina raised her head and saw the trail turn around the hill and link to a faraway plateau. The trail looked as if it could reach the ends of earth. A remote and funny memory awoke in her mind. She said, "I have a story to tell you."

"What's it about?"

"About a country fellow from a poor peasant's family," she said, images of people in patched and worn-out clothes working in the fields of rural China flitted across her mind. "People from this kind of family are trusted and can get a decent job."

He slowed down to wait for her. "What's this good ol' boy's job?"

"He's a driver of a horse-drawn cart. It was considered a great job, especially when the bus was out of service because most people were involved in the revolution and had stopped working, and many services disappeared," she said. Then she told him about the "three loyalties," which reached its peak in the year 1969.

"'Three loyalties?' What does that mean?" he asked.

"It means to be loyal to Chairmen Mao, the Chinese Communist Party, and Mao's revolution. It's kind of a formal routine people carry out every day. I remember that as a child, I'd learned to shout 'Long Live Chairman Mao' from my first day in kindergarten. Every morning, our work day started with that slogan: 'Long Live Chairman Mao!' In all the newspaper stories, the heroes always call out that catchphrase, in order to show their loyalty, as if it is the last thing they will ever utter in the world." Nina paused to see if Roger was able to follow her.

Roger nodded. "Sounds like the Japanese soldier's way of being loyal to Emperor Hirohito."

"Something like that," Nina said, panting as she climbed a hill. "One day, fully loaded with fertilizer sacks, this man's horse-drawn cart slipped on the wet mountain road. A rain shower had made the road slippery. All of a sudden, an oncoming truck appeared around a bend on the left. The driver pressed the horn to warn the handler of his crazily running horse-drawn cart. Startled by the horn, the animal bounded back. In a blink, the cart rolled over and dropped into the ditch," Nina said, stretching her hand out to grasp a tree branch. "You can guess the rest."

"Did the young man survive?" Roger asked.

"He burst out shouting, 'Long live Chairman Mao!' Thirty seconds later, he opened his eyes. The horse was standing by him, and its sniffing nose made him sneeze loudly."

Roger breathed a sigh of relief. "He must've been hurt, but still managed to remember the slogan. Then what did he do?"

"Then he climbed up and out of the ditch, and went back to his cart," Nina paused, and taking a breath, she let go of the branch she was leaning on and stepped forward.

"Be careful. There's a bridge in front of you!" Roger called out behind her, but it was too late. Nina had slipped. Unable to keep her balance, she tumbled off of the bridge.

Roger came down to her quickly. "Are you all right?" he asked as he bent over and stretched his hand out.

"Long live Chairman Mao!" she yelled, eyeing his face.

Roger hesitated for a second and then replied, "Long live the Red Guard!" He held her hand and pulled her up.

Nina leaned on him as she balanced herself on the skis once again. She laughed until she had tears running down her face, the echo of her laughter resounding in the valley.

"Maybe I understand the Cultural Revolution a little bit more now," Roger said under his breath while a cluster of birds hopped among the branches.

They returned to his apartment in the afternoon. Nina's limbs were sore and stiff after skiing. Instead of exploring the town, they elected to stay home. Nina slumped on the couch and listened to Roger play his favourite songs on his guitar: "Nature Boy" by Eden Ahbez and "All You Need Is Love" by John Lennon and the Beatles.

The melodies, like a creek, flowed down through a zigzag path, woven with episodes of Roger's life in the past: as a

Colombia University freshman, he had recited some parts of Jack Kerouac's novel, *On the Road* and Allen Ginsberg's poem, "Howl;" he had marched among the students' anti-Vietnam War protest; the stoned Roger had made love with his ex-girlfriends and had danced with his friends; and as a passionate journalist, he had interviewed fishermen in different villages and written reports about their lives.

Suddenly, Roger's voice quivered. "*Darling, you're free to leave, I won't stop you. But I hope you'll stay.*" His eyes seemed sad and his ponytail shook slightly.

"What's this song about?"

"I composed it to commemorate 'The Summer of Love' in 1967. You want me to tell you about it?" She nodded, so he stopped playing the guitar to tell his story. It was his last year at university. With his fiancée, a university student, Roger had joined a hippie gathering in New York, and they had played music and taken psychedelic drugs. Inspired by Martin Luther King, Jr.'s speech, "A Time to Break Silence," given that April, Roger and his friends had made public speeches against the Vietnam War. During the gathering, they had also practised sexual freedom. "To me, at that time, sexual freedom meant I could have sex anytime and anywhere I desired. My fiancée and I enjoyed those days together, but because of the drugs, we both went overboard. My girlfriend got together with another man, and, stoned or high, I had sex with a lot of other women. In the end, my girlfriend and I broke up. And it really upset me." He tried to explain that though he had lived through the sexual revolution of the '60s, his natural tendencies actually lay more on the conservative side.

His fingers stroked the strings of his guitar randomly, then suddenly stopped. He returned to the present. "What would you like for dinner?" he asked.

"Anything is fine," she said, her mind still processing everything he had told her.

He ordered some takeout and after supper, Roger cleared the

table and Nina washed the dishes. "You don't have to rush. I'll drive you back. Okay?"

"What if I don't need a ride?" she asked, tilting her head toward him, a smile spreading across her face.

"I'll drive you to the terminal now. Or you'll miss the bus," Roger repeated.

"Or, I could leave tomorrow." Nina was interested in getting to know him more.

Roger's face lit up. "That's great!" he said. "Want to watch TV or play Scrabble?"

"Play Scrabble."

The whole weekend left Nina with sweet and ecstatic memories. She enjoyed everything about him — his words, his wit, and later, his body.

After returning to school, she started to write down the tale of the handler with his horse-drawn cart since Roger persuaded her to do so. He had said that many Americans would be interested to know what was behind the closed door of China. Even though Nixon's visit had left the door slightly ajar, most of life in China was still cast in mysterious shadows.

She finished the writing and sent it to Roger. With his suggestions, Nina made changes and corrections. After polishing it, she submitted her essay to a few local newspapers.

Not long afterward, the Chinese-American librarian told Nina that she had applied for a Chinese visa to visit her brother in China but her application had been rejected. Nina listened and shook her head sympathetically. *The door of China is still closed,* she thought.

Nina had not seen her mother in over six years, ever since she left for the military farm in 1968. She also had no way of knowing if her mother had ever received any of her letters, so her mother might not even know that Nina had moved to the U.S. Nina wondered how much longer she would have to wait for the opportunity to see or speak with her again.

12.

BLUEBERRY PIE

The year 1975 was a turning point for Nina, who had her first article published in *Portland Press Herald*. It was the piece Roger had encouraged her to write about the man and his horse-drawn cart. This boosted her confidence and she continued to write small pieces that she sent out to local newspapers with varying degrees of success. She was pleased to be able to hone her skills and to gain some experience in writing and publishing. In September of that year, Nina started the final year of her university degree, and she threw herself into her studies. She and Roger continued to date, and to slowly get to know each other, although her studies and his work often conspired to keep them apart for longer periods of time than either would have wished.

At the end of the fall term, Roger agreed to take on the position of editor at *The Yarmouth County Vanguard* and he moved back to his birthplace, Yarmouth, Nova Scotia, Canada, which was a five-hour ferry trip from Portland. Immersed in her school work, Nina could not get to Yarmouth often, but they talked to each other on the phone as often as they could.

Nina graduated in April 1976, but she did not apply to enter the Master's degree program even though her professor had encouraged her to do so. She thought she needed to do something practical rather than continue with her studies.

She sent her resume along with applications for many job positions but was disappointed not to even get an interview.

After a couple of months of trying, Roger suggested she move to Yarmouth and stay with him. He suggested that she could try her hand at more freelance writing as she hunted for a job.

On the phone, Roger said, "Don't worry about money. The cottage is my father's gift to me. You don't need to pay the rent until you're making money."

"But I need a permit to work in Canada."

"As a freelance writer, you can try to get your writing published anywhere without a permit. Maybe..."

"Maybe what?"

"Maybe later, you could become a Canadian citizen if you wish to."

Nina could imagine his face beaming and his blue eyes sparkling. She thought about how hard it was becoming to keep up their long distance relationship, and then decided that living together would give them an opportunity to see if they really fit well together. "Yes!" she said to Roger, who replied that she had made him a happy man.

When Roger came to pick her up, she had her B.A. in Political Science tucked into her briefcase, and all her personal belongings inside two small suitcases.

They arrived at Roger's cottage located on the seashore at the end of the Bay of Fundy. The one-and-a-half storey bungalow was surrounded by golden yellow daffodils and wild, white daisies, and at the back, the grassy beach spread all the way out to the ocean. Roger brought her to the bedroom on the main floor. "This room is yours now. I can sleep in the attic. Come on in." They were still shy with one another and he did not want her to think that his offer to live in his house carried any obligations on her part that she might not want to fill. He carried her suitcases into the room and then placed them down in the closet. "Would you like to take a look upstairs?" he asked as he came out of the room and started to climb upstairs.

"Sure." Nina followed him to the attic, which was filled with the light of a golden-red sunset that penetrated through the window in the west wall. Everything looked smoothly glazed. "What a gorgeous view!"

"In the morning, the east window takes in the sunrise, and you can view its fantastic light over the water. Roger led her over to the east window and pointed out to the ocean. "Tomorrow, I'll wake as if in a dream. If…" Roger paused.

"If what?" Nina asked.

"If you are still here." Roger said, turning to cup her face, which glistened in the light of a gentle sunbeam. "If you need me," he whispered gruffly, "we can go to your room."

His hands were warm and his eyes soft and inviting, as his lips bent to hers.

"I need you now," she whispered. They kissed each other long and slow, their hands exploring each other as if for the first time. Once unbuttoned and unzipped, their clothes in a heap on the floor, their bodies joined under the flamboyant light of the sloping sun. Nina kissed Roger's neck and mouthed the words, "I love you," as he groaned against her and covered her mouth with his own.

"I love you, too," he sighed.

Afterwards, both spent and content, legs entwined, Roger gently brushed the hair out of Nina's eyes, and kissed the tip of her nose. Smiling, he said, "Now, how about some of my very special blueberry pie?"

Every day after Roger went to work, Nina would sit down to write. When she needed a break, she would go out of the house and stroll along the beach where seagulls flew over the mirror-like water in search of prey. From the seashore, she could spot the roofs of a few houses in the tangle of woods that bordered the narrow headland and that were home to hundreds of birds. To relax, she would amble to the point and sit on a large rock to watch the currents move and to listen to the cheerful chirping of the birds.

One afternoon, she finished an article about her father's persecution, which led to his death during the Cultural Revolution, and mailed it to several newspapers both in Canada and in the U.S. After she returned from the post office, she felt relaxed and happy. She decided to get started on dinner: tomato sauce and paste added to ground beef in a pot would make a good spaghetti sauce.

When Roger came back from work, he sniffed the sauce in the pot. "It smells so good." Then he took a newspaper out of his briefcase and passed it to Nina. It was folded open to a specific page. "I thought you might like to see this piece in *The Globe and Mail*. Go ahead and read it. I will finish dinner." He filled a pot with water and placed it on the stove.

Nina sat down at the kitchen table and scanned the story about the visit of some Chinese-Americans to China. "This is interesting," she said, her face shining with excitement.

Roger dropped two handfuls of spaghetti noodles into the bubbling water and covered the pot with a lid. "They got their visa from the Chinese Embassy in Ottawa instead of the one in the U.S. You could try that, too." More excited than Nina, Roger tapped a long wooden spoon on the lid. "Don't worry about money. It's not a problem," he said as if he had guessed what was in her mind.

"I'll write to the embassy and request an application," she said. A flicker of hope appeared in her eyes as she looked over the article once more. It would take one or two months to get a visa, so she had some time to make some money and plan for the trip.

That evening, Nina imagined visiting China and finding her mother, Dahai, and Rei whom she had left behind seven years earlier. When she thought about seeing Dahai, her heart felt heavy. *What should I tell him? Should I tell him I have a lover?* They had sworn to each other that their love would never die. As the Chinese saying went, "The heart remains the same even if the ocean dries out and the stones crack."

But Nina knew that she had changed tremendously. She was not even sure if her mother would understand her now — she who had made love to more than one man and was currently in a premarital relationship. In China, such was considered immoral. Sometimes, people lost their jobs or reputations as a result of such behaviour. She tossed and turned, and had trouble falling asleep.

The next day, that same thought haunted her as she wrote to the Chinese Embassy and her eagerness about the possibility of going home and seeing her beloved ones lessened.

Roger noticed her despondent mood when he returned from work. Assuming she was worried about not getting a visa, he said, "Honey, don't worry about something unknown."

"You're right. I should enjoy the time we're together."

"What? You sound like it's the end of the world," said Roger. His hand stretched to the table calendar and turned it to face her. "Today's Friday. Let's go to a movie."

"Why not?" Nina said, trying to smile.

They decided to watch the musical, *Funny Lady,* the new sequel to *Funny Girl.* The story of the comedienne Fanny Brice cheered Nina up, and by the time they returned home she was feeling lighthearted again.

That night, when she and Roger made love, all she could see were the faces of Dahai and her mother hovering over her. Her body stiffened involuntarily and Roger's hands on her back loosened. "What's the matter?" He caressed her face and saw a flash of discomfort. "Did I hurt you?"

"No, no," she said, stroking his shoulders. "I am just worried about something," she said, then told him what had been bothering her.

Roger listened to her carefully and said, "Let me ask you some questions." He sat up and leaned his back on the headboard. "Do you enjoy sex with me? Tell me the truth."

Seeing Nina nod, he asked another question. "Does that hurt anybody?" Nina shook her head. Roger went on. "You think Dahai is hurt. Do you know where he is? Are you his wife? The answer is no. Is having sex with a lover against the laws or social norms? The answer is the same. So you don't need to feel guilty about your sexual relationship. You're an adult living in Canada now. You loved Dahai and promised him something, but under the circumstances, you don't even know if he's still alive. You can't wait for him forever. There're some things beyond our control in this world."

"Understood," answered Nina, who appreciated his candour. When he spoke, his hand moved as if he were scribbling in the air; his chest muscles vibrated along with his hand and his blonde hair fell over his forehead. His sinewy body reminded her of Michelangelo's *David*, and she reached out to touch him, pulling herself out from under the blanket to sit up next to him. "When you make love to me, don't you feel guilty about your ex-girlfriend?"

"I loved her then, but that's history now," he said, wrapping his arms around her. He pulled her onto his lap. "I've never cheated on any woman. I always trust my own feelings, too." He gently cupped her breasts in his hands. "We both enjoy each other. It doesn't hurt anyone. Your body tells me that you enjoy being touched by me." He bent his head and pushed away her shoulder-length hair. His warm lips caressed her neck, and his thighs trembled under her. Feeling herself melt in his arms, she turned and wrapped her legs tightly around his waist. Her guilt slid into the darkness that belonged to an invisible and remote world.

Nina learned to make blueberry pie from Roger and decided she could earn some money by selling the pies at the farmers' market on weekends.

On a Saturday morning, Roger helped Nina make pies from scratch. He blended flour and Crisco to make pie pastry while she followed a recipe to make the blueberry filling. By the time the second load of four pies came out of the oven and joined the first pies on the kitchen table, half a day had already passed. Hungry enough, Nina felt she could eat up two pies by herself.

After lunch, Roger picked up a calculator. "Let's see how much money you can make." While he looked at the recipes, he keyed in all the costs. "Altogether it costs us fifteen dollars to make the pies, plus free labour. Tell me how much a home-made pie sells for."

"About two dollars," answered Nina. "So, if we sell eight pies we will make sixteen dollars. Oh well, our profit is one dollar if we sell them all."

"Plus the few hours you may spend in the market." Roger snapped his fingers. "Do you still plan to sell them?"

"Definitely not!" Nina picked up a knife and sliced a pie into four pieces. "Let's enjoy them by ourselves."

"Yes!" Roger jumped up from his seat. He took two small plates from the cupboard and placed them on the table. "We'll freeze some for next week."

"Maybe I should think about preparing some Chinese food instead. That might sell well."

"For example?" Roger mumbled as his mouth was full. He took a tissue to clean the purple stains off his fingers.

"Chinese-style ravioli. Dumplings, really."

"I love it. Maybe your Chinese-style ravioli might actually make more money than your pies."

"What do you mean 'my pies'? We made them together."

"No matter what we sell, pies or ravioli, many people will think, based on gender stereotypes, that it's you who make them. So though your pies aren't authentic, your so-called ravioli will be."

"You're sexist and racist," Nina laughed, lifting her hand and pretending to slap his face.

"I most definitely am not!" Roger grabbed her hand. "You look sexy when you're mad. Now, give me a kiss to thank me for all my hard work."

Nina happily obliged.

That afternoon they went to a couple of grocery stores to find the ingredients they would need. Finally, from an Asian food store they bought wonton wrappers that they would use to make the dumplings, which would be filled with ground beef and minced celery. They worked all night.

The next morning, they drove to the farmers' market and filled a table with their homemade Chinese-style ravioli. It was a beautiful morning and the market was full of shoppers. By noon, they were sold out. Back at home, they counted the money they had made, and their profit was six dollars. When Roger told her that amounted to an hourly wage of $1.50, Nina clapped her hands and sighed. "I guess we're what you would call oh so cheap labour."

"It was fun though," Roger said. "We can do this again, and see how it goes. It can be our weekend activity for now." He placed the bills and coins in a box. "This is your capital for next weekend. Let's take a break now."

That night, when Nina went to bed, she fell asleep right away. When she woke up, she walked to the bay window in the living room and looked out. At sunrise, the bay looked as if it were covered by an orange-red carpet, dotted with white seagulls looking for their morning food.

Another beautiful day had started. She suddenly remembered the pies they had made Saturday morning, and a delightful thought crossed her mind. She pulled open the fridge door and took out a blueberry pie. After cutting it into several pieces, she laid one slice on a plate and took a bite. When she imagined Roger saying, *Blueberry pie for breakfast?* she smiled and thought, *the pies we made together are the very best.* Then she put another huge slice on a plate and decided to surprise him with breakfast in bed.

13.

THE FALLEN RED SUN

ON SEPTEMBER 8, 1976, Nina arrived at the Baiyun Airport of Guangzhou — her hometown. Riding on an airport bus and with her eyes wide open, she eagerly looked out the window. Everything looked grey — the buildings, the streets, people's clothes, even the trees, as if dark clouds had been cast over the city for too long. *Does Mother still live in the same building?* When she alighted at the Liuhua Bus Station, she located a phone booth and dialled the number of the Guangzhou Children's Hospital. "May I speak to Dr. Liao?"

"Who's calling?" The person's response sounded impatient.

To avoid possible trouble, Nina said, "I'm her relative. May I speak to her?"

"It seems she has more and more relatives now," the woman said in a louder and more irritated voice. "She's busy. She can't answer the phone."

"Could you please tell the doctor that Nina called?" she asked. "Does she still live on Yuexiu Street North?"

After hearing Nina's politely persistent tone, the person on the phone softened hers. "Yes. I will." Then the line went dead.

Nina decided to go to the old address under the assumption that her mother still lived there. A crowded bus reached the stop where Nina was waiting. She lifted her luggage and stepped on the bus, jamming herself in with all the standing passengers. The air was so sticky and hot that she wished every stop were hers. By the time the vehicle reached her destination, Nina was soaked in sweat. The shade cast by a four-storey brick building on the street in front of her seemed to beckon. She recalled that seven years earlier, she and Rei had paced back and forth in front of the building until she finally had seen her mother's figure in the window. Her steps quickened, and she slipped through the entrance and went slowly upstairs. The mixed odours of food cooking and laundry stirred old memories — Nina and her mother had lived in this building in a one-bedroom apartment. They had been forced to move out of their three-bedroom apartment after her father had been jailed. Half a year later, her father had committed suicide, and her mother had been placed under house arrest. Then Nina had been dispatched to a faraway military farm in Yunnan Province.

Nina mounted the entire flight of stairs to the top floor and laid her suitcase down and against the door to make a seat. In that humid hot afternoon, she perched on the edge of her suitcase, then slid and leaned her back against the door. The clamour of vehicles and bicycle bells came in from the street, and unclear human voices echoed against the building's walls. Soon, she slipped into slumber.

In her dream, she felt like she was being held in somebody's arms. She also heard breathing near her head. Nina opened her eyes and gradually the face before her came into sharp focus. "Mother!" she called out. "Joyful tears trickled down both their cheeks. After eight long years, they were finally in each other's arms again.

"Sweetie!" Her mother pulled Nina to her feet and opened the door. "I don't believe my eyes."

"Did the woman in the office tell you I'd called?" Nina asked as she moved her suitcase into the room.

"Yes, but she didn't say your name." Mother motioned Nina to take a seat. "Are you hungry? I bought some food on the way home," she said, taking three containers out of her tote bag. As she opened them, the aroma of shredded pork with peppers, fried green beans, and plain rice spread into the room. She also removed two buns from another package, which she placed on the kitchen counter for her breakfast the following day. "I'll make some noodles if this isn't enough for us," she said, a wide and happy smile on her face.

"It all smells great," Nina said as she squeezed her mother's arm. She couldn't believe she was finally here, at home, with her mother. She pulled two bowls from the cupboard and two pairs of chopsticks from the wooden holder on the side of the cupboard. She was amazed that she still remembered where everything was after so many years.

"I should've bought some soup too," her mother said, sighing. "I didn't imagine it was you who had called. Nor could I have imagined this wonderful surprise of having you here! I will cook for you tomorrow."

Sitting around the table, the daughter and mother enjoyed the meal that they had not been able to share together for ages. "Did you come from Hong Kong?" asked Mother.

"I came from Canada," Nina said, knowing then that the letters she had sent had never reached her mother.

"Canada? How? In September, 1969, I received a letter from your farm that asked for you to return. I knew something had gone wrong. You hadn't come home..." her mother said. The wrinkles on her forehead seemed to have smoothed. Seeing her daughter again made her eyes beam. "I didn't know the details until a year later when Rei finally got out of jail. He said you had fled to Hong Kong."

Nina was instantly relieved, Rei, her cousin, had survived the shooting during their escape. "How is he?"

"He works in a small factory. Got married a couple of months ago." Mother paused. She placed some more pork and green beans in Nina's bowl. "Eat some more, please. Don't starve yourself."

"I'll make my long story short," Nina responded. "In Hong Kong, I was granted political asylum to the United States. Later,

I moved to Canada. I guess none of my letters ever reached you."

"No, never." Tears trickled down her mother's face. "I only prayed that I would see you one more time before I died."

Nina learned that after her mother's release from house arrest, she had not been allowed to resume her work as a doctor. First, she was asked to work in a factory and then she was sent to work as a caretaker in the hospital where she had worked previously as a doctor. She worked as a caretaker for years as part of the obligatory labour reform, until a doctor shortage meant she was finally permitted to practise medicine again.

They had so many stories to share and so many questions for each other that they talked until well past midnight. Their chat was like a creek flowing through a dark wood till it reached open land and then a hillside; sometimes there were sighs under the moonlight, and sometimes there were loud cheers in the sunshine.

The following morning, Nina's mother went to work as usual. The revolution did not allow anyone to take personal leaves. Serving the country was everybody's priority. Intellectuals had to reform their ideology and behave more carefully. Nina's mother left a key to the apartment on the table before leaving for the hospital.

After getting up late, Nina prepared a bowl of noodles for a western-style brunch. Then she went out for a walk. There were not many people on the street, but in the shade under an apartment building's portico, several elderly people perched on wooden or bamboo chairs were waving their fans. A group of children played noisily around them. In the food and vegetable stores, there were the usual line-ups. Most of the people Nina saw were still dressed in dark colours: dark blue, grey, and military green. Occasionally, Nina saw toddlers wearing bright red, orange, or colourful floral prints. None of the girls or women walking by were wearing skirts. She was glad then that she had made herself unnoticeable by pulling on a navy blue T-shirt and grey slacks instead of her usual summer attire — a pink blouse with a white skirt or shorts. In addition, her two shoulder-length braids not only made her look younger, but it also mirrored the fashion of the other women she saw on the street.

She strolled over to Yuexiu Park where the air seemed clearer and cleaner somehow. There were some elderly people doing Tai Chi or standing under trees swinging their arms back and forth — a sort of exercise. Even though several young women were pushing baby strollers around the flowerbeds, Nina could not shrug off the sensation that many of the elderly persons looked at her as if she were an alien. The few young people in the park suddenly reminded her that most people her age were supposed to be working at some kind of a revolutionary post instead of loitering in a park.

On her way home, she went to a grocery store and joined in a line-up at the meat counter. On her turn, she said, "One pound of ground pork and a half pound of fish fillet, please."

"How many ration coupons do you have?' the clerk asked. "We don't take one and a half coupons. Where have you been living lately?"

Nina looked up at the clerk's blunt face, and only then remembered that, because of the Cultural Revolution, ration coupons were used to buy meat, egg, sugar, bean noodles, and even soy sauce. "Sorry. I've forgotten to bring coupons," Nina mumbled and then left the counter.

"Next!" the clerk said, rolling her eyes.

Maybe I should make a vegetarian supper, Nina thought as she walked to another grocery store although she did not have a bag or basket. After paying for the vegetables she selected, she tied them together with abandoned straw ropes she had found in the store. With one hand, she held a bundle of long string beans and green peppers and with the other she held a bunch of eggplants. She then strolled home. When she reached the building, the elderly people and children were not there anymore since the shade had moved away. The sun was inching westward in the bright sky, but the place looked empty, dead.

Up on the top floor, she opened the door. It was about three o'clock. Still groggy from the jet lag, she decided to nap.

Suddenly, a loud rapping on the door woke her up. She jumped out of the bed. "Who is it?"

"Open the door!" someone shouted.

It was about five o'clock; she wondered what the emergency was. *Fire?* She sniffed but did not smell any smoke.

The knocks resounded, and she rushed to the door. One of her hands slid the metal bar loose; she pulled open the door with the other.

Two seniors stepped in, a man and a woman. Both wore black bands on their left arms. *Poor couple.* A black band on the arm was a sign of death. *Has something horrible happened to their children?* Nina wondered. Before she could say anything, the grey-haired woman spoke. "I'm Zhang. He is Li."

Puzzled, Nina looked at them. "Do I know you?"

"On behalf of the Residents' Committee, we're here to check your residency permit and must ask you a couple of questions. I saw you arrive yesterday," the woman said as she glanced at the man who held a notebook and a pen. Then she stared at Nina. "Who are you? What's your relationship with Dr. Liao?"

When she realized they were here to interrogate her, Nina told herself: *This is China. You have to obey these Residents' Committee members.* "I'm Dr. Liao's daughter. I'm here to visit my mother."

"Why haven't you visited your mother before?" the woman committee member asked. She pulled the arm of her fellow worker and asked, "Have you seen her before?"

"I saw her nine years ago before she left for Yunnan. I haven't seen her since," the elderly man answered, turning to Nina. "Where did you come from?"

"I came from Canada."

"Is it an imperialist country?" the woman asked, her eyes alert. She turned to the man. Then her gaze fell on Nina.

The man sized Nina up, and then he patted his partner. His voice suddenly filled with excitement. "My dear comrade, do you remember Dr. Bethune?" he asked, turning his thin-haired head back and forth between Nina and his comrade.

"Oh," the woman lowered her voice. "Please show your I.D."

Nina went back to the bedroom and returned with her passport. She handed it to them.

The woman looked at the image of an eagle. "Is this a Canadian passport?"

"No. It's American."

"Is Canada in the U.S.?"

"No, but I live in Canada with an American passport," Nina explained. And then she looked at the old man. "Do you remember President Nixon?"

"Yes," the man answered. "Four years ago, Nixon shook hands with Chairman Mao. She is from his country."

The woman turned to the page with Nina's photo and examined Nina's face. "The photo is hers," she told the man, "but I don't understand these foreign words. I can read the numbers though."

The man took the passport to examine it. "It's smaller than our resident booklet. I think our booklet should have a photo on it, too." Then he gave it back to Nina. "Why did you go to America?"

"I visited my uncle." Nina had to have a cover for her escape.

"What does your uncle do there?"

"He's a factory worker."

"Ah, he's like us, working class." The old fellow was pleased. "Is he married?"

"Yes, his wife is black." Nina found herself good at telling white lies.

"Wow! She's our sister from the same class." The senior

woman was contented, remembering how Mao had said that two-thirds of the people in the world lived a miserable life, and that the black people were discriminated against and exploited by capitalists. "Can they speak Chinese?"

"Yes, they only speak Chinese," she answered. A funny feeling rose in her, but she had to stifle it.

"That's good. They still keep our culture. I know it's not easy. I'm glad to know that overseas Chinese work with President Nixon." The woman patted Nina's shoulder. Her voice was filled with sorrow. "Our red sun has fallen. We must be watchful in case any enemy attacks our country at our weakest moment. Do you understand?"

Nina knew "red sun" referred to Mao. *When did he die?* she wondered, but she dared not ask and only said, "Understood."

"We'll come again. We like your mother. She's a trustworthy and revolutionary doctor." The woman and man turned to the door. Their footsteps gradually disappeared from hearing range.

As soon as Nina closed the door, she turned on the radio. The announcer's voice rose along with a dirge: "Our dearest, greatest leader and the reddest sun in our heart has passed away today...."

She drew a deep breath and plopped down in a chair. A thought crossed her mind: *China's last emperor has finally gone West.*

The next day was Friday. Nina went shopping and with ration coupons from her mother, she bought a box of egg cakes, a packet of soft candy, and a silk quilt cover that she would bring with her on her visit to see Rei.

Anxiously and feverishly, Nina had to wait till the evening to visit Rei since he and his wife worked long hours during the day. She took a bus and then headed to a one-storey building where they had had to live with Rei's grandmother since the couple had no chance of being allotted an apartment. The door opened, and a man with a light beard and crew-cut hair stared at her as if he had seen a ghost.

"Rei! It's me! Nina," she whispered.

"Is it true?" Rei murmured. Then he turned and called out with joy. "Grandma, look who's here!" He gestured Nina over to an elderly woman who sat in an armchair.

"How have you been doing for all these years?" Rei's grandmother pointed to a chair near her. "Sit down. Rei said you have been in Hong Kong. Is he right?"

"Yes and no." Nina held one arm of Rei's grandmother. "Grandmother, did you ever get any of my letters from Hong Kong?"

"Never," the old woman said.

"They must've been stopped somewhere," Nina said, placing the boxes of cake and candy into her lap. "I hope you like these."

Nina turned to the smiling young woman who had finished preparing the table. "Are you Rei's wife?"

The woman nodded. "I'm Ahua," she said, arranging some cups on the table. "Help yourself to some tea."

"I hope you like this quilt cover," Nina said, handing Ahua the package. As she did so, she noticed that the red paper cutting with the Chinese character "double happiness" under a portrait of Chairman Mao on the wall had faded a little. "Is that from your wedding?"

"Yes, Grandma likes that word and intends to keep it there for good," Ahua explained.

"It's very nice. Congratulations," Nina said and then turned to Rei. "I have been so worried about you all this time, wondering what might have happened to you that night I heard gunshots. Did you get shot by the military patroller?"

"A bullet grazed my arm. I was lucky. The PLA solders didn't know you were with me. I lied and told them that I'd lost direction when I rowed the boat for fun. They didn't believe me but couldn't find anything suspicious since I'd dropped all my stuff into the water before they reached me. Anyway, I was still put behind bars for a year."

Nina told him her own brief story, and Rei listened in amazement. When they talked about Mao's death they quickly realized they shared the same sentiment. "I'm sure things will change soon."

Rei told her about his wife. "We're both working at the same factory now. Back in high school, she was two years my junior. She returned to the city after getting her re-education in the country." Rei's face glowed under the light. "We're expecting some opportunity before we're too old."

"What opportunity?" Nina asked.

"Not sure. Maybe the opportunity of going to college. It seems impossible though. I have a criminal record. Ahua's father is still a revolutionary target."

"Grandma wants to go to bed," Ahua called.

The old woman said goodnight, and with Ahua's help, she shuffled to her bed in a corner.

"It's eleven-thirty." Rei looked at his watch and told his wife he would walk Nina to the bus stop and be back soon.

Nina could not decline Rei's offer and went with him to the bus stop. They waited for a while, but no bus came. Rei decided to accompany her all the way home. He did not think it was safe for her to walk alone at night. "I've been practicing kung fu. I know how to fight if needed."

By the time Nina reached her mother's building, all the windows were dark except for the one in her mother's room. The light made her heart swell with warm feelings. *Mother's waiting up for me,* she thought. She felt as if she were a little girl again, yearning to be home after being away all day long. Nina waved goodbye to Rei and hastened up the stairs.

14.

LOST SHEEP

WHEN NINA SAID she planned to visit the former military farm in Yunnan where she had laboured years earlier, her mother offered to pay for a berth on the train. Booking that type of seat required an approval from the authorities, and it was usually unavailable to ordinary passengers.

Mother said, "I have savings of seven hundred yuan that can pay for ten such trips."

"I didn't bring any money to you. How can I use yours?"

"Silly girl." Mother chuckled. "What else can I use the money for? I have more money than I need. In addition, I get some compensation for your father from the naval academy."

Nina looked into her mother's shining eyes and was touched. "Thanks."

"You're my only child. My extra money is yours."

Several days later, Nina boarded an express train to Kunming City. When she located her sleeping car, three passengers were already sitting on two of the lower bunks. Hers was at the top of triple bunks in the compartment. She greeted the people and placed her travel bag under the lower bed since all the higher berths were still folded against the wall.

The other passengers were middle-aged and well-groomed. Two men in white shirts and dark blue pants were seated next to a woman who moved inward to leave some space for Nina to sit. "You have a nice T-shirt," she said to Nina with a smile

"Thank you," Nina said, noting her neighbour's white blouse and olive green skirt. "Do you work in the army?" she asked.

"Yes," the military woman said, nodding and smiling. When the other men went outside, she asked, "Do you speak English?"

"Yes. Sure," Nina answered in English, astonished. "How did you know?"

"I gathered from your T-shirt and from the way you spoke," the woman said in a hushed voice. "I studied in the U.S. thirty years ago."

"Are you a doctor?" Nina asked, wondering about her life in China since then.

"You guess right, too," the woman said with a grin. She pressed a few loose hairs under a black hair clip on the right side of her head. "I survived the Cultural Revolution. At the beginning, I was treated as an outcast because of my training in the U.S., and then confined, but later they realized they needed me to do medical research. Therefore, I've been sheltered from the political chaos. Are you a student in the U.S.?"

"I graduated this year. I've come back to see my mother, who is also a doctor."

On the same wavelength as Nina, the woman was open about her own past. From the conversation, Nina learned more about the treatment of people who were trained in the U.S. during the Cultural Revolution. Like her father, they had all been deemed potential enemies of the State or obstacles to the revolutionary cause.

When the other passengers returned, they stopped speaking in English, and started to converse in Chinese, chatting pleasantly about weather and daily life.

In the evening, two more passengers joined them. They managed to open the upper berths and Nina climbed to her top bunk and read a book.

Two days later, the train finally arrived at Kunming. The army doctor gave Nina a note with an address. "We have a military hostel in the city. It's safe and inexpensive. Tell them

I sent you. The person in charge is my former student."

"Thanks so much." Nina shook her hand. "I hope your dream of revisiting your alma mater will come true."

"Thank you for refreshing my rusty English. I do hope to visit my alma mater in New York someday. Who knows?" The doctor strode to a soldier waiting for her on the platform. Because civilians and soldiers wore such dark colours, the doctor quickly merged in the crowd and disappeared.

Nina found the hostel the doctor had recommended and got a single bedroom. The following morning, as planned, she arrived at Spring City University to look for the address of Dahai's mother, Meihua Wei. She used to be an art professor at the university before being incarcerated in a labour camp. Even if she was not out of the camp, at the very least Nina might be able to meet with some of his other family members, from whom she could learn, hopefully, Dahai's whereabouts. On her way to the administration building, some of his words ran through her mind again: "If I die, find my brother and sister. Tell them my story." Her heart tightened, and her steps became heavier. *I'm here to find out about you, Dahai.*

At the front desk, she was redirected to a clerk in an office at the end of the hallway. Nina walked up to the reception and politely introduced herself. "Good morning. I am Nina Huang. Could you tell me if Meihua Wei or her family still live on campus?"

The woman stared at her. "Who are you?"

"I'm her former student," Nina answered politely.

"You don't sound like you're from here," the clerk said in an unpleasant voice.

"I came from Guangzhou," she explained. "I have a business meeting in Kunming. I'd like to have a brief visit with her." She selected her words carefully, not wanting to cause any suspicion.

"You must have a high-paying job in order to travel this far," the woman said, sitting back. "You graduated from here?"

"No. She tutored me when I was a child," Nina said, aware that lying about being a graduate might cause trouble.

After looking Nina up and down with the scowl on her face, the clerk finally shrugged and turned to look through a pile of booklets she withdrew from a black cabinet that towered against the back wall of the office. She pulled one of the booklets out of the pile and laid it on her desk, then leafed through it quickly. Finally, her gaze fell on a specific page. She was curt. "The Wei family lives at Apartment 202 in a five-storey staff dormitory that faces a basketball court."

Relieved, Nina's heart returned to its normal beat. "Could you please tell me the name of the building?"

"Number Ten." The clerk closed her booklet.

Nina exhaled, thanked her, and left. High-spirited, she walked and prayed that Dahai's mother had been released from the labour camp.

Finally, she found Number Ten, and entered the building. As she stood in front of Apartment 202, she took a deep breath. Hesitating for only a second, she lifted her hand and knocked on the door. The door opened and an oversized woman appeared, her wrinkled forehead covered with wispy grey bangs. "Who are you looking for?"

"Is Professor Wei at home?" Nina asked, remembering what Dahai had told her. "I think you are Yao."

"Yes. Who are you?"

"I'm an old friend of Dahai's."

The grey-haired woman looked her quizzically. "A friend?" She shook her head with astonishment. "After all these years?"

"Is he here?" Nina asked, a gleam of anticipation in her eyes. She wiped the beads of sweat off her forehead, and smiled politely at the older woman.

"Come on in."

Yao turned around, her two thick grey braids, ends tied together, swishing softly against her back. Nina followed her inside and sat down on the closest chair.

Yao set a glass of hot tea on the table. "Help yourself," she said, and then added, "You're his friend, but don't you know what's happened to him?"

Every nerve in Nina's body tingled. Holding her breath, she asked, "Is he all right? We have been out of touch for some time."

"I am sorry, but he is dead," Yao said, wiping her eyes with the hem of her apron.

The last thread of hope snapped. A black balloon had suddenly popped in front of Nina's face and all went dark. Her hand reached out and took Yao's arm. "How?" was the only word she could sound out.

"Many years ago, a young man from Burma brought me Dahai's last letter," Yao said, rubbing her forehead lightly with her fingers. "I remember now. It was 1971."

"Was that fellow named Wang?" Nina remembered Dahai's plan.

"Yes, yes," Yao said. "His name was on the tip of my tongue. My memory isn't as good as yours."

"Do you have the letter?"

"His mother has it. You need to wait for her."

Nina wept. Yao patted Nina on her shoulder while her other hand continued to pull the hem of her apron to wipe the tears pouring down her own face. Nina nestled her head in her arms on the table, and the sorrow she felt was accentuated with every pat of Yao's compassionate hand. When the door opened, Nina lifted her head and watched a woman enter the room. Yao stood and shuffled over to her, speaking to her in soft tones.

The woman looked to be in her early fifties, but her shoulder-length hair was greying, and her face was covered in spidery lines that spoke to a life of worry and hardship. Nina gazed into her deep-set, light-brown eyes, and right away she recognized Dahai. "Mrs. Wei?" Nina assumed she was Dahai's mother. "I was Dahai's friend. Yao has told me the shocking news."

The woman nodded and gave her a slight smile. "Let's go out for lunch. We can talk about Dahai. I don't want my other children to overhear us as I don't want them to be upset. Knowing less is better for them, and makes things easier for them at school too."

"Yes, of course," Nina said, rising from her chair.

"Wait a second," Mrs. Wei said, as she went into another room, and then quickly returned with something that she slipped into her bag.

Nina followed her to a restaurant that served rice noodles. Since it was early for lunch hour, they got their seats right away. "The beef noodles are a delicacy in this city," said Mrs. Wei, who ordered two large bowls. "It's my treat."

As they ate the rice noodles, Nina started her story from the moment she had discussed her escape plan with Dahai. Despite the fact it was her first time meeting Dahai's mother, Nina felt as though she had known her for years, so she also told her everything that had happened to her in Hong Kong as well as her experiences in North America.

When Nina mentioned taking her citizenship oath in front of the American flag, she could hear the first line of the American national anthem resound in her ears: *O! say can you see by the dawn's early light, what so proudly we hailed at the twilight's last gleaming....*

Dahai's mother listened attentively to the description of that solemn event, and the last lyric of the anthem, "The Star-Spangled Banner," flashed through her mind as well: "*O'er the land of the free and the home of the brave.*" She had told Nina that she had actually been born in America and that she had come to China to find her father and then never left. She missed America but felt happy for Nina: *This brave girl has reached the free land.* Slowly, Dahai's mother took out a sheet of paper from her purse and gave it to Nina. "This is Dahai's letter that Wang brought to Yao five years ago. I didn't have the chance to meet him as I was in jail then."

"I know Wang. He and Dahai planned to join the Vietnam War together," Nina said, "but I don't know why they ended up in Burma." Holding the page with her trembling hands, she read it and learned that Dahai and Wang had not reached Vietnam, and had instead joined the People's Army led by the Communist Party of Burma, and fought to liberate the Burmese poor people. In the letter, Dahai had told Yao, and his brother and sister, that if he died, his blood would wash away his parents' anti-revolutionary crimes. After reading it twice, Nina stared at the date of on the page: March 22, 1970, and the memory of an old nightmare came suddenly to mind. It was a dream she had had on an Easter Sunday night, years ago, a dream about a fallen lamb, its face stained with blood and its feet struggling to stand. "I understand my dream now," she said to Mrs. Wei.

Mrs. Wei said, "According to what Wang told Yao, that battle started on the Thursday. Dahai fell on the Sunday." She pulled a handkerchief out of her pocket and dabbed her eyes. "I know the 1970 calendar by heart. One week after Dahai wrote this letter, it was Easter Sunday. And that is the day he passed away. Don't you see? Your dream predicted his death."

Shocked at the realization that her vision of the dead sheep coincided with Dahai's death, Nina shuddered. Something had happened beyond her understanding. Her nightmare six years earlier had been a sign of Dahai's fate, but she had not accepted it until now. She looked at Mrs. Wei and saw a mixed facial expression. To comfort her, Nina explained, "Back then, us youth, we were easily and stupidly fooled by all the propaganda. We were duped. And not many of us knew what we were doing."

"I wish he'd fled with you," murmured Dahai's mother. Touched by Nina's words, she added, "We of the older generation were and even now are also mixed up." She stretched out her hand to Nina. "Forget Dahai. Enjoy your new life in Canada."

"What about you? Do you plan to return to the States?" Nina placed the letter back into Dahai's mother's hand.

"I have so many matters to deal with," Mrs. Wei explained. "I am still looking for my Chinese father and hope to find him some day. My mother still lives in Boston. She planned to visit us last month, but her visa was rejected." She sighed audibly, and patted Nina's hand. "Now after Mao's death, things may eventually change. Then we shall see."

Nina nodded. In hesitation, she asked, "Can I meet Dahai's brother and sister? I promised him."

"Sure, but please don't mention Dahai. Stay with us for supper. I'll introduce you as my former student."

Nina agreed but she needed to go back to her hostel before visiting with Dahai's family later that afternoon. After saying goodbye to Dahai's mother, she walked to a bus stop. Through the branches of the tall fir trees, she looked up at the sky which was a clear and beautiful blue. A few white clouds clustered together seemed to take the shape of a flock of sheep standing at the foot of a mountain. *The lambs have grown up into sheep. Mao is dead, and the dark days will go away entirely,* she thought with relief.

Roger popped into her mind and she wondered what he was doing. She took a deep breath and smiled as she realized that she could now love him wholly and deeply. In Guangzhou, she had called him once at the general post office to tell him of her safe arrival, but she hadn't spoken to him since, and now she missed him. She decided to send him a postcard and tell him what she had learned. He would be happy, she thought.

Her next destination was Jinghong County where the Number Five Military Farm was situated. A long-distance bus took her to the county bus terminal.

In the dusk, she strode to Tiande Village to find Zeng, who had helped her escape years earlier. Under the moonlight, she groped for a tall oak tree and turned right. Then a walled yard appeared in front of her. The yard gate, which was made from various tree branches, was ajar. From the opening, she saw someone sitting by the door of the dimly-lit house. "Is Zeng at home? I'm a friend," she called out.

"She moved out a while ago," answered a teenage boy. "Where are you from? I'm her brother."

"Earthy, it's Nina. Are your folks at home?"

"Hello! Come on in. I remember you," the seventeen-year-old boy said, turning around to beckon his parents who were inside the house.

Zeng's parents were surprised and pleased to see Nina. Zeng's mother kept telling Nina that her mother's medical team had visited the village in 1952. "You know, she taught me how to write and read. Is she still as tall and healthy as before?"

"Yes, she is." Nina took a few packages from her satchel and laid them on the table. "These gifts are for you, from my mother."

Nina discovered that Zeng had married and now lived in an apartment allotted by her husband's work unit. Earthy promised to take her there the next morning.

Zeng's mother cooked some noodles and fried eggs for supper, and Nina accepted their invitation to stay overnight. The air was heavy with the odour of pig feed, but it did not bother her, and she slept soundly.

The next afternoon, Nina finally met with Zeng in her new home. They greeted each other warmly and held each other's hands, jumping up and down like two excited children. "Is it true? You are really here!" Zeng screamed with joy, her eyes brightened, and her long braids shook on her chest. She pulled her two-year-old boy to Nina. "Call her Aunt Nina." The boy raised his head, mumbled a few words out of a partially toothless mouth, and fidgeted with a broken wooden train. When Nina placed a piece of candy in his hand, he forgot the train. His fingers pulled the wrapper and saliva trickled out from a corner of his mouth as he smiled at her gleefully.

Zeng told Nina that she had gotten married the same year after Nina left. Her daughter was a first grader and in school. "I'm a lucky woman. Then I had a son who is as strong as a calf," Zeng said, a satisfied look on her round face.

Nina was happy for Zeng who seemed content with life. They reminisced for a while and Nina confessed that she yearned to hear about her former workmates. "Have you heard anything about the Number Five Farm?"

"Not too much." Zeng scoured her memory. "Wait a second. A couple of years ago, a young man was executed."

"Why?"

"He was caught sneaking across the border into Vietnam. You'll find out the details when you get there."

Nina's heart skipped a beat, and she sighed loudly. *Another lost sheep.*

After Zeng's daughter and husband come back, Nina had supper with the family. Zeng persuaded Nina to stay overnight. "My hubby can sleep on the temporary bed in the living room."

Zeng also passed along a message to her neighbour, whose truck passed by the military farm every day, about Nina's plan to visit the farm on the following day. He would let Nina's co-workers know she was coming.

Excited about the get-together with her former co-workers, Nina prayed that no trouble would arise.

15.

REMOTE CORNER

EARLY THE NEXT MORNING, Zeng left her children in the care of her husband. The two young women cycled over to the Number Five Military Farm, and Zeng led the way through fields of different crops.

Tall and dense, each corn stalk carried two or three ears of corn. Some of the fields were filled with tomato plants, which bore egg-shaped or apple-sized fruit. Some were covered with weeds and bushes; the scent of numerous and nameless wild-flowers penetrated the air. *Across mountains, rivers, and an ocean, I am back here. And right here, on this land, many youths have shed their blood and sweat.* Nina's thoughts drifted back to seven years earlier and then to the present. Many memories of labouring on this land flooded her mind.

Nina and Zeng approached a large brick structure that was finished with a mixture of mud and straw as its roof. Zeng said it was the place for their get-together that day. Two gas-powered tractors stood in front of the building, and stacks of large baskets, bamboo shoulder poles, and hoes lay or stood against the walls. Nina remembered that the building had once been a dormitory for thirty workers. Zeng told her that the building was now used as a garage to keep tractors and store tools.

The ringing of their bicycle bells brought a couple bustling out of the building. "Welcome back, you lucky dog!" said the man, who then pointed to his companion, and announced, "My wife."

"I remember you both! Huguo and Dongfang," Nina said. "I admired your bravery." She shook hands with Huguo and hugged the woman, Dongfang.

The lovers finally formed a family. Nina recalled that the couple had once been criticized for falling in love with each other. Nobody on the farm was allowed to have love affairs. But that had not stopped them, nor had they tried to hide their secret. Nina had always insisted on meeting Dahai secretly so as to avoid detection. Thinking about that ridiculous rule now, Nina sighed and shook her head.

Dongfang held Nina. "You haven't forgotten us, old friend. We heard a rumour that you vanished."

"We were here earlier to clear out the place for our gathering today. The other friends will join us soon," said Huguo.

"I'll leave you here and come to get you this evening," Zeng told Nina. She waved her hand to the others. "Enjoy yourselves."

"Nina will stay with us at least until tomorrow. If you're interested, you're welcome to join us tonight," said Dongfang, who then looked at Nina for her consent.

"Go look after your family, Zeng. Tomorrow I'll come back by myself," Nina said, waving her hand to say goodbye.

"Don't worry. Nina is under our care now," Huguo said, popping out his muscular arms. "I can fight if I have to." Zeng laughed, waved back, and turned her bike around for the journey back to her home.

Nina followed the couple into the garage. A girl of three sat on a stool and clutched a stick, which she trailed across the floor. "Mama, I'm helping the ants find their home."

"This is our daughter," Dongfang said to Nina. She turned to her daughter, and said, "Yaya, come say hello to your American auntie."

"Why am I introduced this way?" Nina asked, looking surprised.

Dongfang said, "You're from the American continent, right?"

Nina, thinking about her American citizenship, chuckled at

her new title and said, "Okay." She then pulled a paper bag out of her satchel and laid it in Yaya's hands "Yaya, this is yours."

"I've never seen you before, American auntie," the little girl said, looking up at her. "Is America far away?" She held the package. After taking a look inside, she took out a few pieces of candy and gave them to her parents.

"Take the whole pack," Nina persuaded.

"Mama always tells me not to be greedy. I'll get one more." Yaya put her hand into the package.

Touched by her words, Nina said to Yaya, "Well, you can share some of the candy with the other kids when they get here."

Yaya nodded and clutched the package in her hands. "Thank you."

Soon other people, twelve of them, from Shanghai and Chongqing, joined them. Some of them brought their children. One woman, Kali, had two kids; the younger one was cradled in her arms. She turned to the middle-aged man following her, and said, "Leave your vegetable basket here. You can go home now. My friends will take care of us."

Dongfang said to Nina, "Kali's husband is a local peasant who always follows her everywhere. He's afraid she'll leave him if he isn't with her." She laughed out loud as she ushered Kali and her children to some chairs that had been set up in a corner of the room.

Nina went over to speak to Kali, pulling up a chair beside her. The peasant husband loitered around for a while and finally left.

Whole chickens were steamed in a huge wok, corncobs were roasted in the bonfire, fish soup was reheated, and vegetables were stir-fried. Everybody got excited since they had not had such a festive occasion together for years. Some of the children were experiencing such a joyful gathering for the first time in their lives. The cheers, singing, and kids' babbling almost blew off the thin roof.

Nina handed one hundred yuan to Huguo. "Can you use the money to buy some useful stuff as my gift to everyone? I don't know what to buy."

"I can't take it. You have a long journey. You need money."

"Compared to you guys, I have an easy life. I beg you to have it. Otherwise, I won't eat the dinner."

"Whoa, hunger strike?" Huguo shook the bills. "This is a monthly salary for more than three workers."

Nina laid on the table two bottles of wine she had bought in Kunming, a red and a white.

The wine was poured into ceramic mugs and the group toasted each other. "For Nina's visit, for our wasted youth, and for our sorrowful past," offered one friend. For the second toast, Huguo quoted an ancient catchphrase: "Let's get wealthy, but not forget one another." This well-known phrase was from the peasant uprising led by Chen Sheng and Wu Guang in 209 BC. After overthrowing Emperor Qin Shi Huang, Chen Sheng and Wu Guang became emperors themselves. Every adult remembered the countrymen's uprising, which had been taught in elementary school, so they repeated Huguo's toast with giggles.

"I'm no longer a naïve city teenager. I'm a peasant making a living with a hoe in my hand, dependent upon the heavens," a man said in a mocking voice.

"We've been working here on the farm for eight years," a woman said with a sigh.

"We may never get rich, but we won't forget each other," Dongfang said.

"That's right," many in the group shouted out together. "Nina still remembers us."

As she pondered the uprising almost two thousand years earlier, Nina was struck by a thought. *Is China going to experience another uprising after Mao's death? Isn't Mao himself the leader of uprising peasants?* In history, when peasants suffered and felt desperate, they rebelled. If she had been among those countrymen, she would have joined in their riots. But she wondered if the uprising was successful, would another ruler enforce a similar regime? Would history repeat itself? She asked herself these questions, but did not have any answers.

While they devoured the festive food, the chatter was lively and numerous stories were shared about old friends who had left the farm. One person told what he had heard about Dahai and Wang, those two daredevils. Nina did not mention what she knew about Dahai's death. Since nobody else had known about their relationship, she did not need to show them this scar or drop such a bombshell, but a sadness like an invasion of invisible flies did battle all over her skin.

"I remember a rumour about Dahai and Wang. I heard that after they ran away in August, 1969, they earned medals from a battle in Vietnam. Even I thought about crossing the border to join in the Vietnam War, but I dared not. Jingsheng did, but he got caught," one person said.

Jingsheng? Nina searched her memory. She remembered him as a medium-built young man with glasses whom everyone had nicknamed "Ancient Poet" since he could recite many poems by Li Bai and Du Fu. She asked, "What happened then?"

"You want to know?" Huguo said. "I'll never forget it. Jingsheng was arrested on the border by the People's Liberation Army's patrol team and sent back to the farm to be denounced. Do you remember Chairman Yang? He organized a denunciation meeting, but none of us said anything against Jingsheng. Even though we were warned that we would lose our chance of visiting our parents if we didn't cooperate. Yang found his authority challenged, so he contacted the Public Security Bureau and they put Jingsheng in jail.

"A couple of days later, I remember, Yang announced the shocking news that Jingsheng would be executed because he had betrayed the country. When the day came, all of us got up early. We didn't go to work in the field but trudged to the place used to shoot death-row criminals. It was our sympathy strike although we didn't call it that out loud. We told one another, 'The law can't punish everyone. They can't put all of us into jail.'

"The execution spot was at the bottom of a rocky hill that had been surrounded by armed soldiers. Nobody was allowed to get close to it, so we stood with other onlookers to watch the execution. Jingsheng was forced to kneel on the ground. They gagged his mouth with a thick rope and pushed his head down.

"The ruling class always practise the idiom, 'to kill a chicken is to scare the monkey,' but at that moment, we monkeys weren't completely frightened. We had our way to protest. Kill-one-to-warn-a-hundred didn't work that time. Instead, hundreds of hearts and brains came together to protest this cruelty.

"When the gunshots echoed in the valley, Jingsheng fell into the pit in front of him. I still remember his blood spattering on the weeds around his head. I cried, and many watchers cried, even though men were not expected to shed tears. Even now, whenever I think about it, I tear up. Any one of us could have ended up like him. I looked at his body and felt my heart stop beating. Right after the soldiers left, all the farm workers rushed down the hill. Another man and I had brought a stretcher with us. We placed the dead body on it, and four of us carried it away. All the others followed us. On our way home, everyone took a turn in bringing home the remains of Jingsheng.

"In our twelve-person dorm room, we washed Jingsheng's body and dressed him in the best outfit we could find. Everybody chipped in. We used the money to get a casket. We couldn't get his parents here right away as they were far away in Beijing, but we did everything we could on behalf of his family. We read his favourite poem by Li Bai, 'Long Yearning.' Anybody remember the poem?"

Many voices responded:

Above the dark night stands the sky
Beneath the green water the tides rise

Along the long path in the endless sky,
my bitter spirit flies
The dream of my soul can't get through as the mountain pass lies
Long yearning
My broken heart sighs.

Listening to the stanza, Nina burst into tears.

Huguo continued. "Jingsheng was buried on the top of a hill, and a tombstone was set facing north. We believed his soul could see his family and vice versa. For the next three days, nobody went to work. We took turns sitting around the tomb because we were ready to fight if the authorities sent people to destroy it.

"We returned to work on the fourth day, and a military truck came and arrested five of us workers. By the time the truck drove the captives away, the news of the arrest had spread to the other 996 workers who arrived at the local court on foot and sat around the building.

"That was the first time we re-educated youth organized ourselves to stand up for our basic right to bury a body. We refused to be treated like ants or flies. We are human beings. We insisted on our human dignity. Guess what happened? More than two thousand other youths from different military farms came, and even some local peasants also joined us. Finally, after the provincial court placed an order, the local court had to release the five jailed workers. We won!"

The story touched Nina deeply, and she felt a shiver from head to toe. She, too, would have been shot if she had been caught red-handed on Defence Road, or caught jumping into the water on that dark night.

From their reminiscences, Nina learned that several years earlier, some dispatched young people had found different excuses for returning to their home cities.

One of the men said, "We all are eager to leave, but Mao's directive wanted us to settle down in these rural areas for the rest of our lives. A man from Shanghai named Ting Huimin is trying to organize a petition to send to the Central Committee of the Communist Party of China in Beijing to allow us to return home. All of us who came here in 1968, like you, will sign the petition."

When Nina thought about the reality of her former fellow workers' circumstances, she felt wretched for the unfair treatment they had received in life. They had not had any chance to choose their own future, such as an education, a job, or even a place to live. What Rei had told her then came to mind, so she asked, "Do you think someday everyone will have a chance to go to college?"

"My dream was shattered when the Cultural Revolution started," a woman said. "But I hope my daughter will have a chance. I've been teaching her how to read and do math since she turned three."

"My city has abandoned me. Hopefully, my son will return there," a man sighed.

"Maybe the sun will rise from the West someday," said Huguo. "Old Man Mao didn't live forever like what we had been led to believe. Isn't that right?" Seeing others nod, he continued, "Let's look on the bright side. Things will look up if we don't give up."

"Right now, let's put the kids to bed. They're tired out," Dongfang reminded the others. As the parents unfolded the blankets on the pallets for their children to sleep on, the moonlight filtered through the windows and mingled with the light emitted from the kerosene lamps in the room.

"Let's sing," one person suggested.

"Look at the full moon outside, bright and nice," another responded. "How about singing the song, 'Dating at Aobao'?"

All of them hummed along. Nina's memory of those lyrics came back, and she joined in the singing: *"The moon on the fifteenth rises in the sky. Why are there no beautiful clouds around?"*

When the lyrics of "The Song of the Sent-down Youth" started, Nina sobbed with the crowd who had lost their green years to hard labour. Tears of lamentation on each face glittered in the moonlight that now streamed through the windows, and each pair of eyes reflected the flame of the kerosene lamps. Originally composed by a young man named Ren Yi, dispatched from Nanjing, the song had been popular among the entire young generation who were sent to the countryside.

We go to the field in the sunrise
We drag ourselves home in the moonlight
To repair the earth we dig with sigh
We even try to change the sky.

Then, they lifted up their voices in the verses they had collectively composed behind the scenes on the Number Five Military Farm.

Born in Red China
We were taught to be loyal to Mao.
As Red Guards in the Revolution
We fought to defend Mao.
From peasants we get re-education
We settle in remote corners now.

These songs had accompanied them everywhere during those unforgettable years. The lyrics had described their wondering minds, their critical thoughts, and their struggling lives, every endless dismal day and starless night.

The moon eventually inched up high into the sky. In a faraway place, the last dog's barking faded. Exhausted, each person leaned against the wall or lay down with her or his own child. Her heart pumping with powerful emotion, Nina felt so close to each person, it was as if she had never left.

Her eyelids heavy, she eventually fell into a deep sleep on a bundle of branches in the corner while the first early rooster crowed in the distance.

16.

AN AMERICAN SPY ON THE RUN

AWAKENED BY THE children giggling and the adults talking, Nina sat up in her bedroll and squinted in the penetrating sunlight to look around. Some of the parents were helping their children dress, while others were feeding their toddlers water and pancakes. Several persons stood around Kali's husband as she fed her two children. Once finished, the husband grabbed his little daughter's hand, while the other was stretched out to his wife who held the baby boy in her arms.

"You made up this story, right?" a man with a brush cut asked, his voice anxious.

"I think what he said is true," said Huguo. "Let's wake up Nina and the others."

"I'm up now." Nina pulled herself up off the floor and asked, "What's happened?"

"This fellow," answered Huguo, gesturing to the local peasant, "came to tell us that the Party Secretary of the village heard about you. He's organizing the militia and coming soon to interrogate you as an American spy. Our friend here wants to take his kids and wife home, but Kali doesn't want to go."

Nina walked up to Kali and smiled at her. "For safety's sake, take your children home." She turned to the others. "All of us should leave here as soon as possible."

"No, we'll see what the militia plans to do to us," the man with the brush cut said.

One woman responded, "Don't forget that 'eggs must not quarrel with stones.' We should evade the militia."

At that moment, many younger farm workers arrived at the gate. "We're here to support you. More will come."

"Thank you all." Huguo turned around and raised his voice: "Listen, everyone. We have nobody from America. Okay? Nina is from Guangzhou. She's our former co-worker, right?"

"Yes. How could an American get to this part of the country?" someone else called out.

Huguo spoke to Nina, "You should leave right now. I'll drive you to the bus terminal."

"I'm sorry to cause this trouble." Nina took her satchel and turned to the others. "My friends, I enjoyed being with you. Thanks for your friendship and time. We'll see each other again." She asked Dongfang to take care of the bicycle and return it to Zeng for her.

Some people cried out, "Goodbye" and "Take care."

After starting one of the tractors, Huguo asked Nina to stand on the bottom step next to his seat and to hold tightly to the metal bar of the seat. "No matter how soon the militia comes, they definitely can't catch up with my powerful engine," he said with a confident smile. The machine then jerked and inched forward on the muddy road.

They arrived at Zeng's home where Nina picked up her bag and hastily said goodbye to Zeng and her family. Then, she and Huguo were on the run again.

At the bus terminal, Nina gave her mailing address to Huguo. "I don't know if your letter can reach anyone outside of China. Here's my mother's address. You can contact her. Don't put yourself in trouble for this 'American spy' incident."

Huguo replied, "Don't worry. I will survive. Winter's gone; spring's come around. Take good care of yourself."

Nina boarded a bus. From the window, she watched Huguo's tractor disappear from sight down the dusty street. Her heartbeat eventually returned to normal.

At the Kunming Railway Station, after lining up for several hours in the booking office, Nina bought a ticket to Guangzhou. When she finally located her seat on the train, she felt as if she had won the lottery. *I'm finally out of the reach of the militia*, she thought with relief when she laid her pack under the seat and sat next to a man whose gaze was fixed on whatever was outside the window. Across from her bench was a couple engrossed in conversation.

Nina noticed the man next to her was wearing a clean but faded blue shirt with several patches. His greying hair suggested that he was in his late fifties. As the train started, the view of buildings in various sizes moved past; streets and roads faded away. Soon, vegetable fields and rice paddies came into view. His gaze never wavered from the window. It was as if he was memorizing every building, every road, and every field that hurried past.

About an hour later, the man finally turned his head to look at Nina. "Where are you going?" he asked.

"Guangzhou."

"That's far away. You're going home?" he asked, his heavy eyes blinking rapidly as they adjusted to the interior of the train after having faced the sunlight for so long.

"Yes. What about you?"

"I'm going to see my son in the country." His face was clouded, but he seemed eager to talk. "He broke his legs during a rock blasting operation," he said, his knuckles gently rapping the table in front of him. "My son and daughter both settled in the countryside in 1968. Last year, in the factory where my late wife used to work, there was a job available for one of our children, who was allowed to work and live in Kunming. My son let his sister take the opportunity. Now with his shattered legs, he has no chance of finding a good job or even of farming well." He drew in a deep breath. "My boy is suffering so much. I'm going to take him home."

"Where is he?" Nina asked, her heart breaking for him.

"Red Water River County. He could've chosen a closer area, but he decided to go there. He told us that during the Long March in 1935, Mao's Red Army had passed the Red Water River. So he was determined to get a revolutionary education there. He's so headstrong," said the man, his eyes shining with pride for his son. "His sister went with him. Two heads are better than one. My wife used to cry because she missed them so much. Now their mother is gone, but my son's still there. My third child, a daughter, is in high school. Hopefully, she doesn't have to receive re-education. I am working class," the man smirked. "She can get re-education from me."

The couple on the opposite seat were listening to his story along with Nina. They shared the story of their daughter who had settled in a nearby village so they could visit her more often. The husband said, "Besides, because I work on the railway, and we have free tickets to travel."

"You are lucky," the grey-haired man next to Nina said. "This is my first time on the train in fifteen years. I haven't been able to afford to buy a ticket. I still have two kids who don't have jobs." He then asked about any possibilities of getting a job with the railway. The couple gave him their names and address. "We're working class. We should help one another. Come to see us when you're back in Kunming again."

The husband checked his watch and said they had about twenty minutes before they had to get off at the next station. "Since we have gotten to know each other a little bit, let me tell you something else." He looked around to make sure no one looked suspicious. "I've been to a foreign country."

The grey-haired man stared incredulously at the younger man across from him. "You don't mean the country across the ocean with high-nosed devils?"

"Not the high-nosed in the West. The people I met were Black," answered the railway man, with a chuckle.

"You've been to Africa, then?" asked the older man, his head tilted toward the storyteller.

"Yes, I was in Tanzania for a year," the younger man lowered his voice. "And guess what?"

"Our Black brothers only had dark bread to eat," the older man replied without hesitation.

"You're wrong, ha!" The railway worker said, his hand slapping his thigh excitedly. "They eat and dress better than us. Their streets are clean. Pedestrians get fined if they spit and litter on the streets."

"Really?" muttered the older man, shaking his head. He was surprised to hear that many ordinary people in Tanzania owned cars.

The railway worker seemed to know what was in his new friend's head. "I wouldn't believe it if I hadn't seen it with my own eyes."

A puzzled look on his face, the older man said, "I thought the people in Africa lived in poverty and needed our help to build their railways." He ran his hands lightly through his hair. "I think we're poorer than them. Why do they need our country to help them?"

"Guess what? Most people there love Chairman Mao just like us or maybe more than us. When they saw me, they had their thumbs up, and they said, 'Chairman Mao is good.'" With a grin on his face, he added, "I bet Mao was the leader of the Third World."

"Let's not talk about this," replied the older man. His head shook from right to left, and then he grumbled, "Otherwise, I might say something that is politically incorrect."

"You're right. Let's not invite trouble."

At the next stop, the couple said goodbye, and two passengers who had been standing nearby plopped immediately into the available seats.

Later, an announcement sounded through the speaker: "Passenger comrades: It's time for supper. Fifty fen for each meal box. Please have the right amount of money ready."

A train attendant manoeuvred a cart with difficulty around

the crowded passengers standing in the aisle. Every few seconds, she would call out, "Please leave me some space!"

Some travellers bought the food, while others opened containers filled with their homemade meals. With her Styrofoam container in hand, Nina was happy to eat even if her meal consisted only of plain rice, two slices of fatty pork, and a couple of shreds of napa cabbage.

A second announcement about the checking of tickets followed. Nina noticed that the two occupants in the opposite seats got up and hurried away. *Maybe they don't have tickets,* she thought, recalling how she had done the same thing years before. Two other persons took the freed-up seats in no time. Eventually, it got dark outside, the light on the train emitting only a dull glow.

Several hours later, threading her way through the crowd, Nina avoided stumbling over the people slouching down in the aisle. She made her way to the washroom and entered with her pack of toiletries. She turned on the tap, but no water came out, so she was only able to wipe her face and hands with the small cloth she had in her bag. Then she went to look for the water boiler in hopes of finding some drinking water, but only a few brown drops trickled out of the tap. "None of the boilers have water at this time," a nearby woman explained.

"What time will the water be available?"

"Try in the early morning. I got some boiled water at six this morning"

Back in her seat, lulled by the successive sounds and motion of the train, Nina gradually fell asleep.

At dawn, the train stopped and the speaker announced, "Guiyang City!" Nina woke and raised her head from up off the table. It was the place where her neighbour needed to transfer to another train. The older passenger had already pulled his bag out from under his seat. Nina helped him get the other one he had placed on the upper rack. "Good luck to you and your son."

The man thanked her and hurried away. As soon as Nina moved to the seat beside the window, another woman sat down next to her. Nina felt so lucky that she was able to stay seated and tried to fall asleep with her head lying on a folded jacket she had placed against the window. There were still many passengers standing in the aisle or crouched on the floor wherever there was room.

A baby's loud wails woke Nina up from a fitful sleep. She decided to get up and stretch her legs. In an unoccupied washroom, there was still no water running from the taps. Back in her seat, she felt even wearier than before. "Have you had breakfast?" she asked the woman next to her.

"It's over. You'll have to wait till lunchtime," the woman replied. Then, in an excited voice, she asked, "Would you like some eggs?"

"Boiled eggs?" Nina was tempted.

"No, fresh ones. Look," she said, lifting a covered basket from the floor, and then setting it on the table carefully. "If you want to buy some, I'll let you see them."

Before Nina could respond, two middle-aged women from the opposite seats asked at the same time, "How much?"

"Ten fen each," the egg owner said, pulling back a corner of the cloth covering the basket. "Very large eggs. You can't find them at this price at the market. How many would you like?"

"Ten for each of us," one woman said after peeking under the cover. She pulled a round metal container out of her sack and laid it on the table. Her friend counted the eggs, her fingers moving deftly around them. After the desired eggs were laid first in the container and then in a plastic basin, the vendor charged each woman one yuan.

More people approached the woman and bought eggs. When the train stopped, the woman got off, her basket empty, but her pocket full of bills and coins. One of the buyers told Nina that the state-owned commercial market did not allow individuals to sell certain goods such as meats, eggs, tea, and peanuts, so peddlers came to sell their goods on the train. She noticed Nina's surprise. "Are you from outer space? How can you know nothing about this popular underground market?"

"I haven't taken the train for ages," said Nina, her mouth curving into a smile.

Half an hour later, the train stopped again at a large station. Nina followed other passengers to get off the car. From one of the food stands, she bought a glass bottle of mineral water and a packet of cookies. She also found a sink with running water to wash her face and brush her teeth.

In Hunan Province, more peddlers boarded the train to sell eggs, cigarettes, peanuts, and sausages. Some even hawked live chickens. As the train ambled to the next station, the vendors paced the aisles up and down, trying to sell as much as they could. At the next station, the vendors would detrain.

Once the train stopped, many teenaged girls and boys appeared under the windows with fruit, steamed buns, bottled water, or juice in their baskets. They raised their goods up to the passengers. Without getting off the train, buyers purchased food and drink through open windows though both seller and buyer had to work hard to stretch their arms across to each other. There was more than enough food for travellers to choose from different station platforms. Nina bought her meals through the window, too. The boxed food served on the train no longer attracted anyone.

Nina contemplated what Mao would have done if he had been alive and known about the peddling business taking place in his birth province of Hunan. His policies had forbidden private enterprise.

She also wondered whether she would interrogated or arrested if it was discovered that she was from North America. She was comforted by the thought that people seemed more attentive to business than to the revolution. *They are all jumping at the chance to live a better life.* And that put a smile on her tired face.

17.

AT DAWN

NINA DISEMBARKED AT the Guangzhou Railway Station on Friday at noon and boarded a bus to Yuexiu Street. But ten minutes into the ride, the bus came to a sudden stop at the corner of Yuexiu Street North. The driver turned his head to the passengers and announced: "A parade is ahead of us on the road. This is as far as we can go for the time being." Nina followed the other passengers and got off the bus, their collective feet scuffling along the street. A crowd of people from the parade turned onto a side street. Some of them held up framed portraits of Mao dressed all in black, while others lifted portraits of a middle-aged man in an army uniform. A red banner lifted high among the heads in the crowd had the slogan: "Support Chairman Hua Guofeng!" on it. She realized the day was October 1, China's National Day. Three weeks had passed since Nina had first arrived back in China.

It was a short parade with demonstrators calling out a few catch phrases: "Chairman Mao lives with us forever!", "Follow Chairman Hua!" and "Carry on Hua's Revolutionary line!" Eventually the demonstrators merged with the onlookers, the posters held high over their shoulders, and the crowd started to thin as people made their way home.

Nina reached her mother's dwelling and bounded up the stairs. She couldn't wait to see her mother again, and she knocked lightly and rapidly on the door, hoping her mother was home. She was. When she opened the door, her face was shiny, and welcoming. As Nina entered, her mother nodded to a pleasant-looking man, who seemed to be in his fifties, seated gingerly at the kitchen table. "This is Dr. Tang from my hospital."

"How do you do?" Nina greeted him.

The man's handshake was firm. "I dropped by for a brief visit with your mother," he said gently. His voice was soft and his eyes, almost black they were so dark, and kind. Then he smiled at Nina's mother and turning to leave, he said, "Nina needs a rest after her long trip. I will see you again soon."

Her mother saw him to the door. When she turned around, she blushed at Nina's smiling eyes.

"You've made a great choice," said Nina.

"This is his first visit," Nina's mother said, her cheeks still pink. "We're just friends, nothing else."

"Mother, it is wonderful that you are seeing someone after all these years," Nina said with enthusiasm. "Is he available?"

She sighed. "His wife died last year from illness. His two dispatched kids just came back from the countryside. They're still looking for jobs," her mother said, going into the kitchen to throw together a meal.

"Is he interested in you?" asked Nina, who enjoyed playing at the role of mother.

"Yes, but if he married me, it would be harder for his children to find jobs."

"Do you mean because of my father's suicide?" Nina asked.

"Yes, for that reason, as well as for others. Your father has stains on his record. As you know, he graduated from West Point and he was an officer with the Nationalist Army. Such stains affect all his relatives." Nina's mother took a breath, and her hand reached out to hold Nina's. "Never think about coming back to China permanently. If you lived here, I'm sure you would never have a normal life."

Nina's mother turned toward the stove and began to prepare a soup for the two of them to share. While she was chopping vegetables and tossing them into a broth that had already started to simmer, she continued. "After you were sent to Yunnan, because I was considered a traitor's wife, I was forced to work in a factory where I glued paper matchboxes for years. I don't know if that information ever reached you. It was a difficult time."

"I'm sorry I was not here to share these hardships with you all those years," Nina said. "But things are changing now in China. I noticed differences during my trip."

"What's changed?" asked her mother, tossing some noodles into the bubbling pot.

Nina placed two bowls on the table, and described what she had seen. "People are starting to think and awaken," she said.

Nina's mother raised her eyebrows as she carried the soup to the table and carefully ladled the noodles and broth into the bowls. "You should be careful during your stay. I've gone through too much trouble, and I don't want anything more to happen to you." So many images overlapped in her mind: Red Guards burning books found in her home; her husband's bloody head hitting the ground; being pushed to kneel down for her denunciation; and, the nightmares over her daughter's disappearance.

"I will be careful, Mother," Nina said. "Now let's get back to Dr. Tang? Do you like him?" she teased.

Her mother shook off the haunting memories and nodded. "I do."

"So, you should consider marrying him as soon as his kids find jobs," said Nina, her hand holding her mother's.

"Yes, my little mother," her mother chuckled, thinking about what Nina had told her the relationship between her and Roger. "Now I have a question. What about you and Roger? Will you marry?"

"I'm not sure. It depends on many factors."

"But you've been living with him," her mother added, hesitating a little; she did not intend to cause a dispute.

"I know what you are thinking. And maybe I shouldn't have told you about him. I know that according to Chinese tradition, a premarital relationship is considered sinful. But I don't need to follow Chinese ways anymore. I live in a free country now." She did her best to explain. "I like the fact that in America we are given free choices. By living together, Roger and I can discover and learn if we are suited to each other."

"It will take me some time to understand it," Nina's mother said in a gentle tone. "How is Roger? Can he speak a little bit of Chinese?"

"Maybe he can say two phrases: 'how do you do' and 'goodbye.'"

"I will only be able to speak a few words in English, too, if I ever meet him," he mother said with a grin. "All right. Let's promise each other. We'll each take care of our own personal relationships, but we will tell each other about them as well." They smiled at each other companionably and finished the rest of their soup in silence.

Nina then cleared the table and started washing the dishes in the sink. Her mother tugged her arm, and pulled her from the sink. "Let me do it. You should rest."

"I'm not tired," Nina said, though she was not able to stifle a yawn.

That night, she fell into such a deep sleep that her exhaustion from the emotional and physical stress of the past few days melted away.

On Sunday, Nina took her mother to the Friendship Store — a store for foreigners to buy certain goods that were unavailable in any other stores. She wanted to buy a television.

The red double door was open, but compared to other stores along that street, there were fewer customers coming and going. *Good. We don't need to lineup here,* Nina thought, quickening her steps.

A middle-aged doorman, with a dour look on his face, stood

on the flagstone steps leading into the store. When he noticed Nina heading into the store, her mother behind her, the man asked brusquely, "Where are you going?"

"To the store," answered Nina, wondering why he asked the question. "We want to have a look around."

"Not just anybody can browse in this store. Do you have money? I mean, do you have U.S. dollars?" the doorkeeper smirked.

"Yes, I do," she answered, and from her wallet, she drew out a ten-dollar banknote.

"Do you have an American passport?" asked the man. "I bet you don't." He was suddenly gleeful.

Before Nina could say anything, her mother pulled her back. "Let's go somewhere else."

"I'll come back another time," Nina tossed back at him crossly. She did not have her passport with her or she would have stomped angrily by him. Just then, a couple of Westerners stepped past the doorkeeper, but he did not ask them a single question. He smiled and greet them politely, "Welcome."

The following day, after her mother left for the hospital, Nina went back to the Friendship Store, this time with her passport. When the same doorman examined her document, his face displayed a disgust that looked familiar. Nina knew that behind these eyes was the unspoken thought: "An American running dog!" She shivered a little, knowing that with a label like that upon her, any perceived misbehaviour could see her put behind bars.

Nina bought a twelve-inch colour TV for her mother, who had never even owned a black-and-white one.

When her mother saw the gift, she gasped and wrapped her arms around Nina in a warm embrace. "You shouldn't have wasted your money on me," she said, wiping her tears. "Just seeing you again is enough."

"You need some entertainment even though many of the programs you have here may be boring political stuff," said

Nina. She picked up the remote control and showed her mother how to use it. "Live well and enjoy life as much as you can. You deserve to."

The next afternoon, Nina arrived at an address that Rei had given to her. She found a three-storey building labelled Number 4, entered Unit 1, and then knocked on the door of Apartment 101. A girl her age opened it and gaped at Nina with astonishment. "Oh! Is it you, Nina?" she asked, her face pale, and her voice quivering.

"Liya!" Nina held out her arms, and Liya pulled her in. They were thrilled to see each other.

"It was rumoured that you were shot dead when you sneaked across the border to Vietnam. I've cried for you many times." Liya's voice trembled. "Where have you been all these years?"

Nina told her the true story and before the two former high-school mates knew it, the clock on the wall struck five. "I'm supposed to cook supper for my parents now." Liya went into the kitchen and started to boil some rice and wash a bowl of soybean sprouts. Nina helped to slice the eggplant. "Have supper with us," Liya said, "but don't tell my folks you came from outside of China. They're timid as mice."

"How about it if I take you out to dinner instead?" Nina suggested. "Then we can continue talking while we eat."

Nodding, Liya answered, "Yes, that sounds great. My night shift doesn't start until ten o'clock, so we'll have lots of time to catch up some more." After supper was prepared, Liya left a note on the table for her parents, and the two girls went out and found a quiet restaurant.

They ordered chicken congee and fried buns and picked up where they left off. Their memories harkened back nine years when they were both eighteen. Liya had been able to choose a re-education location closer to home since her parents were middle-school teachers without any so-called political problems. So, in 1968, she had moved to Hainan Province. Seven years later, like most of her counterparts, she returned to the city, and found a job in a small factory that produced pots and pans, where she still worked today. Recalling her years in the country, Liya shivered. Many times she had been bitten by black flies and wasps and suffered their poison for several days without receiving any treatment. Frequently, she had to work in the rice paddies hour after hour. Even when the blood from her monthly period trickled down her legs and stained her pants, she did not have the time or a place to change the pad.

Liya told her about an incident that had occurred the previous October. More than 100,000 sent-down youths had gathered on Baiyun Mountain in the suburbs to share their experiences and make complaints about the government. Some people had even sold maps containing a secret route to Hong Kong to those who planned on escaping. The Provincial Public Security Department had dispatched a large number of policemen to disperse the crowds but failed to find out who had organized the rally. "I was there, too. Because that was the Double Ninth Festival for mountain climbing, so all of us said we were climbing Baiyun Mountain to celebrate the festival," Liya added.

Then she smiled shyly and told Nina that part of the reason she had gone to the rally was to try and meet up with a former co-worker that she had found attractive. She had debated whether to talk to him during the rally, and maybe get to know him a little. But when the police had arrived, he had run away with some of the other young men, and she had never found out what had happened to him.

Nina told Liya that at Number Five Military Farm they had not been permitted to have relationships with other workers. "Were young people allowed to have a boyfriend or girlfriend where you were?" she asked.

"At that time, nobody was allowed to make friends with people of the opposite gender. I generally followed this rule," Liya said. "And the only time I considered breaking it ... well, you know what happened. Maybe this is why I don't have a boyfriend even now." They finished the hot congee and paused to sip some tea. With a tissue, Liya cleaned the lenses of her glasses that had misted with the tea. "You know, I work with a bunch of older people. I don't get many chances to meet men my age. At work, 'Spinster' is my nickname." Liya grinned. "At first, I cried because I was ashamed of this nickname. But now, guess what? I don't care anymore."

Slowly and calmly, Liya told Nina her story as if it were the story of some other person. "Reading a lot of banned literary works in my spare time has become my great pleasure. Maybe books are better than a boyfriend. As long as I have books to read, I'm happy," she said. "Sometimes, I think we were born in the wrong place at the wrong time. But at least you were able to leave China. Tell me about your American boyfriend."

Nina talked only about Roger. The fact that she had slept with two men might spoil her friend's impression of her even though Liya had read many novels by Western writers.

"You have an admirable sweetheart," Liya said, excited for Nina. "When are you going to get married?"

"Maybe soon," Nina lied — a white lie — so as not to disappoint her friend. According to Chinese morals, a good girl should get married. She did not want to have the same conversation with Liya she had had with her mother. Not everyone would understand. She tried instead to comfort her friend. She knew how important marriage was in Chinese culture. "I'm sure you'll meet your Mr. Right very soon. Don't give up hope. You need a person who understands you and also enjoys the books you read."

"You're the first person who has listened to my stories with interest. Most people our age have much similar, dismal life experiences. They can't bear more. Someday, I'd like to write my stories down, though I don't know where I'll find readers who will be interested in them.

"I'm sure there are plenty of people, like me, who'll want to read your stories."

"Really?" She smiled brightly. "My folks say I have shut my eyes to reality. They think I'm in a rut. But I can hope, can't I?"

Nina smiled back at her and then told her what she had learned on her trip to her former farm.

"Interesting," said Liya. "At least I know there are people like me who are still striving even though we don't know what'll become of us. You know what I'll do? I am going to contact a couple of my acquaintances who have returned from the military farm in Hainan Province. Like you did with your co-workers, we too can re-connect and share our personal experiences with one another."

The following week, Nina went to look for Yangcheng Foreign Books, the only bookstore in town that sold books in languages other than in Chinese, and she finally located it in a narrow lane with a small plate on the door. It looked as if it were hidden there to evade trouble. She stepped in and noticed a few visitors meandering among the bookshelves that lined the walls. Some rummaged through stacks of books in cardboard boxes marked, "On Sale."

She browsed around. Most of the books were in English. Some were in French, German, Russian, and Japanese. Most of the English titles were versions of eight model plays supported by Madame Mao, as well as recently published novels and poems by contemporary Chinese workers, farmers, and army men. There were also English versions of Chinese magazines such as *Beijing Review*, *China Today*, and *People's China*. Entire volumes of Mao's work, poetry, and booklets occupied many of the shelves. Nina smiled to herself and thought the place should be called, "The Bookstore of Chinese books in English." She looked at a newly published, thin pocketbook titled *Mao Tse-tung Poems in English* and wondered why the translator had not placed an apostrophe and an "s" after Mao Tse-tung's name.

She walked over to the shelves with the most people around

them. These shelves held English textbooks and dictionaries. A young man in his early twenties stood by one of the shelves with an open book in his hand. When he noticed Nina's pocketbook, he asked, "Do you like Mao's poems and understand them in English?"

"I'm trying," she said. "What are you reading?"

He showed her the cover of his book. "English 900 Sentences. It's American English."

"Do you listen to the Voice of America?"

"Sure. I enjoy its English 900 teaching program. Do you?"

"I did," Nina spoke in English.

"Wow, your English is so cool," the young man said. "You sound like a perfect English teacher."

"I'm not. Are you a student of English?"

"I wish. I'm receiving re-education in the countryside and am self-taught. How about you? Where did you learn to speak English?"

To avoid attention, she only said, "I started learning English from the Voice of America actually."

"Then?" the young man craved to know more.

"Then, from some teachers."

"I dream someday I can speak English as well as you do."

"Why are you trying to learn English?"

"I love English novels. Hopefully, I'll be able to read the originals."

"Doesn't reading Western books cause you trouble?"

"I haven't gotten into any so far. Except for a couple of friends, nobody else knows about my interest in this."

"I'm sure you will speak good English if you keep trying," Nina said. She could see, through this young man, how her generation yearned to see beyond the tightly closed door that was China.

The day Nina left, her mother saw her off at the airport. She wiped the tears on her mother's face with a handkerchief and hugged her once more. "When will I see you again?" her mother asked, her voice trembling.

"I hope it won't be too long," Nina said, and kissed her goodbye. She looked back once to wave then joined the other passengers and boarded the plane.

18.

THE SUN RISES FROM THE WEST

NINA TOOK THE ferry from Portland to Yarmouth and spotted Roger, in jeans and a tie-dyed T-shirt, standing by the exit, anxiously scanning the passengers as they stepped down onto the dock. When he finally saw Nina, Roger breathed a sigh of relief.

An hour later, they were at home, nestled together on the couch with a platter of cheese and two glasses of red wine on the coffee table in front of them.

"I am happy now," Roger said, his hand reaching for his goblet on the table.

Nina raised her glass to him, and smiled warmly, "I am glad to be home." They spent the rest of the night catching up, with words and with their bodies.

The following day, when Nina woke up, Roger had already left for his office. She decided to go for her customary walk along the beach. The soft red sunlight came through the thin fog over the water. It looked as though red wine had filled the bay. Seagulls and eagles slid through the air as if drunk from the wine.

It was a sleepy, peaceful morning, but the images and visions of the people and events during her journey came to haunt her, one by one. As she strolled, she drank in the ocean and shoreline in front of her, and the air, which tasted of sea salt, cleared her nose.

When she returned home, she made herself comfortable at

her desk and continued with her writing project. Her mind was immersed in memories until Roger's voice sounded behind her.

"Your essay got into the *Portland Press Herald* again," he said, handing a newspaper along with an envelope to her. "I just got this letter from our mailbox. It's from the *Herald*." Nina looked at the title of the article in the paper, "My Father." She had submitted the piece just before her trip. Inside the envelope was a cheque for $20 as payment for the piece. She shook the cheque playfully under Roger's nose and grinned. "Come on! I'll take you out to dinner. Let's celebrate!"

"By the way," Roger added, helping her to her feet. "Your postcard from China reached me. It means the mail is getting through, so I think you can write to your mother and she will probably get the letter."

That Friday, they went to a nice restaurant and feasted on lobster and very good Bordeaux. When she looked at Roger's contented face, she remembered the evening with her fellow farm workers enjoying the food they had made underneath the moonlight. Roger listened attentively as she told him all about it.

Later, in bed, her legs wrapped around his, his mouth on hers, she thought of Liya and she shivered. "Honey, is something wrong?" Roger lifted his head.

"I'm a little preoccupied. I was thinking about one of my friends in China."

"Get the story off your chest. You'll feel better." Roger held her in his arms while her head nestled on his chest.

"I think I would like to sing a Chinese folk song instead, and see if you like it."

"Do you need to dress up for this performance or do you prefer to remain naked?" he asked, a cheeky grin on his face. He stroked her hair playfully.

"Just like this. Since you're my only audience, I don't even need to stand up," she said laughing.

"Wait, let me get my guitar." He jumped out of bed and

rushed upstairs. When he came back, he leaned against the headboard next to her. With his fingers on the strings, he said, "You start. I'll follow you."

"The song is called 'Flowing Stream' she said, then cleared her throat and started:

The full moon rises high
My admirer is on the mountain
Like the moon shines at night
Age emits sparkling light

At the foot of the hill
A brook bubbles under moonlight
The silver ray blankets the summit
Age brightens my sight

I miss you, my true love
The breeze blows from the heights
My faraway Age,
Can you hear my chant?

Roger's guitar melody blended easily with Nina's lyrics and their music filled the room. ""It's a love song, right?," he said, putting his guitar by the side of the bed. "Tell me what 'Age' means."

Nina's face glittered under the glow of the lamps. "'Age' literally means 'brother.'" Sensing Roger's confusion, she added, "But it has nothing to do with love between brother and sister. In Chinese folklore, a person calls her/his sweetheart 'brother' or 'sister.'"

"Nice, but very odd. How could I tell whether this 'brother' is a sibling or a 'lover'?"

"The word 'brother' has a few different meanings. For the most part, in a song or poem, a brother or sister means 'lover,'" she explained. "If you understood the language and culture, you would understand the meaning of the word from the context."

He pulled her into his arms. "I can't imagine calling you 'sister.' I don't feel like thinking of you as my sister."

Nina giggled. "This is a cultural difference. When I hear a song with the word, 'Age,' I envision a girl in love. When I sang this song with my old friends at the military farm, all I could think was how much I missed you."

"You look beautiful when you sing, my darling. Call me 'Age' if that arouses you," he whispered into her neck as his hands explored her smooth body. Nina sighed as she wrapped her arms around him and met his lips with her own.

November 25 was Thanksgiving Day. Nina took the ferry to Portland to visit with Eileen and Bruce. Nina sat on the old couch in the living room, remembering her time in the house five years earlier. Eileen entered the room with some tea and biscuits, placed them on the coffee table, and then sat down next to Nina. "You look wonderful, Eileen. Your face is so smooth and lovely, and you don't even have any wrinkles," Nina said.

Eileen laughed, pleased at the compliment. "My secret is drinking lemon juice."

Bruce ran his fingers through his greying hair. "I don't think the same can be said for me," he chuckled. "I am getting greyer every day, but I think I can still climb up on the roof and repair the shingles."

Nina pulled some packages from her pack. "These are sticking plasters my mother suggested for you, Bruce. They should relieve some of your joint pain and the ache in your muscles. Inside, I have translated the instructions on how to use the plasters into English."

"Thanks," Bruce said and opened the packet with curiosity. "I want to try one right away."

Nina handed another packet to Eileen. "And this is for you. I hope you like it."

Eileen opened the packet. "Oh, it's a beautiful silk blouse," she said, caressing the smooth fabric with her fingers.

"I hope you like the colour, Eileen. There were only a few choices in the store." Nina remembered that most of the department stores she had visited in China were half-empty. She had finally found the pretty blue blouse in the Friendship Store.

Eileen asked Nina to tell them more about her trip to China. Fascinated by her experiences, Eileen asked, "Can you come to our church's party tomorrow? I'd like more people to hear you about your trip."

"Sure, I can do that," Nina said. Then, with a delicate sniff, she added. "Is that wonderful aroma coming from a roasting turkey?"

"Yes, dear. It's almost done," Eileen said. "By the way, we've invited a family to join us for dinner. They are refugees from Laos."

"Let me help you prepare the dinner."

"Can you make a stir-fry?" Eileen asked. "I have some green beans, some carrots, and bok choy."

"Do you have chili?" Nina asked. "I think Laotian people like spicy food." She followed Eileen into the kitchen and the two busied themselves with the final preparations for their meal.

When the family from Laos arrived, Eileen introduced the Tsheejs to Nina. She was surprised to see their ten-year-old daughter, Nou Kha, dressed in a multi-coloured tubular skirt and top, and wearing a silver neckband that sported several tiny, jingling bells. Nina said, "Your clothes resemble that of the Miao people."

"'Clothes'?" Mrs. Tsheej mumbled and turned to her daughter for help. The daughter interpreted for her mother and then replied in English, "Mom said, 'My daughter's clothes are homemade.'"

"What you are wearing is very pretty." Nina said slowly. "I saw similar clothes being worn by the Miao people in Yunnan and Hainan provinces. The Miao also live in other southern provinces of China. Girls and women wear many pleated skirts one over the other." After Nou Kha interpreted this for her mother, Nina asked another question: "Do Hmong men play music with reed pipes?"

"Yes, we play," Mr. Tsheej said in broken English. "Our ancestors are from China. Perhaps, the Hmong and Miao are the same people."

The host and guests began their meal and talked amiably about the similarities between the two cultures. Nina's stir-fried vegetables and Mrs. Tsheej's sticky rice cakes added some exotic flavours to the traditional American turkey dinner that Eileen had prepared. When the Tsheejs learned that Nina had recently graduated from a university, Mr. Tsheej said, "We hope our daughter can go university."

"I'm sure she can if she is willing," Nina said.

Mr. Tsheej told them about his parents who had helped the Americans in the Vietnam War, and a year later were killed when the communists, Pathet Lao, occupied Laos. Like many of the Hmong people, the Tsheejs went to Thailand to the refugee camp there. Many Western countries, like Canada, had accepted them as refugees and they had chosen the United States. "I was a child and I saw the Americans. I hear about their country, so I was very happy about moving here," Mr. Tsheej said.

That's very interesting. You should write about it someday."

"I wish I could," Mr. Tsheej said. He made a gesture of holding a pen. "I need to learn to write."

Before the family left, Nina gave her pen to Mr. Tsheej, and said, "Please accept this pen as my gift to you. You can learn how to write, and I will look forward to reading your work."

"Thank you and see you all again soon," Nuo Kha said, waving goodbye.

Back from her visit to Maine, Nina continued to write about her experiences in China, and Roger helped her polish her writing. She was hoping to sell several other personal pieces to the local newspapers. She had sent a couple of pieces that she turned into travel articles to various travel magazines in the United States and in Canada, and was thrilled when they were accepted. When she wasn't writing, she poured through newspapers and journals looking for news and information on China and its political affairs. Her life was simple, but she found it fulfilling and she was content.

Just before Christmas, Nina was delighted to receive a letter from her mother.

Nov. 28, 1976
Dear daughter,

I'm writing to you even though I haven't yet received a letter from you. I hope you will get mine.

You may've heard from the news that the "Gang of Four" — Wang Hongwen, Zhang Chunqiao, Jiang Qing, and Yao Wenyuan — was thrown out of the Chinese Communist Party. Everything looks up now. Smiles appear on everybody's faces.

In short, thanks to the TV you bought for me, I watch the news daily, no matter how busy I am.

Does Roger like the sweater I knitted for him?

Merry Christmas!

Love,
Your mother

Even if her own letters were still going astray, at last, the first letter from her mother in China had arrived! A breath of air had finally managed to slip out of that tightly closed door. Nina was certain now that her letters would reach her mother someday soon, too.

A year slipped away. In November, 1977, Nina learned that the Chinese government had reinstated university entrance examinations. After years of absence from school, the youth who had gone through the government's arranged re-education in the countryside, would now have the opportunity to study at college or university. She remembered Huguo's words: "Maybe the sun will rise from the west someday." *His odd dream is coming true. The sun rises in the West. Something that was once impossible, that was once just a dream, is now happening,* Nina thought.

Several months later, she received a thick envelope with some photographs from her mother, including a letter from Dongfang.

Her mother's letter read:

March 5, 1978
Dear Nina,

I'm glad to know you've published some articles in newspapers and journals. However, as a freelance writer, you must not have a regular income. Why don't you find a permanent position that can secure your financial future? Writing could be your hobby but not a real job. Don't you think so?

I have some good news. After passing the entrance exams, Rei was accepted at Peking University. He is studying in the Law Department.

Dr. Tang's children have both started school, one at college, and the other at university. Many of my colleagues are extremely excited and busy these days. Almost each family has a child that has been accepted to a college this year. One family even has all three children going to university. The age difference between the oldest and the youngest is ten years.

Many young people didn't get a chance for higher education during the past ten years. All of them took the exams at the same time! You can imagine how keen the competition was!

Tang and I have decided to get married on June 17. We'll have a simple wedding ceremony. A couple of relatives and close friends will come over for happy candy. I assume you can join us.

I have also heard some news through the grapevine. It seems that wronged cases during the Cultural Revolution may get corrected. Hopefully, this means your father's name will be cleared.

I'm awaiting good news from you and Roger.

Enclosed is a letter from the Number Five Military Farm. It arrived here last month. I hope I didn't delay it for too long.

Love,
Your mother

Nina opened the second enclosed letter and smoothed it out before reading.

Jan. 28, 1978
Dear Nina,

How was your trip back to Canada? I should've written to you earlier. In fact, I started a letter before but didn't finish it.

You might be interested to know a little more about the American spy incident during your recent visit. After you and Huguo left, we cleaned the garage. The brigade leader with his militia arrived shortly afterward. They asked where the American spy was. We told them we didn't even see one hair belonging to any American, but we had a visitor from Guangzhou who had come to Kunming for an important meeting with the municipal government. Then we explained that our visitor had just left for the meeting.

The leader asked, "Why did she ride on the tractor without her own car and driver if she is that important?'

Our answer was, "She didn't intend to show off. Remember, Chairman Mao rode a horse in Yan'an. Dare you think he isn't important?"

The leader hesitated. He might have remembered seeing Mao on a horse in a movie. But he still asked, "Why did people say she was from America?"

We said, "Rumours always make things intriguing and mysterious. You're very knowledgeable and have a wonderful memory. Do you remember Chairman Mao shaking hands with the American President Nixon?" At this moment, Kali's hubby—you may still remember that local peasant — knelt down. He said, "My wife's friend is gone. Could you let my wife go? I swear I heard them sing the songs of Mao's quotations yesterday. If my wife leaves me because of you, my children will have to call your wife, 'Grandma,' and they'll go live with you."

The leader then looked at him, dismissed his group, and they went away. It was a miracle.

Since Mao's death, earth-shaking changes have taken place. The Gang of Four was arrested. Many of us sent-down youths had a chance to take the entrance exams last December. Huguo got accepted to a college in Kunming. I'll try next year.

By the way, we've heard that Wang lives in Hong Kong now. It is said he's been doing foreign trade business in Shek O. He may become a millionaire. That'll be our pride.

I'm sending the letter to your mother's address. Hopefully, you'll read it someday.

Yours truly,
Dongfang and Huguo

That evening, Nina and Roger sat in the living room. She interpreted the letters for him, and he listened with interest.

He commented on the story from the letter. "It's interesting about his kids calling the leader's wife, 'Grandma.' Is that a kind of curse to make a woman older?"

Nina smiled. "In rural areas, a grandmother has a duty to take care of motherless kids. The leader didn't want his wife to take on the responsibility of raising the offspring of that peasant.

"A very smart guy," Roger nodded. "And what does 'happy candy' mean?"

"It's some nicely wrapped candy that people use to treat guests at a wedding. Offering it means to tie the knot."

Roger remembered reading something about Chinese wedding traditions, so he asked, "As a bride, will your mother sit in a palanquin?"

"No, that's an old tradition. Mao and his Party abolished that custom."

"Will she hold a wedding reception?"

"No."

Roger grinned. "Well, then, I guess your mother is having a hippie wedding, simple and informal."

"Maybe," Nina smirked. "I'm thinking about going back to China for my mother's wedding. Also, I can do some more research for my book."

"China is at an important historical turning point," said Roger. "It is probably an exciting time to go. If I understood and spoke Chinese, I'd go with you."

Nina sensed Roger's concern. "I'll be okay."

"Is your book going to be a memoir?" he asked

"No, not really. I want to write about my generation's ups and downs more than about myself. Many of those who lived in Mao's society are still not free enough to write about their lives during that regime. Still today, people are not allowed to complain about the Cultural Revolution or the Communist Party. But I have the opportunity to do so and these human stories must be told." Nina softened her voice. "I'm sure someday you will see China in person."

"Maybe it's not too late for a thirty-three-year-old man to learn the language."

"Where there's a will there's a way," Nina said. "I can teach you if you're interested."

"Don't expect me to write in Chinese." He chuckled. "I'd be thrilled if I could understand some basic Chinese. In case..." He paused and looked at her.

"In case what?"

"So, I won't be in the dark when you speak Chinese to your child."

"What child? Where?" Puzzled, she looked into his face.

"Will you marry me?" Roger asked, getting down on one knee. "In other words, shall we give out our own happy candy?"

"Oh, Roger, of course I will marry you," Nina said, throwing her arms around his neck. "But I need to go back to China first," she said, holding both his hands. "I would like to collect the firsthand information I need for my book. I hope that's okay with you."

"Well, I don't want there to be any chance of me losing you," he said, wrapping his arms around her waist. "You know, just in case you meet a male hippie during your trip. At least you will travel as my fiancée." With a smile, he lifted her in his arms and carried her into the bedroom.

19.

BROKEN-DOWN SHOE AND FRACTURED LEG

NINA ARRIVED IN Guangzhou two days before her mother's wedding, but the following day, Dr. Tang and her mother would still go to work. There were some changes in her mother's apartment. The walls had been repainted limestone white; two new wicker chairs flanked a small rosewood table; a framed photograph of the couple lay on the dressing table.

Nina's present to the newlyweds was a microwave, which she had brought with her. When her mother returned from work, Nina helped pack the happy candy in small plastic bags, which the couple would pass along to their colleagues when they returned to work after a three-day wedding leave.

On Saturday evening of the wedding day, Nina's mother invited her nephew, Rei with his wife, and Rei's grandmother — her only relatives in the city — to join them. The other guests were Dr. Tang's two children, his sister, and her husband. Both Nina's mother and Tang did not intend to make a fuss over their wedding, so they had each invited only two friends. It would be a simple celebration with family and close friends.

At the end of the ceremony, the new couple stood and held hands. The bridegroom had a wide smile on his face that smoothed away his wrinkles. The bride wore a pink silk flower clipped to her short hair, and her eyes beamed. Together, they sang a song from 1950s, which Nina remembered hearing as a child:

The revolutionary man is forever young
Like a pine tree green all year around
No fear for the thunder that shakes the ground
He stands straight even if rocks rebound...

The couple smiled at their audience. The song had spoken of the fullness in their hearts, which had survived ten years of hardship and depression, and were now filled with joy. Nina thought the ceremony had been simple and beautiful, almost revolutionary-style. *Was it also hippie-style like Roger suggested?* Nina wondered.

After the gathering, Nina went to stay at Rei's grandmother's home. The newlyweds had only three days for their honeymoon, and Nina did not want to disturb them.

The next evening, she visited Liya, but she was not home. Liya's parents told Nina that their daughter had become a student in the Department of Chinese Literature at Pearl River University and was currently living in a dorm room on the campus.

The two friends met on the university campus and held each other's hands as they swirled about on the lawn. Liya showed Nina around her university and explained everything that had happened since they had last seen each other. In the reading room of the university library, Liya turned to a page of the *Sheep City Evening News*. "This article may interest you," Liya said, looking at her watch. "Hang around here and read this over. I must go to a student meeting now. I'll be back in an hour."

The headline was "Student Suspended." The author started the story with questions: "How was Fangren Li (pseudonym) caught red-handed? Why did she steal the forbidden fruit?

"Li was a student from the Department of Chinese Language at a local university. According to her classmates, the quiet Li has always kept her distance from others. She had no close friends. Often, her bed was unoccupied. Her roommates merely assumed that she frequently went back to her parents' home in town.

"One afternoon, a woman in her late twenties trudged into the main office in the university's administration building. In a dark blue, floral-print blouse and baggy pants, she carried a piece of baggage and a wicker basket in each hand. When the woman visitor inquired about Lutou Chu's address at the front desk, the office worker asked her, 'Who are you?'

"'I'm his wife,' answered the visitor.

"'What are you talking about?' Flabbergasted, the clerk said, 'He is single.'

"'He's married. I'm his wife.' Gasping, the young woman's round face was long and red. She raised her voice, 'I have a child with him, too.'

"'Okay.' The worker gave her a pen and a sheet of paper. 'Please write down his name. In case I mistook your words.'

"The unknown wife jotted down her husband's name and said her husband worked in the admissions office.

"The clerk examined the name written down by the visitor, then she copied down his address on a slip of paper. A contented look on her face, the woman loaded the heavy canvas pack on her shoulder and grasped the woven basket with her hand. She trekked across the campus looking for the address the clerk had given her. An hour later, she located the three-storey building. Despite the tiring journey, the wife became excited when she reached her husband's apartment — also her home. Two steps at a time, she mounted the stairs to the top floor without stopping though her shoulder ached from the pressure of the fully loaded pack, and her legs were sore from the long walk.

"She knocked on the door, knowing how surprised her husband would be to see her there. Just thinking about being in his arms thrilled her from head to toe. But no one answered the door. After she laid her pack and basket on the floor, she sat down to wait. Light radio music wafted through the air; as she listened, she became convinced that the music was coming from inside her husband's apartment. *Is he sick and can't get up?* she thought and got worried. She stood and pressed the side of her head against the door. What did she hear? The giggling of a woman and the voice of a man — it was her husband talking from the inside.

"She immediately thought something was wrong and so she banged on the door with her fists. 'Open the door! Lutou Chu!' she hollered.

"The door of the next apartment opened. A woman's head came out. She asked, 'What're you doing?'

"The mad wife ignored the question. She started to kick the door. Then the door opened a crack. Chu stretched his head out. 'Who is it?'

"The woman picked up her pack and basket and pushed her way in. 'It's me, your wife,' she said loudly.

"Chu collapsed on the floor.

"The wife saw a younger woman sitting on the edge of the bed trying to fasten the top button on her blouse. Rage turned the wife's face a livid purple. She threw the bag at her husband and grabbed an egg from the wicker bin she'd just placed on the floor. She hurled the egg at her rival and the younger woman ducked. It cracked against the bed's headboard and the splashed yolk dripped onto the bed's sheets. Meanwhile, the angry wife slapped the young woman's ashen face. 'You broken-down shoe! How dare you sleep with my husband?' She thrust her head into her rival's breasts, like a bull with horns pushing against its opponent. She hated to imagine her husband's hands on the broken-down shoe's breasts instead of hers.

"The girl was caught red-handed. She pushed the wife away, crying out, 'I don't believe he's married to such a barbarian.'

"The woman picked up a bra on the floor and used it to whip the captive. 'Sell your giant ass to other men!' roared the enraged wife.

"Chu pulled himself up from the floor and grabbed his wife's arm. 'Let her go. It's my fault,' he begged.

"The defeated young woman darted out of the room, her face hidden under her uncombed hair. She pushed through the onlookers and hastened away.

"An elderly neighbour recognized her and spat with disgust. 'A student! A broken-down shoe! An unmarried girl lives with a cheating husband. Despicable!'

"Like a skeleton in Chu's closet, Li was exposed in public. But this isn't the end of the story. As an author, I am warning any daredevils who challenge the law and commit bigamy. For a violation of the Marriage Law of the People's Republic of China, Chu was sentenced to two years in prison. The adulterous student was suspended from school forever based on the rule that no student is allowed to have a love affair nor is any student permitted to cohabit with another. In addition, the premarital relationship was immoral."

The author, it seemed to Nina, thought every female student should learn a big lesson from this story. It was a moralizing "tale" to reinforce the value of marriage and came off as salacious rather than news worthy.

Nina felt some empathy for Li but wondered why the author focused more on the moral lesson and not on the unfairness to the suspended student, She thought about the punished young woman, and sighed. She knew an unmarried woman in a sexual relationship was considered a "broken-down shoe." That label might stick with Li and affect her forever.

By this logic, Nina herself was a broken-down shoe. Goosebumps appeared on her arms.

Nina wanted to interview this young woman for her book. The subsequent morning, with Liya's help, Nina met the disgraced woman, Fangren Li, whose real name was Qing, in a dim sum restaurant.

Nina ordered a few dishes from the waitress. "Help yourself," she said to Qing. "It's my treat."

Qing was in her mid-twenties and had short hair. Her bloodshot eyes stuck out in her pale face. Her fair skin made it hard for Nina to believe she had survived the hot and harsh winds of the rubberwood for five years.

"What else do you want to know about me? The newspaper story has told everyone everything," said Qing, picking up her chopsticks to eat. "You're from America where there's sexual freedom. There both men and women have the right to choose their lovers, right? He doesn't love his wife. He chose me."

"You should defend yourself, not him. You do have the right to choose, but Chu doesn't because he's married." Eyes locking on Qing's, Nina continued. "I'm concerned about you. Do you wish to go back to the university?"

"Yes, but how?"

"Do you think the suspension is fair to you?"

Qing did not answer. With a blank look on her face, she bit into a shrimp dumpling. "That tastes good." Then she looked at Nina. "Do American students have the right to love whomever they want and get married?"

"Yes, they do."

"I broke an unfair rule. But I shouldn't be completely suspended from the university. I didn't commit a crime."

Nina nodded. She told Qing that Liya and some other students disagreed with the university's rule. They wanted to support her. However, Qing needed to speak to the Student Association. They could help her deal with the university authorities, and this unfair regulation could perhaps be changed.

Nina asked, "Can you tell me about yourself? I promise that if I write anything about you, I will use a pseudonym."

"What am I afraid of? Everybody who's read the paper already knows my reputation." Her rising brow suggested she did not care about her reputation. "I'll tell you what I went through in the past. It is now an old scar."

When Nina listened to her story, she remembered bits of her own life from eight years earlier.

At the age of sixteen, in 1970, Qing was sent to a farm in Hainan Province. Like other girls, she had experienced many hardships: poor nutrition and an unsanitary environment, labour-intensive chores such as planting rice and carrying heavy manure loads with a shoulder pole, not to mention illness and lack of food and sleep.

One evening, Fang, the new leader, asked her to meet him in his office to discuss her new assignment with a performance group to spread Maoism. Pleased to be chosen for this easy job instead of cutting the barks of rubber trees to collect latex or labouring in the field, she put on her best outfit: a short-sleeved green blouse and a pair of grey pants — the only garments she had with no patches.

Lighthearted, she walked into the office. Middle-aged Fang sized her up, his heavy-lidded eyes half open. "You have a nice figure. I'll teach you how to use it." He blew out the oil lamp and pulled her into him. Before she screamed, he warned her, "If you don't go along, I'll tell my superiors that you seduced me." He pushed her down onto the floor and raped her. After it was over, she sat on the floor, weeping silently in the dark. Fang patted her on the back. "I'm sure you can dance well. Come join the team tomorrow morning."

Fang had raped several girls using the promise of participating in the performance group, but nobody dared to report him. Once a week, he asked Qing to meet him in his bed. In return, he arranged light workloads for her or assigned her to indoor work. After all, he told her, he liked her best. To evade the more labour intensive work, she had agreed to sleep with him. Later, the boyfriend of another abused girl reported the crime to the higher authorities. Fang was sent away so that Qing and other victims were freed from his control. But even after he was gone, her fellow workers avoided her. She had earned the name, "broken-down shoe."

"Then some men came to the farm to meet me, thinking that I would be an easy conquest. Well, I guess I needed a man too. After I was accepted into the university and arrived on campus, I met Lutou, and we kind of liked each other right away. I could tell he had affection for me, and he was much better than other men. He doesn't love his wife, he loves me," said Qing. She took a sip of tea.

"If Lutou's marriage was unhappy, he should have divorced his wife before he started a relationship with you. A married man living with another woman is treated as a bigamist. It's against the law, but this is his problem. Remember? Your purpose is to return to the university."

"You're very helpful." Qing looked at Nina. "Have you slept with any men?" She was eager to know about Nina's life.

"Not with any married men. I sleep with my husband-to-be," answered Nina. When she tried to fit herself into the Chinese tradition, she felt as confused as Qing.

From Ahua, Rei's wife, Nina heard the story of a young man who had returned to Guangzhou from Xiangxi, the poorest area in Hunan Province. Injured and unemloyed, he lived with his parents. His mother worked with Ahua in the same factory.

One day, Nina followed Ahua into a crowded room of this man's home in Guangzhou. The man sat on a bench with heaps of small pieces of fine cardboard and colourful labels lying next to him on the floor.

When Ahua introduced him to Nina, the young man said, "Welcome. My mother has told me about you." He pointed at some wooden crates near him. "You can sit on any of them."

"Would you mind if I record our conversation?" Nina asked as she pulled a small tape recorder out of her satchel. "This will help me remember the details of our discussion. I promise it won't bring any trouble to you."

"What trouble can be more than what I've got? In fact, I hope everybody knows my story."

"Good. Can you start with your leg injury?" Nina asked as she turned on the machine.

"It happened six years ago, in 1972. Before the winter came, we had to cut tree branches and bushes for use as wood fuel. It was dangerous working around a steep mountainside, but we went there because it was a wooded area so we could find what we needed easily. We called our team of eight, 'Commando.' One day, each of us was carrying a full load, about a hundred pounds. One the way home, when we passed a dangerous section, a downpour suddenly started. Rocks on the mountain slid down. I dropped my shoulder pole and tried to find a place to hide from the falling stones. The guy in front of me froze at that moment. I called out, 'Run! Drop your bundles!' I don't know if he couldn't hear me or if he didn't understand. He kept on carrying his load though he couldn't move very fast. A falling rock smashed his head. His blood stained his pole and firewood packs. His life ended in a blink of an eye.

"I was hit by rocks, but not on the head. My legs wouldn't budge. Another guy's arms were injured. The survivors carried the dead body and us two wounded fellows back to the brigade. The authorities did nothing about the incident. We didn't get any medical treatment. The reason was they had no money for us. The dead guy couldn't get buried right way because his parents belonged to the 'Five Blacks' categories. Hopeless and helpless, all the sent-down youths in the area worked together, and made a rectangular case as a coffin out of large tree branches. We buried the body. Some of my fellow workers used herbal remedies to help cure our wounds.

"I survived the incident, but my right leg was seriously injured, has remained numb, and is now shorter than my left. The other fellow had both his hands ruined. I followed Mao's directive to live in the countryside but finally woke up and saw only a dead-end street in front of me.

"For a couple of years, many of us continued to demand fair treatment. We also asked for medical benefits. Last year, all the farm workers who had died while officially working were finally recognized as victims of work-related accidents, and their families got some compensation. We two were allowed to return to the city. I limped with my left leg or walked with the aid of a crutch. Because I was handicapped and without skills, I couldn't find a job, so I lived on my parents' meagre income. Now at least I can make some money by gluing matchboxes but not enough for a woman to marry me."

Before leaving, Nina offered him ten yuan for his help. He declined the offer. "I have a better life now than I did in the countryside. I don't need your money. But I'd like to have one yuan as a keepsake. I can show others. I'll tell them there's hope in this world. Even a stranger cares about me."

Her throat tightening, Nina said, "My heart goes out to you. I admire you and what you've accomplished." She handed him one yuan.

The man folded the banknote and placed it in his shirt pocket. Then he turned to Ahua, who had been sitting quietly beside Nina and listening to his story. "By the way, Ahua, my mother says your husband's studying law at Peking University. Tell him to do well. Maybe he can make the justice system work for all of us."

20.

RUINS OF YUANMINGYUAN GARDEN

NINA INTERVIEWED TWO more people during her stay in Guangzhou. Then, she boarded a train going north for Beijing. With Rei at Peking University, she had the opportunity to expand the scope of her research in the north. After travelling for a day and a night, she arrived in Beijing and then boarded a bus to Peking University. As she stepped through the gates of the university, she was struck by the way the glazed yellow roof tiles on the temple-style buildings sparkled in the sun. She took a leisurely stroll around Weiming Lake in the center of the campus; admiring the gentle sweep of willow branches draped along the shoreline. She breathed deeply and thought that all in all the campus looked the same as it had on her first visit twelve years earlier.

Nina had joined the Red Guards in June, 1966. A month later, a period of revolutionary networking started during which students were encouraged to share their experiences with other students from different places and participate in revolutionary activities all over the country. Everyone, including teachers, could book train tickets free of charge to anywhere they desired to go. Mao's first meeting with a million Red Guards in Tiananmen Square on August 18 had helped increase the feverish desire to catch a glimpse of their helmsman. The catchphrase "Sailing the seas depends on the helmsman.... Making revolution relies on Mao Zedong Thought," became popular and was sung across China.

Nina and her ten fellow Red Guards had joined the Revolutionary Networking crowds, yearning to see Chairman Mao. In a fern-green uniform with a red armband, Nina had reached Beijing by train.

Received by the Red Guards from the middle school affiliated with Peking University at the station, Nina and her group had been accommodated in a classroom on the university campus. Red Guards from various cities and towns had occupied almost every corner of the campus. Tables, benches, floors, and even lawns became the visitors' beds. Everything was free including food, drink, and classrooms. It seemed communism had become a reality — everybody shared things with one another. Many Red Guards had even adopted the same name: "Yaowu," which meant, "seeking armed conflict." At his first meeting with the young revolutionists, Mao told the Red Guard leader, Song Binbin, that "Yaowu" was a better name than "Binbin," since "Binbin" indicated civilization and gentleness, so Song Binbin had promptly changed her name to Song Yaowu. Afterwards, many young students had followed suit. So many names in common had sprouted like new buds in spring: "Weidong," which stood for "defending Mao Zedong"; "Weihong," which implied "to protect the red"; and, "Weige," which meant "one intended to fight for the revolution." Some of Nina's fellow Red Guards had criticized her name for being too foreign, so Nina had considered adopting a new name but had not been sure which one she should use.

On August 31, Mao was to show up in Tiananmen Square for the second time. The news, like alcohol, had run in the blood of the Red Guards, and everyone across the campus was drunk. Flustered, Nina had tossed and turned on the table bed in the classroom. The night breeze had come through the open windows and cooled her a little bit. And just when she had fallen asleep, whistles blew and shouts spread across the campus. Nina had jumped out of the makeshift bed, followed the others, and hastened to Tiananmen Square. A green canvas handbag over her shoulder, her hair uncombed, and her face unwashed, she had been among the thousands of thrilled Red Guards from various parts of China. Most of them had been high-school students while some were from colleges and universities.

The swarm of people ahead of Nina had arrived at an alley, unable to move forward since the road was jammed. Apart from her schoolmates, Nina had been with a different crowd on the dimly lit street. She wondered where she was. A girl near her had said, "We're in a corner of Tiananmen Square." After standing for a while, Nina had sat down on the ground like some of the others. Fatigued and sleepy, she had leaned on the girl next to her and dozed off.

A couple of hours later, the melody of the song, "The East Is Red," had blasted from the high-volume speakers. Shouts and screams had forced Nina awake. The waiting youth had pulled one another up from the ground. Nina had stood on her toes and rubbed her eyes. The sea of students with their red-banded arms had moved like currents up and down, though the platform at the Tiananmen Tower was empty, and Mao was seen nowhere. The human waves had still moved forward. As one of those half a million little dots, Nina had inched her way in the throng toward Tiananmen Tower. Some people had tripped and fallen onto the ground because they were pushed by others who were fervent to get even closer to the Tower. The cries of "Help" from those who had been pushed down in the moving crowds mixed with wild cheers and shouts of "Long live Chairman Mao!" Frenzy and commotion surrounded Tiananmen Square.

Hold on. Don't fall! Nina had told herself. She had not wanted to die before seeing Chairman Mao. Her knees had been so weak that she had to hold onto the arms of others to remain standing. An hour later, a few vehicles in a line inched along in the distance. One man in an army uniform had stood in an open Jeep and waved his red-banded arm to the roiling crowds. Overwrought and overwhelmed with joy, all the Red Guards had blubbered. Like the others, Nina's tears, mixed with sweat, had cleaned her unwashed face. She had been hungry and weary, and yet, she shouted in a husky voice filled with revolutionary enthusiasm. She had been willing to devote her own life to the revolution, never expecting that in two weeks' time, she would be outcast from the Red Guards because her father would be branded as an enemy of the revolution.

Now, here she was once more at Peking University. She got directions for the Department of Law and then made her way around the campus till she found the right building. Classes were currently in session, so she simply waited outside until she caught sight of Rei among a throng of students emerging from one classroom. "Rei!" Nina raised her arm and waved.

Rei had arranged for her to stay in a dorm room furnished with eight bunk beds. All the girls were law majors, and half of them were sent-down youth from the countryside. The oldest one, Luja, had already turned thirty. After so many tough years, she had finally become a student in one of the top universities of China. Nina enjoyed talking with her and admired her experience and knowledge.

Nina asked Luja how it came to be that she aspired to study law and recorded what she said: "During the Cultural Revolution, like many other people working in the justice system, my father lost his job as a lawyer. He was subsequently jailed as he'd been labelled a 'rightist' because of his open opinions in 1958. Sent down from Beijing to Xinjiang Province, I lived in the rural area until I recently got accepted by the university.

"My father's case made me wonder why expressing one's beliefs was considered a crime. According to our constitution, a Chinese citizen has the freedom of speech. Anyway, because of my father's plight, I became interested in everything related to law and crime. In the countryside, I saw and heard too many horrible stories from my co-workers or from the local peasants. One thing that happened in the village really scared me.

"The newly appointed Party Secretary to my commune, a forty-year-old bachelor, raped a fifteen-year-old girl in his office. But the girl dared not to tell it to anyone because her grandfather was a former landowner, the enemy of the revolution. Besides, even if she had told someone, she was certain nobody would have believed her. The only thing the girl could do was to avoid him, but she failed. One day, the girl was assigned to cut hay in a field. The Party Secretary found her. He pushed her down into the bush and started raping her again. At that moment, some people walked by. They heard the girl's scream, so they ran over and the rapist was caught on the spot. The three witnesses reported it to the commune committee. Guess what? The Party Secretary wrote self-criticism in the form of a letter to his supervisor, admitting his guilt. Then, the authorities transferred him to a new position in another brigade. He received no punishment at all.

"Another day, the same girl who had been raped by the Party Secretary was beaten to death by some poor peasants. Their reason was that she had seduced the revolutionary leader. The girl's parents, at the same time, were forced to confess their crime as they did not stop their daughter from seducing the leader at a denunciation meeting. So they dared not even bury their poor daughter. We sent-down girls found her body and wrapped her in a used bedsheet. On a starless night, we dug a hole and buried her under a tree. If anyone had found out what we'd done, we would've been labelled as the 'enemy.' The anti-revolutionary hat would've then been ours.

"I read many books in secret: history, philosophy, and literature. It seemed the word 'revolution' covered all the violence and crime, but punished innocence. A real criminal could go free during the revolution. A victim deserved death because her grandparents committed a so-called political crime. What crime? Was it because her grandparents owned some land before the communists' takeover in 1949? This thought has haunted me. I was scared by my own ideas, which could make me a political criminal since my conclusions were opposite to that of Mao's ruling class.

"Why did I choose to study the law? For all of these reasons. My personal interests are criminal law, family law, and land law, but the compulsory courses include the History of the Chinese Communist Party and Current Politics with the Documents of the Central Party are compulsory courses. We have to waste a lot of time on them."

Nina also met other undergraduates and talked with many of them. She learned that some students from the Department of Chinese Language and Literature planned to start their first literary magazine. At that time, in 1978, all the magazines were still under the management of the government. Sick and tired of the monopolistic voice in the media, directed and controlled by the Communist Party, those students aspired to express their true feelings and opinions. They yearned to share their life experiences through creative writing. The pioneers planned to launch an underground literary magazine in September, which they had decided to call, *Our Generation*.

Students in Law, Political Science, History, and Literature initiated several after-class discussions, which Nina attended with avid interest. As she listened, she thought, *The ten-year Cultural Revolution has ended. But it will take many years to clean up its mess and for people to recover from all the damage it has caused.*

Nina wrote in her notebook that the "peaceful evolution" had begun. The passionate and committed students she met at the university helped her envision an enlightened sunshine illuminating China. She recalled years earlier that the newspapers and radio had repeated Mao's directive: "Basing themselves on the changes in the Soviet Union, the imperialist prophets are pinning their hopes of 'peaceful evolution' on the third or fourth generation of the Chinese Party. We must shatter these imperialist prophecies." As she thought about Mao's words now, she smirked. *Human evolution may be interrupted, but it cannot be halted by any dictator.*

One afternoon, Nina and Rei decided to revisit Yuanmingyuan Garden located to the north of Peking University. After passing through a campus side gate, they then wound their way along a path that cut through fields and blooming vegetable gardens. They enjoyed the expanse of clear blue sky above and the bees and dragonflies that accompanied them as they walked in companiable silence. Nina linked her arm to Rei's, then turned and asked, "Do you enjoy your studies at the university?"

"Very much. I have time and a chance to reflect on my past," answered Rei. "Twelve years ago, I was an eighth grader. When school was cancelled because of the Cultural Revolution, I was quite happy."

"Twelve years ago I came to Beijing for Mao's meeting with the Red Guards. I was so excited at that time," said Nina. "I had no idea about what really was going on."

Rei had also been a member of the Red Guard. He remembered one day when he joined others to arrest the principal who had been branded as a reactionary and an academic authority, thus unquestionably *against* the revolution. The Red Guards had taken the headmaster to the auditorium to denounce him. When the captive refused to confess his crime, the student leader had asked Rei to kick him in order to test whether Rei was loyal to the revolution. Rei had closed his eyes and raised one leg to kick the headmaster. Suddenly, his grandmother's words had rung in his ears: "Teachers and headmasters are like your parents. You should always listen to and respect them." Also, the memory of receiving a Student Award for Excellence had run through his mind. His standing leg had started to shake, and then his lifted foot stamped on the floor instead of the headmaster. As a result, Rei had lost his balance and fell down.

The lead Red Guard had pushed him off the stage. "Get out of here! You coward!" he had shouted with palpable disgust. Other Red Guards had lifted their legs or raised their arms to hit the principal. Unable to stand any longer, the captive had collapsed onto the stage.

"I'm glad I was kicked out. Or I would've done more stupid things," said Rei. "I might've even been forced to capture your father."

"Luckily, we both got thrown out of the Red Guards at that time," Nina said with a grin.

When they reached the Yuanmingyuan Garden, the European-style Imperial Palace, built in 1709, Nina stopped to admire the stone arch of the palace's wreckage. "Look at this graceful structure. I like this part best."

"Don't you think these ruins are evidence of the historical crimes of the Western imperialist invaders?" asked Rei.

"Yes, I agree, Nina said. "But, do you remember in June, 1966, students from the middle school affiliated with Qinghua University gathering here? It was here that they took a serious oath to protect Mao's red regime. That started the Red Guards' movement."

"Yes, they were patriots with hatred against Western imperialists. This was why they thought these ruins were the shame of Red China. In terms of patriotism, they weren't wrong," Rei responded.

"In my point of view, Mao used the Red Guards to defeat his political rivals solely to ensure his grip on absolute power."

"Well, I am not sure I totally agree with you about that." Rei pointed at the stone arch. "In 1860, the Anglo-French Allied Armies occupied the area. You know they set fire to the Garden. Forty years later, the Eight-Power Allied Forces destroyed the Garden completely. Maybe eating too much beef in America has made you forget these facts," he said with a chuckle. "I have mixed feelings whenever I visit here."

"Don't you mean Eight-Nation Alliance?" said Nina. "I

hope someday you can read history from a different source and angle; you may find something opposite to what you were taught to believe." Sitting down on a stone, Nina wiped the sweat on her face. "For the damages to Yuanmingyuan Garden, we can put the blame on the imperialist powers. But we also have many heritage sites that have been damaged by our generation." She reminded Rei that the Red Guards had burned the cemetery of Emperor Yan built in 967 in Hunan Province. In Shanxi Province, they had desecrated the tomb of Emperor Yao, which though originally built between 713 to 741, had subsequently been reconstructed during different dynasties. Other Red Guards had also vandalized Confucius's tomb, built in 1331, and crushed his statue in the temple at Shandong. She looked at Rei. "Rampant vandalism took place all across China during the Cultural Revolution. Should we blame the imperialists?"

"I need to think about that," Reid nodded. "Tell me why you think North America is better than China."

"The people in North America have a better life because of the democratic system," Nina said. "I think their political system is a key factor."

"I will admit there are big gaps in our legal system," Reid responded. "If we can improve it, maybe fewer people will go to jail because of their political beliefs. All in all, expressing one's opinion or beliefs shouldn't be considered a criminal act."

Nina was glad that Rei's concerns lay with how to amend current laws. She felt certain that something constructive would come out of the destructive storms of the Cultural Revolution. At the moment, she sat back and enjoyed the gentle rays of the sunset shining golden on the ruins of Yuanmingyuan Garden, while the cool breeze from the fields caressed her skin.

Some day, will the term, "political crime," finally disappear from Chinese criminal legal system? Nina wondered.

21.

FROM SANDRA'S CHIPS TO CHICKEN SOUP

AS THEY HEADED BACK to the university, Nina asked, "How about if I take you to a supper?"

"Why not?" Rei said. "There's an American fast-food diner near the campus. It opened a couple of months ago."

Nina smiled. "That sounds interesting. Let's go, then. What do they serve?"

"French fries and chicken drumsticks."

Rei led the way along a laneway paved in flagstone to an older building. An entrance with a red banner that announced "Sandra's Chips." "Here it is," Rei said.

Nina followed him inside to the counter. The small room was filled with square, black tables and benches. On each table was a bamboo container with chopsticks. Most of the customers looked like students. The aroma told Nina it was authentic American fast food.

She joined Rei at the counter and ordered. On an unoccupied table, they laid their plates of fries and drumsticks and sat down. Nina picked up a French fry with her fingers and dipped it into the tiny ketchup cup. "Hmmm, these are good," she said, licking her fingers. A plastic fork in his hand, Rei caught three fries but had trouble dipping them in ketchup. "I'll follow your wild American table manners," he said, pinching a few fries together with his fingers to dip in the ketchup.

"Americans have good table manners when they eat fancy dinners. When they eat fast food they just use their fingers,"

Nina said, grinning. "But note, please, making noise when you chew food is considered bad table manners to Americans, even though to us it means the food is delicious."

"Really? So Americans have opposite notions of eating etiquette?"

"Oh, yes," Nina said, nodding. She remembered that she had seldom used her fingers to pinch food from bowls since she had been instructed not to do so as a little girl. *My habits have changed.* She picked up a drumstick in her hand. *I even enjoy iced water instead of warm water.*

"Excuse me," a woman said in Chinese with a strong American accent when she placed a glass on the table. "My server said you'd asked for iced water. You're the first customer I've had who asked for that."

"Thanks so much," said Nina, smiling at the blonde woman in a Chinese outfit. "You must be the owner," she said, admiring the woman's silk blouse with mandarin collar and pants with floral embroidery on the hems. Then, in English, she added, "You can speak English if you wish."

"I only own a half," the blonde grinned. When she noticed the puzzled look on Nina's face, she continued in English. "My husband owns the other half. By the way, where did you learn to speak English so well?"

"In America." Nina smiled. "It's amazing to eat American fast food in Beijing. Your restaurant must be the first one here in the city?"

"Maybe. If we do well, some day we might even be able to buy a license to open a Kentucky Fried Chicken."

"Interesting. Where are you from?"

"Maine," the owner answered. "Have you been there?"

"I lived there for years. I even graduated from a university there."

"It's a small world! I'm Sandra."

"I'm Nina. Nice to meet you."

"You, too." At the moment, Sandra heard one of the servers

call out to her. "I've got to go. I hope to see you again." She turned and walked hurriedly to the kitchen.

Rei sipped from a glass of soft drink. "I knew every word you said, but I didn't completely understand what you were saying."

"You need to listen to English more often, instead of only reading it." Nina tapped the table lightly with her fingers. "She's from Maine. You know I lived there for many years."

"Come here again. You can chat with her again," Rei said. "You know, students who are majoring in English come here often so they can practise English with the owners. Also, they get to have a taste of American culture."

"Do you enjoy eating the food here?"

"It's not too bad, but it's more expensive than our canteen. Based on the policy, students who've worked for over five years before going to university get paid, so I do get a decent salary. But I need to save for round-trip tickets, so I can see Ahua at least twice a year." Rei stood up.

"You get a salary for studying? Well, that's great," said Nina. "And I am glad you get some time to see your wife too." They disposed of their empty plates and cups, and left Sandra's Chips, feeling satisfied and ready for the next day's research and studies.

When she got back to her room, Nina wrote a brief letter to Roger.

June 27, 1978
My dear Roger,

Did you receive the letter I sent from Guangzhou?

I'm in Peking University now and staying in a girls' dorm room. I've visited a few historic spots. They are fantastic. And I've met some interesting people and recorded some interviews for my book. The research is going well.

Tonight, I had dinner at an American fast food restaurant near the university called Sandra's Chips. It's run by an American couple. What a surprise! Most customers are university students. I'm going to go there again. Can you believe it? I had French fries!

I'll send you a postcard after I get to Inner Mongolia even though I'll probably be back in Yarmouth before it reaches you.

Take care of yourself.

Love,

Nina

Then she sent a note to Liya, telling her about her conversation with Rei's classmate from Hohhot. She explained that Jing would help them meet with a few people in Inner Mongolia so that Nina could record their stories. She let Liya know where she was staying on campus, and that she looked forward to seeing her soon.

The following day, she walked to Sandra's Chips again hoping that she would be able to chat with some students there. As she walked along the flagstones, she thought of the scholar exams that had taken place in Beijing, the ancient capital, over several dynasties. Ambitious, young, educated men from all over China had come and gone along these once cobblestoned streets, anxious figures expecting to pass their imperial exams and earn an academic certificate granted by the Emperor. A person with that certificate would be appointed a civil service officer. Most educated people had spent all their youth preparing for this annual event. She recalled an ancient story about a man named Fan Jin who had failed the exams several years in a row. When he had finally passed and received his certificate, he suffered a nervous breakdown.

She was lost in the thought of the sad tale of Fan Jin when a young man appeared beside her. "Hello, are you going to the restaurant?"

Confused, she asked, "Yes, how did you know?"

The young man explained. "Yesterday, I saw you speaking to the American owner. I go there often."

Relieved that she wasn't actually being watched or followed by any plainclothes policeman, Nina smiled and asked, "Why?"

"I'm majoring in English. This small diner is a real window to the outside. Sometimes, students can discuss certain topics without fear of being reported. In addition, some of us like to practise speaking in English there. We call this place our 'English Corner.'"

Nina was curious. "What do you talk about?"

"Everything. Freedom, love, money, success, passion, and education. You name it, and it's open for discussion."

When they reached the restaurant, the student said, "Please, go ahead." He stopped. "I'm going to the bookstore now. But you may run into Yueming here. She's a top student."

After she bought some potato salad, Nina joined two young women at a table. It happened that one of them was, indeed, Yueming, from Daxing County near Beijing. She had been accepted in to the university by earning high scores on the entrance exams.

"Did you start to learn English at high school?" asked Nina, as she looked at shiny-eyed Yueming.

"I didn't learn much in high school. I learned it from my former English teacher at elementary school," Yueming said. Noticing the puzzled expression on Nina's face, she explained. "In 1973, a fifteen-year-old student, Zhang Yuqin failed an English test, but her words, 'without learning the a, b, c, I still can be a successor...'" Yueming paused, and then added, "She meant a successor to Mao's revolutionary cause." This became a catchphrase carried in newspapers everywhere in China and that school was then heralded as an example of revolutionary re-education. This was further compounded when another student, Huang Shuai, sent a letter to the *Beijing Daily* to complain about a teacher who had punished her, and this led to the criticism of the school system and also led to the demand for revisionist education. As a result, all teachers, especially teachers of English, were criticized by their students formally or informally all across China." Yueming shook her head, and her bobbed hair trembled as if those unpleasant moments had returned. "Of course, English was no longer taught, among many other topics. And, indeed, no students dared express the desire to learn English, but I loved it. I didn't want to give up. So I begged my teacher to tutor me in secret. That enabled me to be accepted at Peking University four years later. My former teacher was just great." Yueming's admiration for her teacher was so contagious that when she suggested visiting her teacher a few days after her last exam, Nina did not hesitate to join her on the trip to Daxing County.

Nina and Yueming took a bus to the small village where Yueming's family lived. They welcomed them with open arms and a small feast for dinner. The next afternoon, they decided to visit Yueming's former elementary school. They waded through the bushes and pushed their way through the taller sorghum plants. Yueming said, "I walked this route to school daily for six years before going to university. When Teacher Gao started tutoring me, I would meet with her every Sunday morning.

"Did she live at the school?"

"Yes. Only a few single teachers lived in the school dormitory. On the weekend, everyone went home except her."

"Why didn't she?"

"She didn't seem to have any family. She never mentioned them."

"Did she tutor you even when you went to high school?"

"That's right. Without her help, I wouldn't be attending Peking University."

Finally, they reached a large field where a scraggly flock of chickens scratched in the weeds, while a variety of small birds hopped on the basketball playground nearby. A one-storey building came into view.

Nina followed Yueming into the building. "Here's Teacher Gao's room," she said, knocking on the flimsy wood door. A short-haired woman of about thirty opened it and greeted them warmly. "Come on in, Yueming," Gao said. Her eyes, huge under thick glasses, fixated on Nina.

"This is my new friend, Nina. She wants to see you."

"See me?" Gao asked, a puzzled look on her face.

"You trained Yueming to be an English major," Nina said, her eyes sweeping past the woman and taking in the scant furnishings. Nina felt like she was witnessing her own past. Nina's heart opened. "Years ago, I was one of the sent-down youths. However, I was able to move to the United States and I have since graduated from an American university. I'm researching the experiences of my generation for a book I intend to write."

"How?" Gao's eyes were wide open. "How did you get to America?"

"My uncle's there. I went to stay with his family." Nina did not want to scare Gao. Sneaking across the border was considered a political crime, so she had to be cautious. If anyone from Public Security were to find out, Nina would be jailed.

"My father also graduated from an American university," Gao said. Her oval face beamed but clouded soon. She gestured for Nina and Yueming to sit on the edge of her bed. Then she boiled water in a pot. The smell of kerosene from the small metal stove spread in the air.

"Where's your father now?" asked Nina.

"As a labelled 'rightist,' my father was sent to a faraway forced-labour camp at Jiabiangou Valley in Gansu Province. My mother divorced him in order to protect me from political discrimination. When the Cultural Revolution started, I was a freshman student in the English Department of Beijing Normal University. Soon, my mother was denounced as a 'stinking bourgeoisie.' Shortly afterward, she killed herself,"

Gao said, her voice quivering. She bent to lift the boiling pot, filled it with tea leaves, and then poured the tea into mugs. She continued to talk about how she was dispatched to the countryside that same year to receive re-education from the peasants. Years later, the school needed teachers badly because they couldn't find any, so she was recruited, but only on a temporary basis due to her tarnished family background. Gao explained that nobody wanted to be a teacher in those years, as they were labelled "Stinking Number Nines." And, in any case, because the universities had been closed for several years, no students had graduated from normal schools or universities, so when schools reopened, they were forced to recruit high school graduates to be teachers.

As Gao spoke, she laid two mugs of tea on a square stool in front of them. Then, she took a paper bag from a desk drawer and pulled out some almond cookies. "Help yourselves," she said, turning to a chair near the stool and sitting down. The sunset emitted a soft glow through the window that reflected off her face. "Every cloud has a silver lining," she said in a wistful tone that touched a chord in Nina's heart.

"Do you have any news to tell us?" Nina and Yueming asked Gao at the same time.

"Yes! I've been accepted into a graduate program at Beijing Normal University." She clasped her hands in front of her chest.

Yueming gripped Gao's arm. "I knew this day would come. I knew it!"

"Congratulations!" Nina got up off the bed and put a hand on Gao's shoulder. "Let's celebrate. Is there a store around?" she asked. Maybe she could pick up a bottle of wine.

"The store is far. And it's already closed by now," said Gao. "But we can make chicken soup."

Nina looked at the newspaper-covered walls made of mud bricks and the old shelves lined with various items. The only table was piled with exercise books to be marked. There was no sign of a refrigerator or a cooler. She suddenly remembered that most people in China did not have a refrigerator. At that moment, Yueming jumped up and ran outside. "We'll have to catch a chicken first!" Gao followed laughing brightly.

Aha! So that's where the chicken comes from! Nina laughed out loud to as she ran with them into the field. With their arms held wide open, they chased a hen, pushing it into the corner of the building where the chicken coop, made of mud and a roof of branches, was located. The hen scurried into the coop. Dust swirled around. Yueming reached out and caught the hen from inside the shelter. The other chickens fluttered their wings in panic.

Some time later, an enamel basin, covered by a wooden cutting board, sat on the kerosene stove. Eventually, the aroma of chicken soup spread over the spacious room. Later, shreds of cabbage from Gao's own vegetable garden were added to the soup.

"It smells so delicious." Nina held up her bowl to her nose and took a deep whiff.

"Maybe I should suggest that Sandra's Chips add chicken soup to their menu," Yueming said, grinning. She passed out some steamed buns she had brought from home to Nina and Gao. "They're fresh, made of this year's wheat."

"What is 'Sandra's Chips'?" asked Gao.

"An American fast-food restaurant near my university. I'll be working there starting next Monday," Yueming said as she ate. "That'll be something new. I'll learn how to make money as a student."

"That's a really new idea," said Gao, exhilaration in her voice. Imagining her future life as a graduate student and thinking about the return to her hometown, Beijing, thrilled her. Her heart was full, and the two young women with her were delighted for her.

As night fell, Gao took three stools from a classroom next door and placed them along the side of her bed. With abundant bedding added over the top of the stools, her bed was now king-sized. The electricity went off at eight o'clock. Gao lit a candle as usual. *No wonder her eyesight is so poor,* thought Nina.

A cool breeze blew in through the window. Starlight also streamed in to bolster the candlelight. Gao's story blended with the dim light. During her first four years in the countryside, she had worked with peasants to grow wheat and soybeans. She had aimed to forget about learning and teaching English and her past as well, with the idea that after the purgatory, she might once again have a bright future. In addition to the physical hardship of work on the farm, she had found her soul was empty despite Mao's directives ringing in her head and revolutionary songs flooding her ears. It was only later, when she started to listen to English on the Voice of America, did her hellish world slowly fade away.

"Now I feel like I'm in paradise," Gao said, drawing in a long breath. "I'll go look for my father right away after school finishes."

Nina asked, "When is the last time you saw him?"

"Eighteen years ago. That was in 1960 when I was a seventh grader. He came back to Beijing to sign the divorce papers. He said he'd always love me no matter what became of him, but from then on, I should exclude his name whenever I filled out any forms. It was a way to let me evade any connection with him. In other words, being related to him could ruin my future. Luckily, I was accepted to a university in 1965 while many high-school graduates were rejected because of their undesirable family background. Only then could I understand why my parents had divorced. I thought I would find my father after my university graduation, but of course, that never transpired. And now, thirteen years have passed, and with those, my dream passed too." Gao sighed. "I hope my father has survived."

Gao's words touched Nina's heart where indelible feelings were deeply buried. "I wish my father had lived to see today." The scene of that downhearted day came to mind: her mother's trembling hands embracing the dark rosewood box that held her father's ashes. Nina had cried with her mother, staring at her father's photograph on the front board of the small casket.

Gao wrapped her arm gently around Nina's shoulder. "I'm sorry to bring up this topic."

"I'm okay. I'll keep my fingers crossed that you find your father." Looking at Gao, she patted her on the back. "Those terrifying days are finally over. I feel relieved."

"So do I. Now tell me about your studies in the U.S."

Nina's stories continued while the candle's flame flickered in the dark and her companions listened attentively. Eventually, the candle's light died out. It was before dawn; the first rooster crowed. Soon, a chorus of cocks would announce daybreak.

22.

IN THE NAME OF THE REVOLUTION

AFTER SAYING GOODBYE and wishing Gao the best of luck, Nina and Yueming returned to Beijing on the Sunday afternoon. As planned, Liya joined Nina on campus.

The following morning, while Yueming started her first day of work at Sandra's Chips, Nina and Liya boarded the train to Hohhot City, the provincial capital of Inner Mongolia, one of the major provinces, to which an influx of youths from big cities had been dispatched. Rei's classmate, Jing, was arranging some interviews for them.

Nina remembered her previous experience of travelling, so she brought plenty of bottled water along with them in case water was unavailable on the train. The morning sunlight flashed through the open windows as the train glided past the open fields, and the breeze that streamed in cooled the warm air inside. The long-distance travellers dozed in their seats while the local passengers moved about carrying heavy baskets and fully loaded sacks. Some of them had just boarded the train, but others were ready to leave.

Liya noticed Nina's look of curiosity. "These people are vendors who go from town to town," she explained. "They buy goods from this location and sell them in another."

Nina nodded. "I saw this the last time when I was in China visiting my mother. I think these people may well be tomorrow's businessmen," she added.

"Maybe or maybe not," said Liya. "Right now all they think about is how to make money by any means possible to them."

"If everybody thinks about getting rich, the whole country may become wealthy. Aiming to be rich isn't necessarily a bad thing."

Liya picked up on Nina's train of thought. "Do you think if people's basic needs are met, they won't be interested in the revolution?"

"That's right. I believe a peaceful evolution is happening right now."

Liya laughed. "It's funny how we can be on the same wavelength even though we're currently walking different paths in life." By the way," Liya said, pulling out a few folded pages from her handbag. "Can you read this and tell me what you think?"

Nina unfolded the cover page. The title, "In the Name of Revolution," caught her attention immediately. She read:

Spring of 1975 arrived with shocking news
Zhang Zhixin was taken to an execution place
Her feet chained, her hands in cuffs
She was a communist and a mother.

Looking into the sky, she opened her mouth
But she was forever voiceless
Her windpipe slashed by the killers
They feared her words.

Arrested as an anti-revolutionist
Because of her critical comments
Decapitation ended her breaths
Darkness swallowed her flesh and bones.

Raised under Mao's red flag
She practised the communist cause

Anti-revolution and opposing Mao were her crimes
I do not understand the puzzle of this.

Here, tears blurred Nina's eyes, so she pulled a handkerchief out of her pocket and wiped her cheeks. Then she continued.

Who slit her throat and forced her death?
The Communist Party and her comrades.
I have figured it out at last:
She wasn't allowed to have opposing views.

Dare I ask Mao and his Communist Party?
I fear my throat will be cut into two pieces
In the name of revolution, for thought crimes
Such questions can turn me to ashes.

I am asking mountains and oceans
Scouring the sky for answers
In the name of righteous justice
But the world is wrapped in silence.

If telling the truth is offensive
Then everyone is a felon.
If everybody dares not tell the truth
What kind of the nation is this?

If an honest citizen should be slashed
The People's Republic of China is dangerous.
If the communists have to destroy innocents
I must disagree with this practice.

Did her family dare to weep those fearful days?
Have her children survived the savagery?
Tears wash my face while my heart bleeds
In the name of humanity, my dignity awakens.

Nina's heart sank deeply as she read through the poem. She lay the pages on the table, and, with trembling hands, refolded them. "Touching and powerful," she said. "Can you tell me more about this slaughtered woman?"

"Yes," Liya said, and she glanced at the people in the seat across from them. A man in his late forties rested his forehead on the table, napping. The other man, who looked like a peasant, sat back, a bamboo pole leaning on his shoulder. His two hands busily flipped through a bundle of ten and twenty fen bills.

Liya lowered her voice and started the story. "Zhang Zhixin was jailed three years ago because she doubted in Lin Biao, Mao's successor. She didn't want to admit she had committed a crime, so she was executed. Her husband was even forced to divorce her."

Nina felt as if all her old nightmares about the red terror had returned. *Such political oppression has been dealt to my father, to Dahai's mother, to Gao's father, to millions of fathers and mothers, sons and daughters. They've been persecuted and slaughtered in the name of the revolution and under the red flag of Mao's regime.*

Nina imagined Roger would widen his eyes if he were listening to the story. His fingers would freeze on his guitar strings. "Your poem is very impressive, but you have to be careful," she whispered as she placed the pages into Liya's handbag. "You don't want to get into trouble for that."

"Don't worry," Liya whispered so that only Nina could hear. "A group of my fellow students are getting ready to launch a literary magazine named *New Buds*. Such poems and short stories will be in the inaugural issue in October. Students from other universities are doing the same. Freedom of speech has been written into our constitution for a long time. We'll see if this freedom can be put into practice."

"I feel excited about your magazine. The students at Peking University plan to run a literary magazine called *Our Generation*," said Nina as she thought about all those who had been punished for expressing their different opinions, or for telling the truth about what had occurred during the political movements since 1949. She added, "I only wish that such persecution would never happen again."

"People are learning and awakening. If we don't speak up, who will?" Liya clenched her hand into a fist. She envisioned thousands of university students holding up various copies of the new underground magazines, enthusiasm and wisdom on their faces. Nina could see the desire for freedom on her face, and she shivered, knowing that the price of such freedom could be high.

"Ladies!" A loud voice erupted out of the mouth of the sleepy man. "You should obey Chairman Mao's will!"

Nina raised her head. The middle-aged man from the opposite seat had pulled a cigarette out of his front pocket. He casually lit it, and then said, "The revolution continues." He took a hard, deep puff, drew in the nicotine, and then let the smoke escape from his nostrils. "You bourgeoisie can't change the world. Anti-revolution is a crime! Am I right, my peasant brother?" He nudged his neighbour's shoulder. "Wake up, my brother, and speak!"

"I'm not against revolution. Chairman Mao was my saviour," answered the peasant, placing a palm-sized cloth pouch on the table. Then he pulled a white slip of paper from his pocket. "But Deng Xiaoping let me earn money. Now my family has enough to eat and wear." Back and forth between pouch and paper, his fingers quickly pinched tobacco shreds and then laid them on the white slip to roll into a cigarette. "Worker Bro, try my cigarette. It might be better than yours."

The worker accepted the cigarette that the peasant had lit. He took a puff, then exhaled. "It is more tasty," he acknowledged, nodding and lightly slapping the peasant's back.

"What's the difference between capitalism and socialism? The students' talk is all mumbo-jumbo," said the peasant. He rolled up another cigarette, this time for himself. "You don't need to bother with them. We know better, don't we?"

"That's true. Chairman Mao always said that intellectuals stink. They should learn from us workers and peasants." The worker puffed hard on the cigarette. "The world changes fast," he sighed, "and not always for the better." Wafts of smoke blew out from his mouth and nose.

Soon, the smoke from the two men clouded the seats and made Nina and Liya cough, but they remained where they were since there were no other empty seats. Nina grabbed Liya's arm and spoke softly into her ear, "We should be more careful. Some people don't even realize or aren't concerned about the problems in the system."

Liya nodded and turned her head to the window. Everything looked vague through the cigarette smoke but a warm breeze blew in and diluted the choking air around the booth.

When the train reached Hohhot Railway Station, Jing was waiting on the platform. She took them to her parents' apartment in a building that belonged to the *Inner Mongolian Daily*. During the summer holiday, Jing returned home to take care of her mother, who was in the hospital. Nina felt fortunate to have this opportunity to meet people in this area through Jing, and they accepted the young woman's invitation to stay in her home overnight. Jing had arranged a meeting with Muying, a co-worker from a military farm, who just recently had been one of the lucky people accepted into a college program. "You'll be very much touched by her story," Jing said.

Nina's heart shrank when she saw Muying perched on the edge of a bed in her room even though Jing had mentioned the burn on her face beforehand. The skin on her face looked like charred bark. Her eyes were two dark holes, and her nose was a knob above an unclosed mouth. In the dim room, her face was almost frightening. Turning her eyes toward the unopened window curtains, Nina suddenly understood that the sunlight might be a discomfort to their hostess.

"Muying, this is Nina and Liya," Jing introduced them to the woman, who gestured for them to sit on a bench near her bed.

"Congratulations on your acceptance to college," said Nina when she shook Muying's outstretched hand.

"Jing told me you were coming. I am happy to share my story with you." Muying started with her past right away.

"I was only fifteen when I was sent to the military farm. I learned quickly how to ride horseback and tend sheep. Besides coping with the changeable weather and insufficient sustenance, we were also plagued with a lack of electricity. Without sanitary paper for our menses, we were obliged to cut our underwear into pieces and use them as substitutes. Did you do the same at that time?" Muying's dark eye holes turned to Nina, then Liya.

Nina nodded. Liya said, "So did I. None of us had the money to buy tissues that we could use during our monthly courses."

Muying continued her story. "But three years later, I got used to the nomadic life. In fact, I already looked like a shepherd girl with my red frostbitten face and sheepskin gown. We grew wheat, cut grass, and tended animals. There were about two hundred student workers like me."

Nina easily pictured the numerous herds of cattle and sheep scattered about on the endless grassland of that northern military farm, and she also understood how that life might even, after a time, become appealing and comfortable. Tragedy struck a fall evening in 1973, when a severe fire had been aggravated by a strong gust of wind and quickly spread to a large sheep pen. A husky voice had shouted, "Fire! Fire!" Some of the young men and women had stopped what they were doing and scuttled over to the burning pen with spades or hoes slung over their shoulders.

Around the tents, the Political Commissar, responsible for the political education of these young men and women, had hollered, "Comrades, we should protect the state property! Chairman Mao says, 'Wherever there is struggle there is sacrifice, and death is a common occurrence!'"

Muying and the other workers had dashed out from different dwellings. Some held pails of water; some gripped brooms. They hastened over to the fire and smoke.

Muying's short hair had still been wet from washing; the warm wind on the grassland soon dried her hair. But before she reached the edge of the blaze, she had felt as though she were being roasted in an oven. Some of the workers in front of her swatted their brooms and spades in the burning bushes in an attempt to halt the spread of the fire. The charred wood smell mixed with the stench of burning animals had choked her breath. Some flames had then engulfed a young girl just in front of her, and Muying leapt to pour the water from her jug on the flames. She had then thrown down the bucket and pulled at the girl's arm to try and get her to drop and roll onto the ground, but the heat from the flames overwhelmed Muying and she collapsed in a smouldering heap on the ground. Realizing her hair was on fire, she had slapped at the strands with her hands, but a fireball rolled over her and it pressed her into a tiny speck of dust, consuming her face.

Three days later, she had awakened in the hospital. Her bandaged head had looked like a white basketball. Her eyes, nose, and mouth had been reduced to four small openings of different sizes and shapes that merely suggested a face. She had only then learned that twelve young men and women had lost their lives. She had been one of three pulled out of the raging fire to have survived. The second- and third-degree burns had confined her to bed for several weeks.

"Besides suffering from the lingering pain, I was anxious about how I look," Muying said, fingering her ear-length dark hair. "Although there're ugly scars over my limbs, I still held out hope that my face wouldn't be destroyed too much. When the bandage was removed, I slowly opened my eyes in front of a mirror. What a shock! My desperation reached a peak at that moment. I felt as if I had been slapped. Stars twinkled in front of my eyes. Scared, I dared not look at my own face again. After that, I didn't want to have any mirrors in my house. I was angry for surviving. Living became a burden to me. Whenever I envisioned my face, I couldn't breathe. The Political Commissar who had ordered us to fight the fire was promoted. The dozen workers who died as a result were recognized as revolutionary martyrs. I refused to give a speech as a surviving heroine because I realized that state property had been more valuable than those twelve lives or my health. The property could be rebuilt, but my fellow workers would never come back to life.

"Afterwards, I was rewarded for my sacrifice — I was allowed to return to the city. I was alive, but I felt like a corpse. At eighteen, I felt like I was eighty. I was assigned a job as a warehouse keeper for the graveyard shift. I was glad nobody would see me. But I deeply missed the sheep and cows that I'd helped raise. I started to read books about animals, which has become the greatest pleasure in my life." Muying paused. A glow sparkled on her face, as if sunbeams had brightened a cloudy sky.

"You asked me how I decided to go to college. That was because of Jing, who persuaded me to apply after the entrance exams were reinstated. I didn't want to because of my horrible face, until this May. Jing's letter about her studies and her student life enlightened my dreary heart and suddenly I felt like I should try to live again. Now I pray I can cope with people's strange looks and reactions when they see me."

"You're brave. People will know you by your heart and intelligence," replied Liya with an admiring tone.

Nina smiled encouragingly. "I think you'll enjoy your new life. As a matter of fact, you can probably also get some surgery to help with some of the scarring on your face."

"If I won't look at myself, who will?" said Muying with a rueful tone.

Touched by her words, Nina wrapped an arm around Muying's shoulder. "Hopefully, you'll feel like a new person at college."

Nina imagined that once Muying was walking on campus, confidence would shine in her eyes and heart.

Before they left, Muying pulled open the always closed curtain. Sunshine poured in through the window. The darkish room was brightened immediately. All of them squinted their eyes, but delight radiated from each face.

23.

GENGHIS KHAN'S TWO HORSES

TUESDAY AFTERNOON, Nina and Liya visited Jing's former high-school classmate Weimin, who had been sent to the Peach Blossom Village in Yuquan District, a suburb of Hohhot, for his re-education. The Tomb of Zhaojun, built during the Western Han Dynasty nearly two thousand years earlier, was located in the area, nine kilometres from the city. According to Weimin, a gulag called Peach Blossom Camp was also located there. One of his co-workers had been jailed in the labour camp after being caught trying to cross the border into the Soviet Union. The same compound confined many branded rightists as well.

Nina and Liya decided to visit the gulag. If they were lucky, they might be able to speak to some people still imprisoned there. After drawing a map of the area on a scrap of paper, Weimin jotted down the name and address of a rancher who lived near the gulag. "He's Mongolian, very kind. He helped me a lot in my years there. Go visit him. He'll show you around."

The next morning, when Nina and Liya reached the bus terminal, Weimin was already waiting for them. He had brought a small packet of sticking plasters with him and asked Nina to pass the packet along to his rancher friend.

Forty-five minutes later, the bus arrived at the stop for Peach Blossom. Nina and Liya got off and followed a path in the grassland, bathed in sunlight, that led them to the Tomb of

Zhaojun. A gentle mist rose from the earth and twinkled over the open field. At the end of the path, a large mound came into view. "That's the Tomb of Zhaojun," Liya said, pointing to it with excitement.

"Are you sure?" Nina asked, wiping the perspiration from her face with a tissue.

"I'm positive. Do you notice that it is green and not yellow?" Liya noted, then said, "That's why people call it the 'Green Mound.' It's said that even in late fall, the plants over the mound continue growing green while the grass and the leaves in the trees everywhere else turn brown and wither.

"I never heard that before. The vegetation on the mound must be evergreens."

"According to the legend, it is because Zhaojun's spirit is forever young." Liya remembered that she had read that in a history book.

"Tell me more about Zhaojun," Nina said.

"She was one of numerous concubines of Emperor Yuan of the Han Dynasty, roughly two thousand years ago. The people of the Han Dynasty and the Huns, a nomadic people in the north, were constantly at war. The chief of the Huns, Khan Huhanxie, travelled to the capital, Beijing, in order to make peace with Emperor Yuan. To strengthen the relationship with the minority group, Emperor Yuan proposed a marriage between the chief and a woman from his imperial family. Zhaojun Wang, considered as one of the four most beautiful women in ancient China, volunteered to marry the Hun to ensure the unity of China. After their marriage, the two nations enjoyed a peaceful and friendly relationship and there were no more wars between the Hans and the Huns.

It took them almost an hour to reach the large cemetery mound, which they explored with interest as they admired the scenery around them. Nina took some snapshots of the tomb. Then, they sat down under a pine tree to rest, and Nina pulled out some apples from her satchel as Liya opened a package of dried apricots. They shared their snacks and drank water from the canteens they had brought with them.

Through the grass, they spotted a herd of sheep ambling toward them. Behind the animals was a young boy wearing a white sleeveless robe and whistling a Mongolian folk song. The melody was both joyful and mournful, and added a gentle note to the fields of grass and wildflowers.

"Hello, young fellow! Could you tell me what you are singing?" asked Liya in a loud voice.

"It's called, 'Genghis Khan's Two Horses,'" said the shepherd. He turned his head to look at them and asked, "Are you by chance named Wang?"

"No, why?" replied Liya.

The lad whistled long and low to halt his sheep, and then walked over to them. "Wang's people come here to pray for blessings. I thought you might be one of them.

"Sit here," Liya said. "Do you need water?" She shook her canteen.

"No, thanks. I have my own." The youngster patted a felt bag hanging on his waistband. He then inserted his whip into the band.

"How about an apple, then?" Nina asked, passing one to the boy.

He accepted the apple and took a big bite. "Tastes good. Thanks. So, why are you here?"

Liya said, "We just wanted to see the Green Mound." She paused, then asked, "Can you sing 'Gada Meilin'?"

"Absolutely." The teenager hummed the tune and Liya joined him in the song. "The young wild goose from the south longs to fly to the Yangtze. I'm telling the story about Gada Meilin. He led an uprising against the tyrannical warlord."

Nina had heard the Chinese version of the Mongolian folk song as a child and remembered some of the lyrics, so she joined them. The boy sung loudly. He held the unfinished apple, his hand waving in the air. Liya could not follow him since she only knew a small portion of the lyrics that had been translated into Chinese. The mellifluous voice of the young singer floated over the weeds and delicately wound around the Green Mound. Nina imagined the spirit of the Mongolian rebel resting in peace, while the song told of his exploits. Ten minutes later, the boy paused. "It would take me a couple of hours to sing this entire song," he said, returning to his apple.

Nina and Liya clapped enthusiastically. "That was wonderful! Where did you learn it?" asked Nina.

"From my parents, my grandparents, and my neighbours. Everybody can sing it. We also sing many other songs. We're Genghis Khan's offspring. We do all the things that he enjoyed."

"Do you go to worship Genghis Khan?" asked Liya.

"We worship him every day. But my family sometimes brings our homemade kumis to visit his tomb. We pray for blessings, just like the people from the Wang clan. They come here to pray at the Tomb of Zhaojun."

"Your family name isn't Khan, is it?" asked Liya.

"No, but we Mongols are all from the same family. Genghis Khan is our oldest ancestor. He's our God." The lad stood up, and pulled his whip out from his waistband. His whip swirling in the air, he waded through the grass over to his waiting sheep. "Ooh!" he yelled, turning to smile at them. Then the shepherd and his sheep gradually disappeared amidst the long grasses.

"Let's go to Dalai," said Nina. Liya stood up and looked in the direction the boy had taken. "His voice was amazing and his songs moved me."

"I too was moved. Ah, I forgot to ask him about which direction to go in," said Nina.

"Don't worry. Let's go back to the path. I'm sure we'll find our way."

At the roadside, Nina and Liya found a sign for the village of Wulanbatu. They knew that the village of Dalai was in the same direction. They had been told that they would find the Peach Blossom Camp near Dalai.

The sun was high in the sky and warmed their backs as they trekked south. Liya interpreted the long and short verses by famous poets in Chinese history, such as Du Fu, Bai Juyi, and Su Shi. "Laments of Zhaojun," which she had learned from a course on the Chinese Ancient Classics, was one of her favourites. Zhaojun had had to adjust to the totally different language and culture of the Huns. The sense of isolation and homesickness in Zhaojun's words from centuries earlier seemed to intensify the heat of the day. Gazing at the endless grassland and edgeless sky, Nina seemed to feel what Zhaojun had experienced thousands of years before. Admiration arose in her heart.

They trudged along for about an hour and finally spotted a sign for Wulanbatu. Following Weimin's map, they turned west and continued walking. They reached an area of large fields, some of which were filled by corn stalks, while other fields had heaps of wheat stalks. They did not spot any yurts, so they wandered around. When they noticed a few poles with barbed wire along a path, they knew they were in the right spot. Nina took several photographs of the poles as they reminded her of her former military farm. She knew these camps were far worse than the military farm where she had lived and worked. The workers in these camps were constantly watched by armed guards. They had no freedom.

The path ended abruptly at the edge of an open grassy field that accommodated a large herd of sheep. They could see two people slouched against a tree. "Hiyo!" a young voice rose from under the tree. "Did you people follow me?"

Nina recognized the boy they had met earlier. "We're just looking around." She and Liya strode through the grass over to them.

"You must know a shortcut," said Liya.

"I know everything here. My cousin does too," the lad said, and patted the other herder's arm. "Look. That's a 'ghost gate', a place where many have suffered and died." He pointed at a wall made of mud beyond a large grove of shrubbery and trees.

Nina noticed the barbed wire on top of the wall and some wild jujube trees by a small gate. "Is that Peach Blossom Camp?"

"Yes. How do you know its name? Some people have been in there for ages. They're my grandpa's age. Our old people tell us that these inmates opposed the Emperor."

Nina understood the boy. She knew that in the Mongols' minds, Mao was the Emperor.

"Do you mean Chairman Mao?" Liya asked with surprise.

"What's the difference? We don't like any emperor. We have our Genghis Khan. Don't you agree, my cousin?" the boy asked. He pulled the arm of his cousin who seemed to be in his early twenties, and completely disinterested in the conversation.

His cousin answered, "You're absolutely right, but we don't want to talk about the Emperor. We don't need any trouble. Gada Meilin upset the emperor fifty years ago and was killed for it."

The cousin nodded curtly to the boy. "Let's enjoy our break." We still have a long way to go."

Nina and Liya waded through the tall grass that led to the wall until they could see the gate clearly. Nina then took aim with her camera and took some photographs of the gate as she tried to imagine what it looked like behind the walls.

Just as she placed her camera back in its case, a shout broke out. "Freeze!" A large man carrying a rifle scuttled over to them.

Nina froze. Liya gripped Nina's arm and hissed, "What should we do?"

"Don't move," Nina whispered, inhaling her fear. "Let's just wait." *What is he going to do? Arrest us?*

As the armed young guard approached them, he shouted again. "Give me your camera!" He then thrust his hand in Nina's bag and grabbed it. Opening the camera, he pulled the film out and then handed the camera back to Nina. "Taking photos is forbidden." He looked over at the two shepherds under the tree, cupped his hands around his mouth, and raised his voice, "What are you two doing there?"

"We-are-herding-our-sheep," two voices answered in a long, drawn-out tone.

"Don't loiter here! Get lost!" the armed man hollered.

"Okay," the young voices drifted away to the melody of "Genghis Khan's Two Horses."

"Show me your I.D.," the guard ordered Nina and Liya.

Liya glanced at Nina and took out a letter-sized page, which stated who she was. The guard hung the strap of his rifle over his shoulder in order to hold the paper flat in the wind with his two hands. He looked at it. The stamp was of Pearl River University. "The letter says you're travelling to view our motherland's mountains and rivers," the man said, his finger passing over the sentences. "But this place is not open for visiting." After he returned the letter to Liya, he stretched his hand out to Nina. "Yours?"

Nina fished into her satchel but pulled out nothing. "Sorry, I can't find mine." She was grateful that she had thought to leave her American passport behind. It would have only caused more suspicion.

"What's in your bag? Let's take a look," the guard said. He pulled Nina's bag open and rummaged inside.

"Inside there are only some provisions for our trip," Nina said meekly.

"Follow me through the gate to meet the warden." The guard returned Nina's bag and patted his rifle.

Liya hooked her arm into Nina's. "I'll go too."

"You don't have to," the guard said.

"We go together," Nina added firmly.

"That's right," Liya said immediately afterward. Their arms linked, they walked through the gate, the guard with the rifle right behind them.

The melody of "Genghis Khan's Two Horses" vanished, but the lyrics still resounded in Nina's head. *His two horses cross the hillside/ Their manes flow high/ No matter come rain or shine/ Genghis Khan's horses never die.* The lines calmed her heart. She thought she was ready for whatever might happen.

As they passed through the gate, the guard moved a few steps ahead of them and then stopped. "Wait here," he said, then disappeared through a door on the far right side of the building.

A few minutes later, the door opened. The guard came out and strode to his post at the gate. A middle-aged woman appeared and her eyes quickly sized up Liya and then Nina. "Come inside. I'm in charge here. Tell me what you are doing here."

Nina had thought about an explanation for her missing I.D. on the way to the gate. She stepped directly in front of Liya, and then clasping her hands behind her, Nina wiggled her fingers slightly at Liya, who understood the hand signal and kept silent.

"I'm from Guangzhouo," Nina said. "So is my friend. When we met in Beijing, we decided to come here to do some sightseeing." Nina made her story simple and clear. She lifted her satchel. "I can't find the letter from my work unit. I think I lost it when I bought buns in a food store."

"A good excuse." Nodding, the warden asked, "Why were you taking photos of this place?"

"I like everything I see here. It's different from my southern province. I just wanted to have some keepsakes from this trip."

"Can you prove it?" asked the warden.

"About taking photos?" Nina was confused.

"No. I mean about who you are." Then, she asked, "Do you know the phone number of your workplace? Come on in here." She led the way to a large desk by a window covered with heaps of newspapers. An aroma of milky tea floated in the room, which made Nina and Liya feel hungry.

"You wait here. Something has to be done," said the warden, looking at Liya. "Can I take a look at your I.D.?" She took the letter from Liya and read it. Then she stared at the glasses on Liya's face, nodding. "You are a university student of the

Chinese Department. You must be a specialist of Chinese?"

"I'm studying the language and literature. I'm not a specialist yet," answered Liya.

"Are you close friends?" asked the woman. "You want to wait for her, don't you?"

"Yes," Liya said. "How long do we have to wait?"

"We'll talk about it later. You can eat your food if you have some with you." The woman pulled a door on her right open. She entered it, and then closed the door firmly behind her.

Opening her satchel, Nina took out some buns stuffed with lamb. "Let's have our lunch," she said.

"Right. I'm starving." Liya took out some Chinese pancakes from her handbag. "I hope they'll let us go soon."

"I wish, but I don't think so," replied Nina, suddenly worried about whether she would be able to catch her plane in four days. When she thought about Roger's shocked face when she did not show up at the airport, her heart grew heavy, but she could not say anything because she did not want the warden in the adjacent room to hear her.

They ate and drank, and then they sat back on the bench. *What will the warden do to us?* Nina asked herself.

24.

PHONE CALLS FROM THE GULAG

THE INSIDE DOOR suddenly opened. The warden came out of the adjacent room, yawning and stretching her arms. "Time to work," she announced as she walked over to her desk and sat down.

Nina glanced up at the clock on the wall. It read two p.m. She had forgotten the routine and daily schedules of the two-hour lunch break in China.

The warden asked for Nina's name and workplace and jotted all the information down in a notebook. "Your work unit should send us a referral letter to prove you are whom you say you are."

"But, we have to return to Hohhot this afternoon," Liya said with panic. "We're supposed to catch tomorrow morning's train from there."

The woman looked at her. "Well, you are free to go. But this is your friend. We don't mind if you wish to stay with her." She turned to face Nina. "Now, tell me why you came here. Your plan was to sightsee, yes? So, you should have had no trouble locating the Tomb of Zhaojun.

"After seeing the tomb, we were on our way to Wulanbatu to visit a herdsman there. We took a wrong turn and ended up here instead." Nina pulled a packet and a slip of paper out of her satchel. "Look at the name on this letter: Temur. A friend of mine asked me to bring this packet with medicine to Temur who has arthritis."

The woman stretched out her hand and grabbed the package, turned it around to scrutinize the instructions on how to use the rheumatism plaster. "Okay. We'll find out about Temur later. First, write down the phone number of your workplace here." She tapped the notebook on the table with her finger. Without hesitation, Nina picked up the pen and wrote down the phone number of Ahua's workshop.

After dialling the operator, the warden asked for a connection to Guangdong Province. About ten minutes later, she got through and handed the phone receiver to Nina. "Direct them to send us a letter," she said.

Taking a deep breath, Nina said into the phone, "May I talk to Forewoman Ahua Tang?"

"Speaking."

It was Ahua's voice. Nina drew in a breath. "It's Nina calling. I lost my referral letter. Can you please write one to prove I work in your workshop? Please send it to me as soon as possible."

In a confused voice, Ahua asked, "What letter? Where are you now?"

"I need a referral letter with the stamp of our Red Star Plastic Factory. I'm being kept in a camp. I'll try to be back at work before Monday. Please help me. I need this letter right away."

Then Nina asked for the address of the gulag from the warden and repeated it to Ahua.

After talking to Ahua, Nina felt some relief; she expected Ahua to immediately tell Rei. Rei would then contact her mother. If she was unable to get back on time, her mother would cancel her plane ticket. If everything went well, a stamped letter would reach here in a few days. Imagining different scenarios, she tried her luck. "Can we leave now, Warden?" She turned to the warden. "You know what I have told you is true," she added politely.

"I don't doubt it. However, according to our policy, you can't leave until we receive the letter from your forewoman."

"That'll take a couple of days." Liya interrupted her. "In that case, can I make a call to a friend?"

"Whom do you intend to call?" asked the warden. Sitting back in her chair, she adjusted herself into a more comfortable position, crossing one of her legs over the other.

"A friend in Hohhot. May I?"

"If I let you make a call, can you do me a favour in return?"

"What kind of favour?"

"Can you help me with some textbooks? We'll pay for your food during your stay here."

"Does the policy allow that?" asked Liya.

"As an acting warden, I know how to implement policy." Her voice was firm. "What's the phone number of your friend?"

"She doesn't have a phone, but I will be able to pass a message to her," Liya answered and opened her notepad. She found the emergency number Jing had given her, which was the switchboard of *Inner Mongolia Daily*, and read it out loud to the warden.

After the phone was connected, Liya asked the operator to pass the message to Editor Li that his daughter's friends could not return to Hohhot that day because they had encountered a small problem. Nina thought Liya's message would not cause any trouble for Jing's father, but at least Jing would glean that they were in trouble because she knew when Nina intended flight back to Canada was scheduled to leave from Guangzhou.

The warden pulled her desk drawer open and retrieved two books. "Here they are." She laid them on the desk and looked at Liya. "I am certain this will be a piece of cake for you," she said.

Liya took a look at the titles. One was *The Modern Chinese Language*, and the other, *The History of the Chinese Communist Party*. She wondered why the warden aspired to study these books, but she did not ask.

"If you like, you can help me, too," said the warden, fixing her gaze on Nina's upturned face. "It's simple. Copy documents for me."

"Why not? I used to copy documents in my factory," answered Nina. Curiosity arose in her: *What documents? It might be something confidential. Maybe inside information!* Her worry about missing the flight lessened as the hope of discovering something useful for her book flickered inside her.

The warden opened a filing cabinet, she took out a thick book and a stack of lined paper. "Here you go." She turned to the page with a bookmark. "I've done some already. You can continue from this page. First, find out who arrived here at the gulag between the years 1957 and 1960. Then copy their basic information onto this sheet." She pointed to a pad of lined paper. "Fill in the blank under each column here: name, date of birth, birthplace, and so on. Understood?"

"Yes, of course," answered Nina, who caught her breath, trying not to reveal her excitement. Liya had mentioned that Hu Yaobang, head of the Central Organization Department of the Communist Party of China, was working on cases of wrongful convictions of rightists during the Anti-Rightist Campaign. Might this be a sign of the start of reparations, she wondered.

"I'll be back soon." The warden went out.

When she returned, she led them to a one-storey building next to the office, and stood by the open door, waving them inside. "This is where you will sleep. It's near the staff latrine at the end of this hallway. Someone will bring you food and water here. You'd better not go anywhere except to the office and latrine. It's for your own safety." Her gaze shifted back and forth between the two girls. "I'm trusting you and letting you stay in the staff dorm room. If you have any problem, you can talk to any guard in the office." She pointed at the watch on her wrist. "But bedtime is nine o'clock. No lights are allowed after that."

Nina surveyed the room. Two beds, each made of a wooden board over two benches, were pushed against the back wall.

A small folding table flanked by two folding chairs stood in the middle of the room. A double-tier stand held two enamel basins. The upper one was for the face, and the lower one, for the feet. Several worn-out towels hung on the top rack of the stand. *Nina thought the room was much better than her dorm in the military farm, but she was undeniably dismayed by the loss of their freedom.*

"It's up to you to stay here or go back in the office. I have some other errands to run. But you can start to work with me at four o'clock," the warden said to Liya and left. Looking at each other, Nina and Liya noticed the other's facial expressions. They were both exhausted, and worried. They did not know when they might be freed, but they were hopeful for a positive outcome.

Ahua was terrified when she got Nina's long-distance call. She wondered how Nina had wound up being held in that camp, but she could not ask any more questions because there were co-workers around her during her phone conversation. She understood she needed a letter with a stamp of her factory to help Nina out of there. *Can I get one through a normal channel? No. Can I get one for myself? Maybe, but for what reason?* Many ideas preoccupied her, and she could not focus on her simple job: to inspect the packages of plastic basins. Suddenly, she had an idea and she marched into the director's office. The door was open, and on the wall across from the door was a large portrait of Chairman Mao. Beneath the image of Mao, sat the director, a cigarette in one hand and a newspaper in the other.

"Director Hong, I need your help," she said.

Hong lifted his head. "Come in, Ahua. Is there a problem in your workshop?"

"No, everything is fine. But I need a requisition to see a specialist in the hospital."

"What's the matter?" he asked. Cigarette smoke came out

of his nose; his face was blurred amidst the smoke. He looked at Ahua, the forewoman of quality control, with concern in his eyes.

"I have a backache. A friend recommended me to a specialist, but the doctor only sees patients who have referral forms stamped from their work unit."

"When are you going?"

"I'll go as soon as I get referred by you. I have trouble bending now." When she lied, she felt her face flush. It was a good thing that the director had started writing on a sheet. When Ahua saw the official red stamp on the lower part of the written letter, she felt like a drowning person who had been tossed a branch. Now she was clutching it with all her might.

Ahua went straight home to speak to Rei. Knowing that Nina wasn't alone, that she was with Liya, made him feel a little bit better. He looked at the letter and wondered if he could find a way to erase the writing and then be able to craft the kind of letter Nina needed. At the same time, he had trouble shaking off the knowledge that it was illegal to fake a government document. But another voice sounded in his heart: *It's not right to retain a person who just wanted to visit a labour camp. Things are terribly wrong with the present legal system.* He had to do something to help Nina out even if it was illegal.

"Maybe we can use vinegar to erase the ink." He grabbed a test piece of paper and scribbled a few words with a pen. Then in the kitchen, he took a bottle of white vinegar from a cupboard and tried erasing the ink on the page. Ahua remembered she had once used cooked rice to discolour an ink stain on her white blouse. She tried that as well. They both worked on test paper for an hour, but they were unsuccessful. The best that Rei had been able to do was remove the ink by scratching it off with a razor blade, but the spot on the paper where they had scratched was visibly thinner and in places slight torn. He decided to go to visit a former co-worker for some help.

He came home at midnight. In their bedroom, out of a manila envelope he had brought back with him, he pulled out a round bar of soap with some carved words on it, and a square metal box that had a red ink pad inside of it. He opened the box and pressed the bar of soap onto the ink pad. Carefully, he stamped the bar of soap, now covered in red ink, onto a sheet of paper. "Oh my," Ahua lowered her thrilled voice. "It looks like a real stamp!"

The following day, Rei mailed out a letter with a fake stamp to the Peach Blossom Camp whose address his wife had received from Nina's phone call. Two days elapsed, and they had heard no further news. Nina and Liya had been detained in the gulag for three days now. Rei started acting on his plan. He needed to see his aunt, Nina's mother, on her lunch break in the hospital. Nina's flight home needed to be cancelled.

Rei found her in the staff lounge. "Aunt, can I speak to you in private?"

"Why are you here?" Nina's mother stood up from an armchair and walked over to Rei. "Follow me," she said and quickly led the way to a window at the end of the hallway. "Is something wrong?" she asked, her voice filled with anxiety.

"Not really," Reid said, taking a breath. "Nina has changed her plans. She wants to stay in Beijing a little longer. She won't be coming home, and she has asked me to bring her ticket and suitcase to Beijing."

"But she's supposed to take the plane here in Guangzhou. What's really happened, Rei?" Nina's mother looked into Rei's eyes.

"Her schedule changed so she arranged to fly from Beijing instead," Rei said carefully, as he did not want to distress his aunt.

"As long as she's okay," Nina's mother sighed with relief. "I'll see her another time. Do you need her stuff right away? Should we go back to the house now?"

"No. I'll meet you at your house after you finish work. That will be fine," Rei said. They chatted a bit more and then he left.

In the late afternoon, he went to the post office and made a long-distance call to the office of Air Canada in Hong Kong to cancel Nina's flight due to a personal emergency. Then he placed a call to the *Inner Mongolia Daily*, and asked for Editor Li. The operator said there was no phone in his office, but she could pass a message to him. Hesitating for a second, he decided not to leave any message. Even if Jing got his message, she would not be able to reach him.

The final step for him was to get on a train to Beijing and then transfer to another train to Hohhot.

The Tuesday evening that Nina and Liya were detained, Jing had prepared a dinner of cornmeal porridge, pancakes, and buns stuffed with lamb. She waited till about eight p.m., but Nina and Liya did not show up. The long-distance bus should have arrived at seven-twenty. She was about to leave for the hospital when one of her father's colleagues passed along a message from the switchboard. It was then that she realized that her friends could not return. Jing wondered where they were and what had happened. It worried her that they had not been able to provide any details with the message they sent. There was nothing she could do and she needed to get to the hospital to replace her father who was taking care her mother and then would go home.

When Jing entered the room, her mother immediately noticed the worry on her face. "Is everything all right?"

Jing told her about the phone message from Nina and Liya. Her mother smiled encouragingly. "Don't worry too much. Your friends probably called from some town's post office. It means they are somewhere safe. Don't you think so?"

Jing nodded, feeling somewhat better. "I'm going to get you some warm water." She took a basin with her to the water boiler and returned with it filled. Her mother had casts on both of her legs, so Jing helped her to sit up in bed and then she gave her a sponge bath.

"Soon, I'll get rid of my cast and be able to do things myself," her mother said as Jing washed her back. "These days, you've wasted a lot of time because of my accident."

"Don't worry. I've had the chance to read a lot of books in here," Jing said to allay her mother's concern. "And, besides, I'm very glad I'm able to take care of you."

At night, most of the patients fell asleep; some patients' family members also dozed off. Jing sank into a chair by her mother's bed. Her eyes were closed, but her mind was wide awake. *Where are they? If they don't return tomorrow, I'll talk to Weimin and see what can be done.*

25.

TEMUR'S STALLION

ON THE WEDNESDAY evening, when Nina and Liya had still not returned, Jing was extremely worried. She rode her bicycle to the hospital and as soon as she had helped wash her mother, she hurried over to Weimin's home.

Weimin let Jing in and gestured for her to take a seat. As he listened, he lit a cigarette, took a long drag, and then pressed it into the ashtray. "Don't worry. We'll find them," he said, looking at Jing's concerned face. After talking over various scenarios that might explain Nina's and Liya's disappearance, they came to the conclusion that the only thing they could do was to visit Temur and ask him for help.

"I can go with you...." Jing said anxiously.

"No. You need to look after your mother. Besides, it's easier for me to go alone. I'll leave tomorrow morning and be back in the evening," answered Weimin. Only one long-distance bus from Hohhot passed by the village of Wulanbatu, and it returned daily.

"Are you sure you can get tomorrow off?" asked Jing.

Weimin was certain his old friend would look the other way.

On Thursday morning, Weimin took the bus to Wulanbatu. After walking for about an hour, he reached a yurt that Mongolians call a "ger," which was set near a grove of pine trees. On the farthest grassland, several more yurts and trees came into view. The door to this ger was open, but nobody seemed to be inside or nearby. He quickened his steps and called out, "Papa Temur!" He followed the Mongolian tradition, in which people call a man of the older generation, "Papa," and a woman, "Mama."

There was no answer.

He heard a woman humming from the back of the yurt, where there was a sheep pen. He walked over to it, and in a far corner of the pen, a small woman sat on a low stool, taking turns petting a ewe and her newborn baby. It was Mama Naran, the wife of Temur. After years of living with herdsmen, Weimin had learned a lot about tending animals. He knew Naran was trying to get the ewe to nurse its baby. Sometimes, a mother sheep rejected its child if it had any scent of a human on its skin. Herdsmen believed that caressing the ewe and its baby as well as humming helped the adult sheep relax. The ewe would feel soothed after listening to the gentle melody and from being petted. In particular, she would get used to the odour of a human on the newborn lamb. Then it could take care of its own baby.

Weimin called out to Mama Naran. Turning her head, the woman saw him and gave him a wide smile. "Hello! Is this Weimin?"

"Yes. Where is Papa Temur?"

"He's outside riding his favourite horse. He'll be back soon. Follow me inside." Mama Naran stopped petting the lamb that lay by its mother. She stood up. A worn silk sash, cinched around the waist of her grey knee-length deel, a short caftan, shone orange in the sun. Now in her early fifties, Naran had been a gleeful grandmother for ten years.

Naran led Weimin into the ger and gestured for him to make himself comfortable on the carpet near a small table in the centre. Then, she walked to a cupboard to get a mug and metal pitcher. Filling the mug with homemade yogurt from the pitcher, she handed it to her visitor.

"Thank you," said Weimin. As he drank the yogurt, the cool

liquid soothed his hot and dry throat. "Have two women come to visit you in the last two days?"

"No," Naran replied, looking at Weimin with curiosity. A smile arose on her face and smoothed away the wrinkles. "Have you found a wife then?" Weimin shook his head. "Oh, you'll find one, soon," Naran nattered. "And, when you do, bring her to see us."

Weimin glanced around the ger and noted three beds set along a wall of animal felt; a large rectangular table separated the beds into two sections. Near the door, a metal stove stood, upon which a kettle sat with steam shooting out of its spout. The aroma of freshly brewed tea soon filled the roomy yurt. Proud of his home, Papa Temur was fond of a particular saying: "Once you close the door to your ger, you're the king in your own domain."

Naran lifted the kettle and poured the aromatic tea into a mug and then handed it to Weimin. "I have one more granddaughter now. She's in bed sleeping. Her folks take her brother with them when they are out tending to their flock of sheep."

Listening to Naran, Weimin remembered the gifts he had brought with him. He opened his pack and pulled out a few packages. "I have some biscuits and tea bricks for you. This packet of candy is for your grandson. I remember he enjoyed hard milky candy."

"You shouldn't have wasted your money on us," Naran said, clearly pleased. Wiping her hands with her apron, she reached out to receive the packages. "I don't have fancy things to treat you with."

"I like the everyday things you cook." Weimin remembered years before, during many stormy nights, in this very yurt, he had eaten freshly cooked cheese pancakes and drunk hot milk tea with this family.

"Ha! Who likes Mama Naran's cooking?" a loud voice called from just outside the door.

"It's me, Papa Temur!" Excited, Weimin jumped up from his

seated position on the carpet, strode over to Temur, and shook hands with him. "I've come to ask for your help."

Temur's strong body blocked half of the door. As soon as he moved aside, sunshine poured into the tent. "Take it easy, my boy," Temur said, hanging his louz, a wide-brimmed hat, and his whip on a hook next to the doorway. "Tell me what I can do."

"Two visitors from Guangzhou came down to this area the day before yesterday. The two women also planned to visit you, but they didn't get here or return to Hohhot. I'm here to look for them."

"Hmm," Temur said, a surprised look on his face. "We haven't had any abductions or crime in the area for years. Can you tell me more?" He sat on a stool and sipped from a mug of milk tea his wife passed to him. He listened carefully to Weimin's story about Nina and Liya's trip.

When Weimin had finished, Temur told his wife, who was sitting by the bed feeding her grandchild,, that he was going to go with Weimin and search for the two women.

Temur walked to the door, picked up his whip and inserted it into his forest-green sash. His hands flapped on his brown deel. With his straw louz on his head and gutal boots on his feet, he was, once again, a horseman.

"Can you still ride a horse?" Temur asked, eyeing Weimin up and down.

"I think so." Weimin followed him out of the ger. A few horses were tethered to the pine trees next to the ger. Temur entered the stable and came out with a saddle that he threw over a piebald pony. "You ride this obedient one. I'll take mine."

A sorrel stallion with a reddish mane stretched its head and shook its ears when it saw his owner coming. When Temur mounted it, the horse whinnied as though expressing its pleasure at having a rider on its back. Weimin patted the piebald pony and hopped on it. By the time they were ready to leave, Naran rushed out of the yurt and passed each of them a sack filled with cheese pancakes and a water bag. The toddler standing by the door waved her hand. "Bye, Grandpa."

Temur led the way to the post office in the village of Nantaishi. When they got there, Temur asked the staff if any visitors had come to use the phone the previous Tuesday. No one had seen the two women. From there, they went to the mayor's office to ask the same question, and where they received the same answer. Another half hour ride northwest brought them to Maolintai. Again, they visited the town's post office and then the mayor's office, but they did not find any information about Nina and Liya.

After they reached Dalai, they decided to take a break and led the horses to the edge of the roadside. The horses nibbled the grass around a poplar tree, while Temur and Weimin sat in the tree's dappled shade. Before they ate lunch, Temur held a strand of wooden beads in his hands and prayed. Their plan was to visit all the surrounding villages after lunch. Weimin hoped they would pick up some clues before they got to their final destination, Xingwangzhuang.

After lunch, they passed the Tomb of Zhaojun and reached the town of Xingwangzhuang, where they once again stopped in at the post office and at the mayor's office, but they had yet to uncover any clues as to the women's whereabouts.

That was the furthest place they had gone to. Even though it pained him to do so, Weimin had to consider the worst possible scenario. He turned to Temur and said, "Maybe they made their phone call from Peach Blossom Camp.

"That is a possibility," said Temur. "That might be our last chance to find them."

Crossing fields of corn and potatoes, they reached the grasslands that surrounded the gulag. Temur asked Weimin to get down from the horse and to wait for him in the field. Then he patted his horse's head and resumed his ride to a mud-made wall in the distance. He hummed his favourite folk song, "My Lasso," to calm himself down.

The stallion pranced on the grass, lifting its hooves in time with Temur's melody as though it understood its master's song." When the horse got close to the wall, Temur dismounted, then with the bridle in his hand, he guided his horse over to the gate. It was closed, but there was a small rectangular opening in the door. When he knocked on the door he could see someone through the opening. "Hello, Comrade. I'm Temur from Wulanbatu, the village where you get your food supplies from."

"What do you want?" asked the guard.

"Two women came here the day before yesterday, didn't they?" asked Temur.

The guard hesitated, then said. "Why did you say that?"

"They were supposed to visit me that day but they never showed up," answered Temur. Feeling surer of what had happened, he asked, "Can I speak to the warden?"

The guard did not say anything but opened the door. "Leave your horse outside, please."

"Thanks a lot." Temur tethered his stallion to a jubilee tree and waited off to one side until the guard pushed open the door and escorted him inside. A moment later, the warden appeared. The guard introduced her. "This is Warden Luo."

Nodding at Temur, Luo asked, "Hello. How can I help you?"

"Dear Warden Luo, I hope you're satisfied with the food supplies from our village. I'm one of those suppliers. You're welcome to visit me if you have any time to come to my village." Temur shook hands with the warden and then asked about the two women. He said they had planned to visit him and had a package of plasters for his rheumatism.

Warden Luo found it hard to deny the fact. She gestured at the door she had just walked out of. "They're here. Please come in."

Stepping into the room, Temur saw two Han women in their twenties, one sitting at the table, and the other on the bench. "Nina and Liya," Temur said, sure it was them. "You're supposed to be at my home. Why are you staying here?"

Nina raised her head from the table. "Papa Temur?" She was amazed.

To Temur, Luo said, "Nina must stay until a referral letter from her workplace reaches us. Her friend Liya is here to keep her company."

"Is that right?" Temur felt relieved, finding conditions better than he had expected. "Can they leave now and come to visit my family as they had planned to?" asked Temur, smiling genially at Luo.

"No," Luo answered.

Nina replied, "I'd love to, but we can't come right now. But I do have a packet for you." She turned to Luo and asked, "May I get it?"

"Sure. Suit yourself," said Luo.

Liya looked up at Temur and asked, "Papa Temur, how did you know we were here?"

"My horse can smell guests. He brought me here," said Temur with a chuckle, and his hand stroked his grey beard.

"Thanks for coming to see us. We're fine. We're helping Warden Luo with a few things." Liya guessed Temur must have heard from Weimin about their disappearance. "Please tell Weimin not to worry about us," she added. "We'll leave here as soon as the letter from Nina's factory in Guangzhou arrives."

"Weimin is with me. I'll let him know."

Nina returned and handed the packet of plasters to Temur. "This is what Weimin had asked us to bring to you."

Temur smiled. "Thank you. Remember, that the grass in every meadow is different, but a friend never changes." He turned to Luo who was sitting at the desk. "When do you think they can come to visit me?"

"When I receive the letter," Luo tried to stifle her impatience. "We still have a lot of work to do."

"Warden Luo, do you have any message to pass along to my food co-op? I can bring it to them." Temur thought he could ask friends in the co-op to help if the two women did not get out of there soon.

"Just tell them we need more butter next time," answered Luo, who stood to see Temur to the door.

Outside the gate, Temur mounted his stallion and rode quickly through the grassland. When he reached its edge, the horse neighed to the piebald pony. Temur told Weimin what he had seen and the conversation that he had had with Nina and Liya. "Don't worry. I'll ask my friends in the co-op to help if need be. Now, hop on your horse. We're going to drink kumis."

On the way back home, Temur sang the folk song, "Sweet Kumis is like Honey." His steed pranced, its head high, and its red mane glowing like a flame under the sunset. *He's always cheerful. Nothing defeats him,* Weimin thought. His pony was trotting after Temur's stallion; the horses were eager to get home. Weimin held the rope tight and leaned on the horse's neck to avoid falling off.

Unable to decline Temur's invitation, Weimin had dinner with three generations of the family. Kumis filled their mugs and served along with lamb chops and cheese pancakes. Knowing people from the city enjoyed fresh vegetables, Mama Naran had also prepared a pot of sliced summer squash. At the end of the meal, Papa Temur took Weimin on horseback to the bus stop.

As soon as Weimin arrived in Hohhot, he went straight to the hospital and found Jing in her mother's ward. She followed him into the hallway, and he recounted the story of how he and Temur had located Nina and Liya in Peach Blossom Camp. Weimin also told her about Temur's rescue option that would involved his co-op friends if Nina and Liya were not released in a timely manner.

"Don't worry too much," Weimin said. "The sky won't fall." At that moment, a Mongolian proverb crossed his mind. "A travelling fool is better than a sitting wise person." He smirked. "I'm like a travelling fool."

Jing patted his arm. "Action is quicker than discussion. The sitting wise girl is appreciative to the travelling fool." They both laughed out loud.

After Weimin left, Jing went back into her mother's room and sat down in the chair next to her bed. She felt as if a stone had fallen from her heart, and she could once again breathe properly. She picked up her book to read, but a question haunted her: *When will we be freed from the gulag?*

26.

THE WIND-BLOWN GRASS

AFTER PAPA TEMUR LEFT, Nina and Liya, locking eyes, knew that Jing and Weimin now knew where they were and would do what they could to help. Liya continued helping Luo with her grammar studies. She told Liya that studying Chinese grammar was much harder than reading any of the documents that were sent to her, but she had to pass two examinations on Chinese language and the history of the Chinese Communist Party. Successful exams were her ticket to becoming the executive warden.

Nina had filled several sheets with the names of the gulag workers and their basic information. She checked all of the individual backgrounds carefully, word by word, since she did not want to miss anyone who had come to the gulag between 1957 and 1960. The Anti-Rightist Campaign took place from 1957 to 1959, but many people who were branded as "rightists" were still being sent down to gulags in remote areas even during 1960, like Gao's father. Before she turned to the next page, she scanned the column and one entry caught her eye. The man's date of birth was 1935. He had university education and had been transferred to this gulag in the year ... but the year was undecipherable. It was possible this person was one of those who were labelled "rightists," so she asked Luo, "Should I copy this name into the sheet? The date of entry to the camp is blurry. I can't tell which year he came here. It could be1960 or 1968?"

"Let me check other documents." Luo went to a cabinet and pulled a drawer out. After rummaging through a pile of papers, she told Nina, "Yes, copy his name onto the sheet."

From Luo's answer, Nina knew she had guessed correctly. As she added that name to the sheet, she thought about not missing any of those branded as "rightists." Her estimation told her that one-third of the one thousand ex-prisoners in this labour camp had been sent here between 1957 and 1960. It meant that all of them could have been labelled "rightists" and might thus be released relatively soon. She would carefully examine the date of birth and education columns of anyone whose entry year was during this period in particular. If the person's birth year was before 1937, and if she or he had a college background, she would add the name to the list. She had heard that so many college students were pushed down during the Anti-Rightist Campaign though she was not aware that twenty thousand of those three million "rightists" were students. Even high-school students did not escape the persecution.

Page after page, Nina leafed through the heavy binder. Another name caught her attention: Gao Haowen, born in Gansu Province in 1921, a university graduate, transferred to the gulag in 1965. The family name and province reminded Nina of Gao, Yueming's English teacher. Gao's father had been sent to a gulag in Gansu, but Nina did not know whether he was born there. It was possible that Gao's father was transferred from Jiabiangou Valley to this camp. She regretted not having asked Gao for more information about her father.

Soon, it was Saturday afternoon. Sunday was the workers' only free day of the week. All the camp workers would be off work. Before Luo left for home for the weekend, she told Nina and Liya that on Sunday they could visit a local farmers' market, popular not only with the local villagers but also with the gulag workers.

Rei arrived at the Hohhot train station on Sunday morning. A bus brought him to the *Inner Mongolia Daily* at about eleven a.m. After finding No. 3 dormitory building, he knocked on the door of apartment 209 and heard Jing's sluggish voice rise from the inside, "Who is it?"

"It's me, Rei," he answered, wondering why she was still sleeping at this hour.

Several minutes later, Jing opened the door.

"Are you ill?" he asked when he walked in, dropping his carry-on bag on the floor.

"No," Jing's gaze fell on his face. "I sleep in the daytime, because I take care of my mother during the night," she explained and then motioned for him to sit on a stool at a table in the living room. "Need some food? I can throw together a simple meal."

"Yes, please," answered Rei, looking at Jing. "You aren't even surprised to see me."

"I knew you were coming because I called your wife," she said, placing a cup of tea on the table. "Help yourself. Give me a couple of minutes."

In a short while, she returned with two bowls of rice fried with scrambled eggs and green onions. After she placed one in front of Rei, she sat on a stool. "My father's in the hospital right now, so there are only two of us here for lunch." She told Rei the little she knew about Nina and Liya's situation, which was not much different from what Rei knew. He told her about the letter. "You didn't have to travel this far," said Jing. "I think they'll let Nina and Liya go as soon as they get the letter."

"I'm afraid Nina might be put behind bars. I just want to make sure she gets out of there and leaves the country without any problem." Hesitating for a moment, Rei then told Jing of his own arrest after his attempt to cross the border into Hong Kong.

His story surprised Jing. She smiled at him. "At least the arrest didn't affect your application for the university."

"There're two reasons for that," said Rei. "I had very high scores. Second, my parents died for the communist revolution. Their old friends in the provincial government helped me. Otherwise, I would've definitely been rejected because of the record of my so-called political crime."

Jing nodded. "It's said there's no such political crime in Western countries. I hope we can learn more about the different criminal justice systems of these countries and maybe adopt some similar laws."

"The library doesn't contain such books in Chinese. Unless we can find the originals and can read them in English, this information will not be available to us," Rei said with a sigh.

After lunch, Jing took Rei to Weimin's place where Weimin would add a folding bed for Rei to sleep on. The two strangers became friends and discussed a rescue plan for Nina and Liya. In their estimation, based on the number of days a piece of registered mail from Guangzhou would reach the camp, they figured they should wait till the following evening. By that time, if Nina and Liya did not show up, they would carry out their two-step plan. On Tuesday, Rei would go to the gulag with another stamped letter saying he was from the Red Star Factory on a business trip. He could prove Nina was from the same factory. If that did not work, Weimin would revisit Papa Temur and ask him to carry out his Plan B.

Relieved, Rei lay down on the temporary cot. Fatigue from the two-day train trip without sleep overwhelmed him, and soon he fell into a deep sleep.

On Sunday morning, Nina and Liya went with the guard named Yuan who had volunteered to take them to the market. They set out along a small path through the grassland and then into the field. Some gulag workers were ahead of them.

That day Nina should have been on her way to Hong Kong; however, she was hiking through the wilderness of Inner Mongolia instead. She had missed her flight, but she had discovered, accidentally, firsthand information about a forced-labour camp. As she marvelled over this thought, she also worried about Roger not finding her at the airport. He would be expecting her this evening. She had no way of calling him and she regretted not having given his phone number to Rei and to her mother. She envisioned Roger's face and his concerned eyes. *When will that letter get here?* she wondered, kicking a small rock on the path, dirt swirling around her feet.

About an hour later, they reached an open area where several yurts were scattered about in a large meadow. Clusters of bushes and trees sprouted at the edge of a large and shimmering lake.

Yuan had been silent all the way along, and the only words Nina had heard from him were "This way, please." But now he seemed excited and raised his hand to shade his eyes against the sun and looked around with a great deal of interest.

"What is this lake?" Nina asked, pointing to the water's shore.

Yuan talked to himself, "More people are here today." Then he turned to Nina, "Pardon me?"

"The name of the lake?"

"Don't know the real name. We call it Bottomless Lake. Every other Sunday is a double market day. Besides the local people coming to sell and buy food and other trifles, ranchers and herdsmen also gather here to trade their animals."

"It's beautiful," Liya said in excitement. "I see sheep standing around the shore. It looks like the scene described in a classical poem from the Southern and Northern Dynasties."

The guard looked at Liya with curiosity. "What's the poem?"

"'*The lofty sky looks deep blue/ The wilderness is without boundaries/ The wind blows grass down/ Cattle and sheep crouch around.*' Have you heard these lines? It was written by an anonymous poet," Liya explained.

"I've heard my eldest sister recite this poem," said the guard, grinning like a child. "But I've never thought about this place in that way. Now the scene in the poem is before me!"

They walked over to the crowds along the lakeshore. Nina noticed that many gulag workers were among the shoppers. Mongolian and Han ranchers were trading lambs and sheep, cows and horses, camels and donkeys. Women and children were selling ears of corn, fried millet, potatoes, and vegetables. The aroma of Mongolian lamb teppanyaki wafted through the air; food venders had set up tables by their stoves. Their customers sat around makeshift tables and enjoyed, along with milk tea or yogurt, the freshly cooked food: lamb soup with cornmeal buns, noodles fried with shreds of lamb, or oat buns stuffed with minced lamb.

Nina saw two men who looked to be about fifty years old enjoying lamb noodles at one of the tables. They wore clean, patched clothes. Their faces were sunburned red, their foreheads full of wrinkles. One of them wore glasses with the temples tied by threads to the frames. *They look like they're from the camp. Is one of them Gao? Do they know Gao? Maybe I can speak to them, but I must avoid arousing any suspicion from the guard.*

Nina called out to Liya, "Do you want some soup?" and walked over to the workers.

Before Liya could respond, Yuan said, "Why don't you try Mongolian lamb teppanyaki? It's a famous local dish." He pointed at another table. "There're more seats over there."

Nina looked at Yuan and understood they were not really free and that the guard did not want them to be in contact with other gulag workers, so she pulled Liya's hand. "Okay, let's try the lamb teppanyaki."

They followed the guard to another table and each of them accepted a plate of charcoal-barbecued lamb chops. More gulag workers joined them. One of them smiled at Nina and Liya. "Are you new here?'

"They're temporary visitors," the guard answered for them, then added abruptly, "It's none of your business."

Everybody fell silent, and only the vender's singsong voice

could be heard: "Piping hot, crispy teppanyaki! Sweet and delicious kumis!"

Later, Nina saw a couple of middle-aged women bend their heads in front of a stand. They were touching strands of brown yarn hanging on a rope. Nina walked over to them and asked, "What's this yarn made of?"

The woman vendor said, "Hand-spun camel wool. It's soft and warm in winter. One skein for seventy-five fen."

A woman shopper bought five skeins of yarn. She told her younger companion, "These skeins are about a kilogram. I can knit a sweater with them."

"I'll learn from you," said the younger woman, who held a yarn ball. "Do you know if this is enough for a pair of socks?"

Nina sensed that Yuan was watching her, so she stopped herself from addressing any of the women who appeared to be gulag workers. .

On the way back to the camp, Yuan said, "The warden asked me to take care of you. I must make sure nothing happens."

Liya smirked. "Don't treat us like prisoners."

"If you were prisoners, you wouldn't have been allowed out beyond the gate without cuffs," said Yuan. Then he became silent again.

In cuffs? Nina shuddered. An image of herself in chains crossed her mind.

They trudged along the path with heavy footsteps because they were against the wind. When the wind shook the trees, the gate beyond the branches of the wild jujube trees came into view. Nina yearned to go home.

On Sunday evening, an excited Roger waited at the exit gate of the Halifax Stanfield International Airport. He watched every female passenger coming out of the gate but did not see Nina. After the final passenger reunited with her family, he realized that something was terribly wrong. At a service window, the staff worker checked with the crew and told him that Nina

Huang was not on the flight. In shock, Roger drove back to Yarmouth. The headlights of his lone car lightened the highway, but his entire heart sank in darkness. *What's happened to her?* The question haunted him.

He got home at midnight. The first thing he did was to find the phone number of Guangzhou Children's Hospital where Nina's mother worked. He dialled the number many times until he heard a woman's voice in the distance. "May I speak to Dr. Liao?" He spoke Chinese slowly, trying to make himself understood.

The voice hesitated. Before she answered, Roger had said it was emergency call from a friend of Liao's daughter.

Finally, the receiver asked him to hold on. A few minutes later, Nina's mother answered the phone. When she realized it was Roger, she tried to speak English. "I thought Nina had told you she could not return to Canada on time."

Roger held the phone receiver tight, like a drowning swimmer clutching a life preserver. "Where is she now?" he said slowly, word by word.

"Rei said Nina will take a plane to Canada in Beijing." Dr. Liao paused and spoke slowly. "Rei took her ticket and her suitcase."

"When?" Roger asked as he suspected something had gone wrong.

"Last Friday she was supposed to go to Beijing." Dr. Liao's voice quavered. "I hope Nina has not encountered any problems."

"Don't worry." Roger comforted her. "I'll work out something for her. You take care." In fact, his mind had gone blank. When he tried to figure out what on earth had occurred, many thoughts crossed his mind.

After the phone call, he uncovered the letter he had received the previous day and reread it. It had come from Beijing and was dated June 27. Nina mentioned she would send a postcard from Hohhot once she got there. *Her mother said she was in*

Beijing, so why hasn't she called me? A scary thought then ran through his mind: *She isn't free to do so! She must be in trouble.* Roger paced the wooden floor, thinking about what he should do. His footsteps in the silent night pounded like a bass played a moody tune.

The next morning, he called the Chinese Embassy in Ottawa and got information about applying for an emergency visa. He was glad he had made a photocopy of the visa application before Nina had filled it out. After filling in the application, he immediately sent it along with his passport to the embassy by courier. Hopefully, he would get the visa in four days. Then, he pulled himself together to map out what to do once he was in Beijing. He would first locate Rei at Peking University or find Sandra's Chips in order to gather clues about Nina's whereabouts.

For the rest of the day, he got to work. He contacted his father and borrowed the money for the trip. Then, after calling a few travel agencies, he found the earliest flight and booked a round-trip flight to Beijing. After he had everything arranged and sat down to sip a glass of water, his vision suddenly became blurry and he felt himself shiver. *Is Nina safe?* With that question on his mind, he leaned back and fell into a fitful sleep on the couch.

27.

CICADAS

ON MONDAY AFTERNOON, having finished making the list for the gulag workers who had arrived between 1957 and 1960, Nina was relaxing in the dorm room, reading a few magazines borrowed from the guardroom. Liya was still working with Luo on her grammar.

Suddenly, the door pushed open, and Liya rushed in, her face beaming. "They got the letter. We can leave now." She could hardly contain her excitement.

"Let's go!" Nina jumped up from the chair and gripped her satchel from the back of the chair. *We are free!* She breathed a long sigh of relief. In the back of her mind, she could hear Roger singing his favourite song, "My Sweetheart."

Before they left the camp, Luo demanded Nina and Liya tell nobody about what they had done there. Then she asked Liya to write down her mailing address in case she needed to contact her.

Like birds freed from a cage, Nina and Liya flew out of the gate and walked as fast as they could to the closest bus stop in the village of Nantaishi. They did not look back once.

Finally, they alighted from the bus at Hohhot's bus terminal, where two familiar faces greeted them. Nina gasped in pleasure. "Rei, how come you are here with Weimin?"

"How did you guys know we'd be coming back now?" Liya asked in joy.

"We tried our luck," Rei said.

"This was the first step in our plan to help you out," Weimin grinned.

Excited about their meeting, the four friends went straight to the hospital to see Jing.

In Rei's opinion, it was better for Nina to leave Hohhot as quickly as possible. But the first thing Nina wanted to do was to call Roger. The post office was closed in the evening, so no telephone service was available. Nina tried to quell her anxiety about getting in touch with Roger, and told herself she would try again the next morning.

Soon Nina, Liya, and Rei boarded the train to Beijing after saying an emotional goodbye to Jing and Weimin. When they arrived in the city early the next morning, Rei went straight to his dorm room to sleep, and Liya and Nina went to Jing's room, which was not being used over the summer holiday as Jing was still in Hohhot. They both slept soundly after the fitful nights they had in the camp. Nina woke at eight a.m. and without disturbing Liya, she left for the post office to make her long-distance call to Roger.

As Nina waited for the line to be connected, she felt her heart pounding. Finally, Roger answered. "It's Nina," she said, almost breathless with relief.

"Where are you, honey?" Roger's voice was tense and worried.

"In Beijing. I'm sorry, Roger, I couldn't call you earlier."

"I'm waiting for a Chinese visa," said Roger. "I've booked a ticket. I was going to fly to Beijing to look for you. I've been frantic with worry."

"I'm so sorry, Roger. I will explain when I get home. You should cancel your ticket. I'll be flying home as soon as I get a ticket."

"Are you free? Are you sure you can leave?" Roger had many questions, but he knew Nina might be unable to answer all of them over the phone.

"Yes, I am. I'll be in touch right after I get my ticket. I promise," she said. Then, just before ending the call, she added fervently, "I miss you."

Nina went to Sandra's Chips, wondering if Sandra had any information about flights to Hong Kong since most of the supplies for the restaurant came from the island. At the counter, she saw Yueming, who was working at the cash register. Yueming was happy to see her and welcomed her over. Nina asked her if Sandra was in. To her surprise, she heard a man from behind the kitchen window speak Chinese with an American accent: "She's not in. You can speak to me." The voice sounded familiar. Nina scanned the kitchen for the face of the man speaking. He was staring at her from the window.

"Bob!" she called out, and her face glowed with surprise. Nina was shocked. She had not expected to run into her former lover in Beijing of all places, although Bob had always said he would have liked to open a restaurant in China. And he did! Nina shook her head in amazement.

"Nina! What are doing here? So nice to see you! How do you know my wife Sandra?" Bob asked as he walked over to the counter, and gave her a hug in greeting.

"I met her here some time ago." Nina said, as she pulled herself free from his arms. "Your dream has come true — you are running a restaurant in China! I am so happy for you."

"What's brought you to Beijing?" he asked, smiling genially. "I remember you telling me that you came from Guangzhou."

"Let me make a long story short," Nina said, noticing that more customers had come in. In brief, she told Bob about her situation and asked if he had any resources or connections to help her get a ticket out of Mainland China.

He nodded and without hesitation went to make a few calls. With Bob's help, Nina had a ticket in her hand the very next day. Two days later, after waving farewell to her friends, Nina caught a flight to Hong Kong.

After arriving at Kai Tak Airport in Kowloon Bay, Nina checked in at the Maple Leaf Guest House nearby. In a phone call to Air Canada's office in Hong Kong, she explained the reason for the cancellation of her flight. A rescheduled flight was offered, but the earliest departure was three days later. She would call Roger right away and let him know. Relieved, she went to the lobby and found a map of Hong Kong's public transportation. While waiting to leave, she planned to see the Gui family with whom she had stayed nine years before.

The following morning, she got on the subway at Ngau Tau Kok Station. Transferring several times on her way, she finally caught a bus to Luk Keng. When she saw a road sign with the name of Bride's Pool on Kwun Tong Road, she smiled, imagining herself as a bride left to wonder about her missing bridegroom.

She got off the bus at the gate of Plover Cove Country Park, which was presently being built. According to the map, there was a path that wound along the Starling Inlet. It was scorching hot, but the breeze over the water cooled the sweat on Nina's face. The fragrance of wild flowers mixed with the odour of salty fish from the bay filled the air. The place refreshed her memory. It was the very place where she had landed on that stormy night after fleeing the black hole of the red terror. She suddenly felt deeply appreciative of her freedom, both then and now, and everything around her, the trees, bushes, grass, rocks, birds, and even the hares, looked sharply beautiful.

She walked for some time before noticing several newly built tea houses, restaurants, and stores. She was sure it was the area where Gui's home and a few other houses had been located. Not far away, behind the buildings, she could see the gigantic boulder the locals called Fish Stone. The stone had earned its name because it was shaped like a fish. The new buildings suggested that the Gui family might no longer be in the area. She went into one of the teahouses and stepped up to the counter. As she paid for a glass of iced tea, she spoke to the store clerk. "I remember there were some houses here years ago. What happened to them and the people who used to live here?"

"They must've been offered apartments somewhere else before their houses were demolished. They must have moved away," the clerk said.

"Do you know how to find them?"

"Don't know. Maybe somebody in the local administration office would know."

"Thanks," said Nina, disappointed. The tin of Oolong tea and the package of waffle rolls she had bought for the family felt heavy to her now. She perched on a bench under a tree to rest briefly. The droning sound of cicadas surged up from the tree — high at one moment and low at another, but always relentless. She sipped the iced tea. Her stomach growled, so she took out the package of waffles from her satchel and ate some. A group of young visitors were picnicking at a nearby table. An elderly man was napping on a bamboo lounging chair bed near the side door of the building. Not far was the clear blue water of Starling Inlet, glistening in the afternoon sun. Gazing at the surface of the bay, Nina recalled what she had felt on that dark night so long ago. That terrifying experience made the freedom she had on this sunny day even more enjoyable.

The following day was Saturday, so she got up very early. The subway took her to Shau Kei Wan. From the bus terminal there, she boarded a double-decker bus, which eventually climbed along the mountain road, leaving the skyscrapers behind and beneath her. Seated on the upper level, she admired the beautiful scenery through the window. *If Roger were here with me, he would really enjoy this.* She sighed. Passengers dismounted at different stops: Deep Water Bay, then Repulse Bay, and Tai Tam Bay — she remembered the names from a novel she had read. Her destination was the last stop: Shek O, the farthest south-eastern point of Hong Kong Island.

Nina wanted to try her luck at finding Wang, Dahai's companion when they ran away from the Number Five Military Farm in 1969. She had read Dahai's last letter, which Wang had delivered to Dahai's family after his untimely death. But she longed to meet him in person and to learn more about their escape. Based on information from Dongfang and Huguo's letter, Wang was supposed to be in Shek O, this pretty beach town on the peninsula.

When the bus finally stopped at Shek O Bus Terminus, passengers dismounted and most of them sauntered along a path toward the beach. Following the throng of visitors, Nina located the Town Planning Board Office where she asked for information about any business related to foreign trade in the town. The worker searched through his files and showed Nina a list of companies. She copied down the phone numbers of all nine companies and thanked him.

She went into a public phone booth where she dialled each number and asked for the name of the owner or manager or assistant manager. Two of them were named Wang, but nobody's first name was Jianzhong.

Jianzhong Wang was a needle in a haystack. It was sweltering, and Nina wiped the sweat off her face with a tissue while she dragged herself to Shek O Beach. Since she was there, she thought she should take the opportunity to see the beautiful beach. The fine sandy beach stretched languidly into the clear water. Umbrellas were scattered everywhere like colourful mushrooms. People in bathing suits looked like small, brightly coloured dots moving over the beach or dropping into the water. Nina breathed out deeply, as if she were blowing away all her disappointments.

She trudged through the crowds of people who were either lying on towels on the sand or perched on beach chairs. In the water, some people waded while others played or swam. The aroma of barbecue drew her attention. She spotted an unoccupied firepit on the ground. Its owner was a young woman, who told Nina that renting a barbecue brazier for two hours cost twenty yuan. With her hand pointing to the left, the renter said, "You can get meat and vegetables as well as sauce and spice from a store on the street over there."

Nina waded past the barbecue rings over to the alley, and among a few food stands and stores along the street, she found a small grocery store. A skinny, black dog sniffed near the entrance. She stretched out her hand to pet the dog but pulled it back right away when she noticed the dog's toothy mouth half-open and its alert eyes. *Mangy mutt*, she thought.

She entered the store and noticed the owner was bent over a chest freezer selecting items for another customer. Various boxes and packets as well as jars lined the shelves along the wall facing the door, and beneath the shelves were another two chest freezers. Several large window freezers stood against a side wall.

Nina reached up to one of the shelves and picked up a small shaker of all-seasoned salt. Then she looked inside one of the freezers. "Do you need any help?" The voice of the owner in accented Cantonese sounded behind her. The voice rang a bell.

When Nina turned her head, she blinked rapidly and cried out, "Jianzhong!" *Miracles do exist!*

"You!" the owner shook his head, blowing his breath slowly. "Nina! Where am I now?" he muttered, a confused and odd look on his face.

"In your store!" Nina laughed, shaking hands with him. "I have been looking for you.

"How come you're here? I heard that you..." he hesitated. "You died."

"It's a long story," Nina said laughing. Another shopper entered the shop, so Nina nudged Jianzhong gently and said, "Serve your customer first."

After helping the buyer, Jianzhong said to Nina, "I'll call it a day now." He grabbed a few packages from the freezers. "You must be hungry. Let's go have barbeque on the beach."

"What about your store?"

"I'm my own boss. I can close without asking for permission." He scribbled a note on a sheet of paper indicating he was closed for the day and stuck it on the door.

He led the way to the beach as he told Nina about his wife and his two-year-old daughter.

"Where are they?" Nina asked.

"On the beach."

They approached a roofed stand. "Mya!" Jianzhong called out to a pretty woman sitting underneath the shelter.

The woman raised her head and eyed Nina with surprise. "You went over there to bring my husband here?" She was the woman who was renting the braziers and who had directed Nina to the store.

"Nice to meet you again," Nina greeted her.

"She's my old pal, Nina, from Yunnan, from the Number Five Military Farm before I went to Burma."

"Pleased to meet you," Mya smiled.

Jianzhong tiptoed over to a reclining chair made of bamboo. "My kid's napping," he whispered, gently moving the hair of his daughter off her forehead. Then he asked his wife, "Can you make a fire over there?"

Nina moved over to the child and cooed, congratulating both Jianzhong and his wife for their beautiful daughter.

Mya nodded happily. She grabbed a metal rack hanging on the side of the stand with one hand and lifted a pack of charcoal with the other. Nina took the plastic bags Jianzhong had brought from the store and followed Mya to the firepit. Mya lit the charcoal and set the grill rack over it. She gestured to a small square table near the brazier indicating to Nina that she should lay the packages there.

Jianzhong in the meantime set three chairs around the table under the shelter. "You can join us," he said to his wife.

Mya waved her hand. "I'm not hungry. So, please help yourselves."

Jianzhong opened up the different packages and laid out pork ribs, lamb chops, beefsteaks, and fish fillets on the grill. Nina added the all-seasoned salt. The delicious scent soon rose up their nostrils. Jianzhong filled two glasses with beer and passed one to Nina. "Cheers to being alive!"

"Cheers!" Nina raised her beer glass. The semi-transparent, amber liquid in the glass shone in the sunlight. As the unremitting and droning call of the cicada sounded off, the breeze over the South China Sea could be heard whispering about the past.

28.

PEACE AND QUIET AFTERWARDS

NINA DID NOT WANT Jianzhong to lose customers though she was longing to hear his story. At her suggestion, Jianzhong reopened his store and resumed service. Customers soon swarmed in the shop. Nina helped with the checkout while he unpacked goods and found items for customers.

After the buyers left, Nina relaxed in a chair; Jianzhong leaned against the freezer, immersed in thought. In response to her question, he said, "Those years I was so poisoned by that international revolution, as was Dahai. Otherwise, we would not have wanted to join the Viet Cong. You know we ended up in Burma because we met a young Burmese by chance. He spoke Chinese and convinced us to join the People's Army run by the Communist Party of Burma instead."

"What did the People's Army do? What did you do with them?"

"They struggled for independence from Great Britain and then fought against the Burmese government. In 1967, Chairman Thakin Than Tun carried out his revolution. I think he copied old Mao." Jianzhong paused for a second, his hand shaking, and then sipped his tea. "In a bloody battle against the Burmese government's troops in 1970, Dahai died. I was injured in a mine explosion. When I was able to walk, I went back to the explosion spot. The hillsides were covered in burnt branches and bush. The land was blood-stained, full of bombed pits, pieces of torn clothing, dark shells, and broken rifles."

Jianzhong's recollection brought Nina to the mound that had been a grave for hundreds of killed soldiers. She envisioned a lanky young man with a bandaged leg hobbling across the scrubby hills to the tomb, around which jumbles of charred plant remains swayed in the wind. Jianzhong had wandered, but he could not find where Dahai's bones had been buried. He had pulled out a piece of wood carved with his friend's name and inserted it into the soil on the mound. Around the marker, Jianzhong had lain several wild flowers he had picked from the nearby fields. When she imagined what Dahai had felt and thought in his last moments, Nina's throat tightened. She still remembered his last words before going to battle — how he was determined to use his own blood to wash off his parents' anti-revolutionary crimes. *He was so brainwashed! If only he had fled with me, he would've seen a completely different world. But, there's no room left for "what ifs."* She sighed.

Jianzhong helped another customer. Then, he came back and sat on a stool at the counter next to her. "I have regrets, but I can't do anything about them. I don't think too much about what's happened in the past." He seemed to be able to read Nina's mind. "Dahai and I thought we could clear away our folks' sins, and prove we were loyal to Mao by joining the international revolution. His death made me rethink the meaning of life and death.

"On the anniversary of the Kyuhkok battle, during which the Communist Party of Burma Army won over the Burmese government in March 1971, I met with many other enlisted Chinese soldiers. They were sent-down youth from Yunnan's rural areas like us. Following the call of the Voice of the People of Burma on the radio, they crossed the border to devote themselves to the revolution. We sat on rocks or patches of weeds around bonfires. We bit into roasted pork and drank wine from coconut bowls. I recalled the Chen Sheng Wu Guang

Uprising. Do you remember? We learned about it in Chinese history class in the third grade. I thought I was a part of a modern version of the same kind of uprising. I asked myself: 'What's our purpose? If the Army wins and the Burmese government is thrown over, can we build a better Burma?' As a matter of fact, after the Chen Sheng Wu Guang Uprising in the Qin Dynasty, China continued to be a feudalistic society for some two thousand years. I think Mao's takeover was just like a peasants' uprising but it was couched in the shiny, sloganistic phrasing of a 'communist revolution.'

"I realized I was living a barbarian's life. After those bloody battles, we cried or laughed like ghosts in the woods. The happy memories of my childhood came flooding back. A sort of human feeling returned to me. Suddenly, I realized that I missed my folks who had been labelled anti-revolutionaries. They were my parents, and they gave me my life. Without them, there was no *me* in this world. Something mysterious in the boundless universe formed me into a living being. I thanked my parents who had given me life. The next month, I asked for a leave of absence to visit my folks back in China.

"I sneaked through the border and returned to Binyang in Guangxi Province. It was a starless night in May 1971. While I groped along a dark alley, I saw that only two street lamps were on. All the other bulbs were broken. I found my home, an apartment in a one-storey building, and thought it was strange that there was no light on inside. I tapped on the door, but nobody answered. Then, the door opened just a crack. Before I could see what was going on, a cat jumped out, fleeing past my legs. I stepped inside the door and called out, 'Anybody home?' No response. A stale odour pushed into my nose. I slid my hand up and down the inside wall near the door to find the switch. I flipped it a couple of times, but no light came on. It was hard to tell if the bulb was broken or if the electricity had been cut. Something was terribly wrong. I retreated quickly. When I noticed a bit of light coming from the next apartment, I rushed to it and knocked on the door. Nobody answered there either. I waited. Then the bulb inside the apartment went off. An ominous sign.

"I left the apartment building and saw a figure on the street striding past. From his gait I could tell that he was an old man. I rushed toward him and asked, 'Could you please tell me where the couple in Apartment 3 are?' The man didn't stop walking, but asked, 'Who are you? Why are you looking for them?'

"I hesitated and then said, 'I'm a relative of the family.' At the same time, I quickened my steps to catch up with him.

"He turned his head and stared at me. A flash appeared in his eyes under the dim streetlight. 'Follow me. Don't speak.' He said nothing more. At that moment, I recognized him as the gatekeeper of the elementary school that I'd attended years earlier.

"I followed him along a laneway to the school. Hobbling to the hut next to the gate, he unlocked the door. 'Come in, Jianzhong Wang.'

"I was surprised that he identified me by name. I remembered him because we schoolboys used to call him 'Old Bachelor.' When the light flickered on, I saw a single bed against the wall. He still lived alone, and he had aged. He gestured for me to sit down on a stool, and then he leaned his wizened body down into a dark brown wooden armchair by the door...."

Jianzhong's story was interrupted when several customers walked into the store. They asked for pork ribs. More shoppers joined the crowd and Nina stood up to help at the counter. It was almost six p.m. The busiest time was just beginning.

An hour later, Mya came into the store carrying their daughter in a sling on her back. "I'll throw together supper," she said to Nina as she made her way past the freezers to a door at the back of the room. She pulled it open and stepped into their living quarters. "Baby, we're at home." She took her child off her back and lay her down on a mat near the door. Nina followed Mya into the room and started to help her with the cooking. The three adults then took turns eating supper, so that someone could keep an eye on the store.

In the evening, after her daughter fell asleep, Mya went back to the beach to look after her barbecue braziers. Jianzhong kept the store open. "I'm going to take some time off tomorrow and show you around."

"Thanks, but you don't have to," Nina said. "Weekends are a perfect time for you to make some money. I don't want you to lose a Sunday. I can stay for another couple of hours just to chat."

Nina left at midnight, promising Jianzhong she would keep in touch with him. After waving goodbye, and asking him to give her regards to his wife, she took the last bus back to Hong Kong Island.

In bed at the hotel, Nina did not fall asleep right away though she was exhausted. Jianzhong's story about his parents haunted her. She was still in shock about the cannibalism that had happened in 1969 — the year Jianzhong and Dahai fled the military farm. According to the school gatekeeper, a militia leader had given a speech at a meeting to denounce the Five Black Categories: ex-landowners, the rich, anti-revolutionaries, evils, and labelled rightists. Then he had suggested that all the revolutionary villagers murder and then eat those enemies. Jianzhong's parents had been repatriated from Guangzhou to Binyang County after they were branded as rightists in 1958. During that barbaric raid, along with other victims, his parents had been beaten, murdered, and parts of their bodies had been cooked and then eaten. The gatekeeper had told Jianzhong to get as far away as possible to hide from persecution.

He had run, but he had not returned to the Burmese army. When he reached a small town called Lashio, he found a job in a restaurant owned by a Chinese-Burmese man. The owner introduced him to his niece, who had lived in Hong Kong and was looking for a husband-to-be from her hometown.

Jianzhong had jumped at the opportunity, which led him to his current, peaceful life.

With Jianzhong's happy ending lingering in her mind, Nina eventually fell asleep.

A few days later, back at home in Yarmouth, Nina lay on a reclining chair on the deck. Sunlight licked the surface of the bay, and a couple of windsurfer's colourful sails floated up and down over the waves. Hopping around on the beach, seagulls cooed or picked out food from the sand. Some small sandpipers hopped up and down the beach, and then buried their heads under their own wings to sleep. The world looked undisturbed and amicable in this corner along the Atlantic Ocean. But the memories of all those struggling souls amidst the turmoil caused by the bloody Cultural Revolution were like rough currents running across Nina's mind. She visualized the darkest period she and her generation had gone through on that faraway land across the Pacific Ocean. *We were born in the wrong place at the wrong time.* Nina remembered that someone had said that to her recently.

As soon as Nina recovered from the jet lag, she started to examine the data she had collected for her book. First, she listened to the tapes she had recorded in her interviews, and then she typed up the transcripts.

Day in and day out, she got up early and stayed up late, burying herself in piles of research. She planned to finish transcribing the interviews before she actually started preparing an outline for her book. She thought of several titles, but she was not sure which one she would use.

It was Friday again. Nina spent all morning typing up the transcripts. In the afternoon, she made notes, recalling the people she had interviewed and jotting down what she still remembered so as to make comparisons with the transcripts.

She remembered something she had learned in a research seminar: Authors have a subjective point of view. *It's true that my descriptions and my opinion, regarding the events, reflect my own point of view.* She kept her eyes on the pile of paper on the desk, checking back and forth between her notes and transcripts. She mulled over being subjective or objective.

Lightning flashed across the sky, and a whirling wind blew outside. A nearby thunderbolt crack woke her from her thoughts. She got up from the chair and walked over to the grand window. Rain was pouring down; the bay looked blurry. Nina felt as if she were hearing calls from the sky, some far and some close, rebounding far across the ocean.

Realizing she was weary, she selected a tape of Chinese folk songs and inserted it into the cassette player. A high-pitched song followed the rhythmic slapping of the rain and wind against the window.

She retreated to the kitchen and started to steam rice in a pot. After slicing and shredding up some ham, she stir-fried it with scrambled eggs, peas, and onions. At last, she mixed the steamed rice with the cooked hodgepodge and then sprinkled it with soy sauce. The delectable aroma spread throughout the kitchen. When she dropped all the shredded vegetables into a pot of soup on the stove, she imagined Roger's smiling face as he walked through the door.

After Nina turned the stove off, she went into the living room and stood by the window again. The sky was once again clear. *My Green Years in the Woods*, the title Liya had given her memoir-in-progress, crossed Nina's mind. Nina needed a title for her book too. She was glad that they had both chosen pen and paper as their weapon to fight for human rights. She went to the office, picked up a pen, and jotted down a few words on a piece of paper: *Voices from the Cultural Revolution: Surviving Mao's Reign of Terror.*

Anxious to know whether Roger, who would be the first person to read her book, would like this title, she sank into a chair by the window and waited for Roger to come home. Dreamily, she looked out the bay window. The bay appeared peaceful after the downpour. Birds glided through the light blue sky, their shadows dissolving into the shiny water's surface. A gorgeous double rainbow arched over the bay and sunshine embraced the world.

Acknowledgements

I am deeply grateful to my Publisher and Editor, at Inanna Publications, Luciana Ricciutelli, and copy-editor Adrienne Weiss, for their dedicated editing and remarkable suggestions that have helped bring this novel to the world.

Thanks also to the readers who have expressed their interest and inquired about the protagonist, Nina Huang, after reading the manuscript "Yearning," or after reading this story from my collection, *Butterfly Tears*. Inspired by their interest and questions, I expanded the story into this novel.

My thanks also go to my critique pals: Marlene Ritchie, Sara Pauff, and Phillis DePore who read the manuscript in its earlier version and provided me with their honest and helpful feedback. I owe personal notes of thanks to Marie Laing, Penelope Stuart, Carol Mortensen, and Dorothy Rawrek who are always there for me.

Last, but certainly not least, I am thankful to my husband and son, Jean-Marc and Shu, for their patience and forever support of my writing.

Photo: Jean-Marc Roy

Born in China, Zoë S. Roy, an avid reader even during the Cultural Revolution, writes literary fiction with a focus on women's cross-cultural experiences. Her publications include a collection of short stories, *Butterfly Tears* (2009), and a novel, *The Long March Home* (2011), both published by Inanna Publications. She holds an M.Ed. in Adult Education and an M.A. in Atlantic Canada Studies from the University of New Brunswick and Saint Mary's University. She currently lives in Toronto, and teaches with the Essential Skills Upgrading program for the Toronto Public School Board.